ONE STEP
Further

FELICE STEVENS

One Step Further
June 2015 Copyright (c) 2015 by Felice Stevens
All rights reserved

Cover Art by Reese Dante
Edited by Keren Reed
Fomratted by Perfectly Publishable

Alex Stern has it all: good looks, charm, a job he loves, and everyone calls him a friend. He lives life to the fullest at a breakneck pace, in the city that never sleeps. But Alex is also a master pretender; not even his best friend sees the pain that Alex hides so well. Alex himself isn't sure who he is or what he's searching for, he only knows that he hasn't found it yet.

As a veterinarian, Rafe Hazelton loves each animal that crosses his path; they don't care if he stutters a bit or that he prefers men. Their love is unconditional, but his life is still empty; they can only give him so much. New friendships convince him it's time to break the wall of loneliness he's hidden behind since childhood and discover what he's been missing.

Alex and Rafe forge a friendship that turns physical, and they both swear that the relationship will last only as long as the fun does. But when old heartaches come to light and secrets hidden for years are revealed, Alex and Rafe discover if they accept what's in their hearts and take it one step further, the greatest reward is waiting for them in the end.

DEDICATION

TO MY FAMILY; BY BLOOD AND BY CHOICE—
YOU'VE MADE IT ALL POSSIBLE.

ACKNOWLEDGMENTS

Thank you to my editor, Keren Reed for making it all come together. To my wine and whine crew: Lindsey, Sandy and Hope-I couldn't have done it without you. To Denise from Shh Mom's Reading-you know how I feel. Thank you for everything, always.

To my readers who love this genre as much as I do, thank you for loving my guys and reading my books. I can't tell you how amazing a feeling it is to hear "I love your books." You are the reason I continue on this journey.

CHAPTER ONE

"Come on, big boy." Alex Stern tickled his best friend, Micah Steinberg, under the chin with the long neon pink straw in his hand. "Have a drink."

The music of Journey pounded from the speakers so Alex wasn't sure Micah even heard his words, but from the horrified expression on his friend's face, Alex knew Micah had seen what he held in his hand. Alex had arranged this bachelor party for his best friend and his fiancé at an all-male strip club, and so far it was a rousing success. A group of around fifty people were busy at the buffet and bar in a private room at the club, while gorgeous male pole dancers were all doing their thing to the '80s playlist he'd given the DJ.

Alex was thrilled Micah had found someone who loved him as much as Josh did. And if that meant he and Micah wouldn't be as close as they once were, well that was inevitable, wasn't it? Life happened and with it came changes. You learned to roll with them or they'd crush you.

The thought of not having Micah as much in his life filled Alex with a stinging sorrow over the inevitable shift in time spent together and priorities. Their friendship as Alex knew it would never be the same, no matter how well Alex and Josh got along. Micah was moving forward, creating a family with Josh that would place Alex at the periphery, not the center of Micah's life. A place where Alex had resided for the better part of fifteen years.

And while Alex didn't begrudge Micah and Josh anything, he suddenly had the need to get completely shit-faced drunk. That would be the only way to deal with not simply losing his best friend, but having to keep a smile on his face all night long.

He downed half his drink in one gulp and offered up the other one in his hand. "Oh please, you know you want to." He put the rubber penis-shaped straw in his mouth and noisily sucked up the rest of his drink, then slowly drew it out from between his lips. "It's nice and soft. Almost like the real thing." He set his empty glass on the table next to them and held out the other one to his friend. "Your turn."

Micah pulled away from him. "Get that thing away from me." He turned to his fiancé, Josh Rosen, and grabbed his arm. "Do you see what he's doing? He's not to be trusted at the wedding. He'll probably show up naked."

Josh glanced at the drink in Alex's hand and broke out in laughter. "Alex, you're impossible."

"A naked best man. Now there's an idea." Wide-eyed, Alex wiggled the straw again so the end jiggled in Micah's face. "I'm your best friend. It's my job to make sure you have a great night and be crazy and do things you've never done." He held out the drink again. "Now come on."

"No." Micah folded his arms. "I won't use that, that thing. You're out of control."

"And look." With a flourish, Alex pulled out two purple sashes with the words "Groom" and "Groom" written in silver, sparkly letters. "Don't you love them? It was either these or tee shirts that said 'His' and 'His.'"

"Alex." Micah took the sashes and tossed them over the back of a chair. "Are you trying to make me kill you before the wedding? Because you're doing a great job of it."

"Oh don't be such a spoil sport." Josh picked up one of the sashes and put it on, over his shoulder, then slipped the other over Micah's chest. "They're fun and Alex is all about fun." Josh kissed Micah, who stopped grumbling long enough to kiss him back.

When it became obvious after watching several minutes of Micah and Josh kissing that they were at least going to wear his sashes, Alex grinned and decided he should finish Micah's drink as well. Yep, he was the King of Fun all right. Good old fun Alex. Still holding his penis straw, Alex wandered off to watch the dancers. One in particular caught his eye and he leaned against the bar to watch him move.

Clad only in a skimpy neon green thong, the young man worked his body, twining his sinuous torso around the pole like a snake. The colored strobe lights played off his glistening dark skin and Alex found himself enthralled.

What normal person could move like that? It was all Alex could do to drag himself to the gym twice a week after hours at the hospital. His stomach tightened as the man threw him a bright smile and switched poles to dance with another, equally pliant pole dancer in a hot pink thong. Their bodies moved in perfect synchronicity as one of his favorite '80s club songs, "Born to Be Alive," started playing.

Sighing, he turned to the bartender and waved his penis straw. "Hit me up, Max. Make it a double."

The dark-haired giant of a man raised his brows. "Didn't I just give you one about twenty minutes ago?"

"The last time I checked I was over twenty-one." He poked the bartender with the straw. "Now pour me a drink."

The bartender jerked away from Alex. "Man, someone needs to take that thing away from you. You are having way too much fun with it." He poured Alex a double vodka. "Here. Drink it slow."

"Yes, Mother, dear." Alex wandered away and scanned the room to see where Micah and Josh were. Hard to miss them, as they were in the middle of the dance floor, moving slowly, despite the fast beat of the music and the wildly colored spinning lights. Josh's blond head nestled in the curve between Micah's neck and shoulder, and Micah held him close, a smile of utter contentment on his face. Both seemed oblivious to the scene around them.

At least that was something he did right, Alex mused as he wandered through the crowd, absently greeting people. From the first time Alex met Josh, he knew Micah needed the man. And Alex was correct; Micah had fallen for Josh without even realizing what was happening. Sometimes love happens organically. It was the way it was supposed to be.

"Damn, this is not the place to go all Zen and shit," he muttered to himself. He looked around and spotted Rafe Hazelton sitting by himself at a table. Alex had met the veterinarian a few times and thought him to be a slightly intense, but perfectly nice person. Quieter than most, but then again he wasn't Alex's friend, he came from Josh.

He raised his glass to his lips, but it was empty. Huh. He must have spilled some walking through the crowd. Well, no matter, there was plenty more where that came from. He moved to the beat of the music, swaying in place. When the room started swaying with him, Alex decided dancing wasn't such a great idea. Maybe he should slow down and sit a while.

Since Micah and Josh were leaving their beloved dog with him while they went to California to visit with Josh's family after the wedding, Alex supposed it would make sense to get to know the vet a little better. He sprawled into the empty chair next to Rafe.

"Hey, what's up?"

"Oh. Hi." Rafe's deliberate way of speaking, though a bit unusual, wasn't unpleasant. There was nothing unpleasant about the man at all. He was very good-looking, only a bit too quiet and uptight for Alex's taste.

And tonight it went beyond a little uptight. Though he was pleasantly buzzed, Alex could still tell when a person was uncomfortable and Rafe Hazelton looked supremely uncomfortable. The man's posture was as rigid as if he was in the army and his wide, gold-flecked brown eyes had a wary, almost hunted look about them. They were pretty eyes, though, Alex thought.

Damn, I must be drunk if I'm thinking about this guy's eyes.

"Why aren't you drinking or dancing or something?" Rafe had way too unhappy a face for being at a gay bachelor party. "Here, put this on." Alex grabbed one of the crowns he'd placed on the table. "I got these 'cause Micah always thought he was King of the World." He huffed out a laugh.

"Now he f-found his Prince Charming, right?" Rafe took the crown from Alex and held it in his hands, but didn't join in with Alex's joking.

"Josh is the best thing to ever happen to Micah. And Micah loves him to death. They're perfect for each other." Alex suddenly felt sober and didn't like the feeling one bit. "You are way too serious, man. Come on and dance or something." Alex stood up, held out his hand and waggled his fingers. "Let's go."

Rafe shook his head. "Uh, I'm n-not really good at dancing. I-I don't go to clubs." An embarrassed flush rose to his face and he looked everywhere but at Alex.

Surprised, Alex shrugged and dropped his hand. "Suit yourself. I'm gonna go and mingle." He walked away, but glanced over his shoulder to see Rafe gazing after him with those big, golden-brown eyes. His wavy, chestnut hair glinted whenever the flashes of light struck it. A powerful surge of lust rolled through Alex, shocking him.

Shouldn't be so surprised. It's been months since you've gotten laid.

Damn he needed another drink. A waiter walked by with a tray of champagne glasses. The toast. Good. It was time for him to make the toast.

"Quiet everybody!" He grabbed a glass from the tray, careful to keep the sloshing to a minimum. The music halted and after all the noise and laughter, the silence seemed almost unearthly. Micah's arm was draped around Josh's shoulders, the two men a perfect unit.

"Don't worry, everyone. I'll be brief so you can all get back to your drinking, dancing and debauchery." He walked over to Micah and Josh and lifted his glass to the two men.

"I've known Micah for almost half my life and he's like a

brother to me. I couldn't wish him any greater happiness than he's already found with Josh. Be good to each other."

They clinked glasses and drank. When he finished he called the waiter over to take their glasses, then placed a hand on Micah's shoulder.

"I love you, man. I couldn't be happier for you. I've always told you, you deserve only the best. And I know Josh is the best man for you."

To his surprise, Micah had tears in his eyes. "Give me a hug, you big jerk."

They threw their arms around each other. So many years together and their friendship stood the test of time—through Alex dropping out of med school and becoming a nurse, and Micah's arrogance and inability to show love.

There were times he now wished he'd shared his own fears and pain with Micah. But tonight was not the time or place for those thoughts. Tonight belonged solely to Micah and Josh.

"I love you, Alex. You know that, right? No matter what, I'm still there for you. I always will be; as much as ever." Micah's voice came out muffled against his shoulder, but Alex heard him. He knew Micah meant what he said in the heat of the moment, when he was full of emotion. Alex knew also Josh was the most important man in Micah's life now and rightly so. Alex wasn't first any longer, and he shouldn't be.

Though he wished he could be first in *someone's* life.

"It's all good, man. I love you too, and you and Josh are going to have the best life." He pulled away and faced Josh, holding his arms open wide. "No kiss for your Fairy Godfather, Alex? If it wasn't for me, you know, you two wouldn't be together."

Josh laughed and pulled Alex in for a hug. "You're the best, Alex; one of a kind, but I see through your bullshit." The last part was whispered in Alex's ear, meant only for him to hear.

Alex stiffened but Josh held him tighter.

"When are you going to give up all the jokes and find someone to love? You deserve it more than anyone."

Swallowing past the ache in his throat, Alex merely kissed

Josh on the cheek and squeezed his shoulder. "I love everyone. I'm good." He pointed to the DJ and called out, "Music, please."

And the sounds of Bon Jovi's "Livin' on a Prayer" burst through the speakers. He backed away from the happy couple and allowed everyone else to move in and congratulate them. Once again he was drawn to the dancers up on the stage. A lot drunker than he was before, and certainly way more emotional than he should ever have allowed himself to become, Alex climbed up on the stage and started dancing with the dancer in the neon green thong he'd admired before.

"Oooh baby, you move nice." The dancer ran his hands over Alex's chest and before Alex knew it, had his shirt unbuttoned and tossed into the center of the room. "Show your body, honey." They continued to move to the pulse of the music. "What's your name, baby?"

"Alex," he said as he twirled and swiveled his hips. He heard some catcalls from below, looked out over the room and saw everyone watching him, clapping and whistling. Micah in particular had a pained expression on his face, so Alex blew him a kiss and wiggled his ass. Josh fell apart laughing, while Micah shook his head in disgust, but Alex wasn't fooled. He'd caught the tail end of a grin on Micah's lips before he turned away. He rocked his pelvis to the beat of the music.

"I'm Vince, honey." The dancer rubbed up against Alex. "I think your man is jealous."

What the hell was the guy talking about? "I'm not the one getting married. He's marrying the man standing next to him."

"I know, silly." The man flashed him a smile as he wrapped himself around Alex's neck like a scarf. "I'm not talkin' about him. I'm talkin' about that fine-looking man, over there." With a long, elegant finger, Vince pointed to the side. Alex followed his direction and found himself staring straight at Rafe Hazelton.

"Him?" Alex laughed but then snuck another look at Rafe. The man wasn't even looking at him; he was busy checking his phone. "He's a friend, and barely that. More like a friend of a friend."

"Well, baby, all I know is Mr. Friend of a Friend was busy checking out your ass and looked like he wanted a piece of what you were shaking." The dancer grabbed a hold of the pole and swung himself around it, resuming his twists and turns. "He looks sad, like he needs to learn to live a little and get some good lovin.' I bet you're the man who could help him do that."

And Alex, who only lived his life in the moment because the past wasn't anything he wanted to remember, couldn't understand why hot tears rushed to his eyes.

"Yeah. I'm that kind of guy."

CHAPTER TWO

Following the same routine every morning provided Rafe Hazelton with that much-needed sense of stability. Shirt first, then pants, socks and tie in that order. Only after everything was in place could he begin his breathing exercises.

He closed his eyes, placed one hand over his stomach and began to take slow, deep breaths. At each inhalation, he imagined starting a conversation. First, Patty, the receptionist at the clinic. She was always so cheerful and happy he rarely tightened up when he spoke to her. That's who he had to concentrate on; nonthreatening, kind people who didn't twist his stomach and nerves into knots.

Breathe deep. Slow. Inhale, exhale.

The tension flowed out of his body and after a few seconds he spoke. "Good morning, Patty."

And then he smiled to himself. There. Perfect. No stumbling or hesitation. Rafe breathed deeply and rehearsed his words, careful to speak with deliberation. He'd been doing these exercises over half his life and he firmly believed they enabled him to conquer his problem.

He continued to converse with himself out loud as he prepared his coffee and finished getting dressed. By the time he was ready to leave for the clinic, Rafe felt sufficiently warmed up to handle the day ahead of him.

He left his apartment building and gazed out over the green

expanse of Prospect Park. The only way Rafe could live in a city cluttered with skyscrapers and concrete was to live near this park; he had to be able to connect with nature somehow. A special kind of tranquility embraced him as he gazed at the lush greenery of the trees facing him. Past hurts and disappointments faded; Rafe felt almost normal and whole.

Walking alongside the walls of the park on his way to the subway centered Rafe, clearing his mind and preparing him to deal with the stresses of the day. He paid his fare and entered the station, glad he didn't have to wait long for a train. He found a seat, slipped on his headphones and let the music carry him away.

Rafe didn't know whether he stuttered because he was shy or he was shy because he stuttered. He only knew that in elementary school all the kids made fun of him because of it, sending him deeper and deeper into his books and his backyard menagerie.

His pets never made fun of him. The stray kittens in the barn were always happy to see him and greeted him with meows and raspy-tongued licks. The dogs too, loved spending time with him and every weekend he and his two mutts, Ben and Jerry, would take a picnic lunch and go exploring. Sometimes he'd sit for hours watching the rabbits hop in the field and the squirrels race up and down the tree trunks.

Eventually they became so used to his quiet presence they'd approach him and he would feed them, thus earning their trust. It was in those fields that he decided he was better suited to be with animals than people. Animals never judged; they loved unconditionally and would never hurt him. They wouldn't tease him about being too skinny when all the other guys had muscles. They loved him even if his words got tangled on his tongue.

Countless secrets were whispered into his dogs' willing ears; they were the keepers of his dreams; the first to know he wanted to become a veterinarian when he grew up, the ones he cried to when his feelings were hurt over always getting picked last for teams in gym class.

The only ones he told out loud he was gay.

Why the vice-like grip he'd kept on his past slipped today, allowing all the sludge of his childhood to stream forth, Rafe had no idea, but it stayed with him his entire forty-five minute ride uptown to the clinic.

Perhaps it was Josh's wedding a week ago that did it. Though happy for his friend, Rafe wished he could find someone to love him as much as Micah Steinberg loved Josh. Rafe had liked Josh immediately; the man was totally nonthreatening and so sweet. Josh was so nice Rafe had done something he'd never done before: after an hour of practicing and hyperventilating, he'd asked the man out. Too late, of course, because Josh had already fallen for Micah, and Rafe retreated immediately, sliding back into the position of friend.

But then he'd met Alex Stern and for a year now he hadn't been able to stop thinking about the man. Good God, he must be crazy.

It's not crazy. You know why you can't stop thinking about him. He's the man you can never have. The one everyone wants, who would never want someone like you.

With his gorgeous blue eyes and messy blond curls, Alex sent Rafe into a tailspin every time he came near. Rafe turned into a babbling idiot, even as his body burned for Alex like it never had for anyone else before. It figured his first crush in years would be the most unattainable man he could've chosen.

Face it. What guy would want someone who had to practice saying hello every morning in the mirror? Certainly not a man like Alex, who could snap his fingers and have whomever he wanted. Rafe was not in the man's universe. He'd been shocked the night of Josh's bachelor party when Alex had asked him to dance.

Rafe inwardly chided himself. *Forget about Alex Stern. He's only after as much fun as he can get.*

The train pulled into the 72nd Street station on the Upper West Side of Manhattan, and Rafe joined the throngs of people exiting. Thankful to breathe fresh air again, he decided to stop at the bagel store on the corner where the veterinary clinic was located and get a self-serve coffee. The smiling woman behind the counter thanked the customer in front of him then turned to him.

"May I help you?"

"Everything, n-not toasted."

She slipped the bagel in a bag and he took it, gratified to feel its fresh warmth seeping into his fingers. He smiled and paid her for the bagel and coffee without saying a word, and left the store. It was almost nine o'clock and Monday mornings were usually the busiest, with people bringing in their pets after any mishaps over the weekend.

He pushed open the door and as expected, the bright face of Patty Rodriguez greeted him.

"Good morning, Dr. Hazelton."

"Good morning." He smiled and walked past her desk. Not so bad. With that simple greeting, confidence flowed hot in his veins. "How is it this morning?"

"Oh, fine. The usual calls about swollen paws, bruises and cuts. Your first patient isn't coming in for another half hour. But first, we have a bit of a situation."

He froze. "W-what is it?"

Her eyes clouded as she caught his expression. "Oh, nothing bad. Only . . . well, come around here and I'll show you." She beckoned him and bemused, he set his coffee on the desk and walked around the U-shaped desk until he entered the open space.

A large black, white and gray rabbit sat in the playpen they normally used to showcase the kittens the local rescue brought by once a month, in the hopes of getting them adopted.

"He was left in a box by the front door. I found him this morning, poor guy," said Patty, her voice rising with her anger. "Who would do that; leave an animal out like the trash?" She bent down to pet the bunny who hopped over to her, sniffed, then hopped around a bit before sprawling out. "He's breathing so fast, Dr. Hazelton, is that normal?"

Rafe nodded. "Rabbits breathe f-faster so while it looks like he's panting, he's fine." Rafe squatted down to the bunny's eye level to get a visual. "Eyes clear and coat is shiny and soft." He spoke more to himself than to Patty, as if taking notes on the animal's condition. "Little guy is good."

"Can we keep him, Doctor? He can stay behind the desk with me, like the kittens do, only he'll be permanent, like our office mascot." Her large eyes entreated him.

Rafe shrugged. "Sure. Order a cage." He picked his coffee up and headed to the back where his office was located. The first thing he did upon entering was to sit in his chair, close his eyes and center himself. Breathe in, breathe out. The deep breathing he'd learned to perfect over the years also helped focus him on the tasks he needed to accomplish.

It only took a moment for his scattered nerves to arrange themselves; Rafe imagined them straight and tall like soldiers lining up for inspection. With his focus steady, he drank his coffee, ate his bagel and reviewed the charts of the patients he was scheduled to see. Outside he could hear the yips and barks of the dogs as the waiting area filled up. The other two vets came in at staggered hours during the day, but since it was his clinic, he always took the early shift.

After half an hour, his phone buzzed.

"Yes?"

"Pebbles is waiting in Room One, Doctor."

"Thanks."

And with that his day was off. Rafe loved every minute of his job. He got to spend his days with the animals he loved, making them healthy, and they loved him back. The owners were usually so grateful to have their beloved pets happy again they merely thanked him and left, not interested in long-winded conversations.

By four thirty he was beat. "Oh God," he moaned, stretching the kinks from his back. In college he'd taken up running, since he knew with his lanky body he'd never be any kind of bulked-up gym rat. He enjoyed the steady pounding of his feet to the ground and how his body relaxed and opened up when he hit his stride. He'd get that high that was almost as good as the infrequent times he'd had sex.

Maybe he'd run a little in Central Park before he went home. He'd seen over fifteen animals today and had barely enough time to drink a protein shake from the juice bar down the block that Patty was sweet enough to buy for him.

"Go on, Dr. Hazelton, go for a run. Dr. Esposito is here and you're not scheduled tonight anyway." Patty stood at the door to his office as he stared at a pair of running shorts and tee shirt he held in his hands.

"Fine, but I'll come back to change and make a final check on the appointments." He smiled at her as she nodded and withdrew, closing the door behind her.

It only took a few minutes for him to strip and put on his shorts and tee shirt. He waved goodbye to the staff, telling them he'd be back in about an hour. His strides ate up the pavement and his anticipation grew as the park drew closer. He crossed Central Park West and entered the park. Rafe found the running path and soon he was pounding his way to mental oblivion, his mind completely focused on his legs and the winding road in front of him.

Almost an hour later, his shirt plastered to his chest with sweat and his hair stuck in damp curls against his brow, Rafe returned to the clinic. He was breathing heavily, but his body hummed with endorphins even as a pleasant tiredness stole through his body. Damn, he missed this feeling.

"Good run, Doctor?" The nighttime receptionist, Sammi, held the door open for him. He made sure not to stand too close to her, as he was hot, sweaty and no doubt didn't smell his best.

"Yes, thanks." He scanned the waiting room and saw only two people, one with a dog and the other with a cat in a carrier. "Any problems?"

"No, Rafe, and you're off duty now."

Rafe spun around to see the smiling face of Jenny Esposito, the veterinarian on duty until midnight. The best thing he ever did after buying this place, after the vet he worked with retired, was keeping it open later hours and hiring great staff. Jenny was a gem. Her husband, Bill, was a hotel manager who also worked nights, and they had no kids, so Jenny was happy to work the five p.m. to midnight shift to keep the clinic open. More importantly, though, Jenny was the person closest to him, the only one he could count on as a friend.

"Yes, Mother." He smirked at her. Jenny was also one of the few people with whom he never had to worry about stuttering. Her smile and genuine caring put him completely at ease. He brushed past her to his office where he wiped himself down with a towel. The thought of getting back into a long-sleeved shirt and pants was distasteful, so he decided to keep his damp running clothes on. Thankfully he didn't wear shorts that were too thin and clinging, so he could ride the subway home without feeling embarrassed.

Damn, he couldn't wait to take a shower. He was sticky and overly warm and a cold beer would taste like heaven right now. Rafe picked up his gym bag and walked back to the front of the clinic, prepared to say goodnight to everyone. His phone buzzed and he checked to see a text from Josh.

Hey everyone. Having a great time here in Cali.

It was a group text, sent to him, Alex and about five or six other people. Below the text, a picture popped up of Josh and Micah looking tanned and happy on a beautiful beach, with the ocean a canvas of blue behind them.

Rafe studied the picture and saw their entwined hands on the blanket, golden wedding bands glinting where a sunbeam happened to strike them. Happy as he was for Josh, Rafe swallowed down his envy.

Would he ever find love?

Rafe already knew the answer to that question—it had been decided years ago in the small town he grew up in. It was embedded in his DNA and in every trickle of blood through his veins. The skinny, plain kid who'd rather spend his days with animals than people was destined to live a solitary life, a spectator of everyone else's happiness.

Only once had he screwed up his courage to talk to his prickly mother.

"Mom. Why doesn't anyone like me?"

He'd thought she'd give him a hug, and make him feel better by telling him how mean the other kids were. Like all the mothers on TV did.

Instead, true to form, she'd folded her arms and stared down at him with hard, black eyes. "You're different. Kids don't like different." Then she turned away to the stove.

Crushed to pieces, that was the last time he ever looked for comfort from his mother. He was only ten years old.

"Screw it," he muttered to himself. Time to go home, take a shower and flop in front of the television with some takeout. In other words, another typical night in his life.

"Rafe?"

His brow furrowed. He must be more tired than he thought. Either that or he was hallucinating.

"Uh, earth to Rafe. Hello?"

With his heart thumping, Rafe turned to meet the handsome, smiling face of Alex Stern.

CHAPTER THREE

The best part of Alex's day was when he took Lucky to the park after work. He'd come home and change, Lucky jumping and barking at his feet. It was nice, Alex realized, to have something alive waiting for him when he opened the door, happy to see him, even if it was a dog and not a man.

So today, on one of those perfect, early summer days in New York City, when the sky shone with a blue as pure as a newborn baby's eyes and the green of the trees in Central Park as fresh and clean as spearmint, Alex spent the better part of an hour with Lucky, tossing a Frisbee for her to chase, and eyeing the cute guys in colorful outfits, running on the path.

With Lucky sufficiently tired out, they left the park, ambling down 86th Street. As they passed Amsterdam Avenue, Lucky stopped and barked. Alex looked up and saw the sign for Rafe's veterinary clinic, *Paws For Care.*

"You want to pay a visit, huh?"

Lucky whined and waved her feathery tail.

Well, why not? Alex had nothing else to do tonight, as usual. Ever since Micah had gotten married, Alex found himself incredibly lonely. In all the years they'd been friends, Alex never thought he needed Micah as much as Micah needed him. Another thing he'd been fooling himself about.

The veterinary clinic was two storefronts down from the corner. Alex pushed the door open and looked around the light and airy office. Only one person sat in the reception area with some kind of animal in a carrier. Lucky whined and pulled on her leash and Alex turned his attention to the front desk. He couldn't be sure if Rafe was even working tonight, but if he told the people behind the desk, they'd certainly give the dog something to drink.

Alex eyed the back of a man, his ass a sweet pear shape in a pair of soft cotton shorts. His body looked tight and lean and his long legs flexed with muscles. Wow. Maybe he should get a dog or a cat so he could come here more often and view these sights.

The man turned around and Alex almost fell over. Rafe Hazelton peered at him through some sexy as fuck black rectangular glasses. The front view was even better than the rear. His hair curled in damp chestnut waves and his face glowed with a healthy sheen. "Rafe?"

Damn. The guy was hot and staring back at him like he wanted to eat his face.

"Earth to Rafe. Hello."

Rafe took several deep breaths. Unbidden, a picture rose up in Alex's mind of Rafe underneath him, long legs wrapped around Alex's hips as he drove inside the man over and over again.

"Alex?"

Alex blinked away the disturbing, erotic images and forced a smile. "Hey. We were in the neighborhood and I thought I'd stop by to say hi."

Rafe blinked a few times. "Oh. Yeah. Um. Hi."

Alex continued. "I was hoping maybe Lucky could get some water? We spent an hour at the park and I'm sure she's thirsty."

Something that might have been disappointment flickered in Rafe's eyes before he glanced down at the dog. "Uh, y-yeah. Of course." He turned and spoke to the woman behind the desk and she got up and went to the back, returning with a bowl of water.

Rafe bent to pet the dog as she drank. "H-how's she d-do-ing?" He concentrated on the dog, not looking at Alex when he spoke.

"She's a good girl. I like taking care of her."

Lucky barked, presumably at hearing "good girl," and he and Rafe shared a laugh. Rafe's golden eyes glowed and his smile beamed warm and bright, with no hesitation. Alex's breath caught in his throat and he swallowed, suddenly nervous for the first time in years.

Before he could think twice, he blurted out, "Want to grab some dinner and catch a movie?"

Rafe's smile faded and he blinked rapidly. "Wh-what?" He stuffed his hands in his pockets and his eyes grew wide and almost panicky.

"Dinner, you know, food, eat?" Alex laughed trying to lighten the odd mood that had sprung up between them.

Rafe's brow furrowed. "W-with m-me?"

The slight stutter hit Alex then. It was something he hadn't noticed before since he and Rafe rarely spoke directly. Watching Rafe struggle, the words giving him such obvious trouble, a wave of protectiveness toward the man rose up within Alex. The last thing he wanted to do was contribute to Rafe's anxiety.

"Yes, with you. And I won't take no for an answer. You, me and Lucky here will hang out in Micah and Josh's apartment. They're still on their honeymoon, so I'm staying at their place while I watch her. We can rent a movie if you don't feel like going anywhere."

Rafe couldn't know how much Alex needed his company. The last thing Alex wanted was to spend another night on the sofa with Lucky. Cute as she was, Alex was a people person. Over the years, many of his long-time friends had become simple acquaintances, due to his demanding schedule and friendship with Micah which admittedly took up so much of his free time. People never understood why he put up with Micah, but Alex didn't need to explain why he did what he did. He knew why and that's all that mattered.

"Um, ok-kay. I guess."

"Don't sound so excited about it." Alex joked in an effort to keep the mood light. "The only time you'd have to worry is if I would say I'm cooking."

Rafe shot him a tentative grin, his golden-brown eyes still somewhat wary. Alex couldn't help smiling back. The guy was so sweetly cute, and with his disheveled, messy hair and perfect body, he was a wet dream come true.

Rein it in, boy. This is Rafe. He's Josh's friend, your friend.

Lucky finished her water and Rafe said goodnight to his staff, then the three of them left the clinic for the two-block walk back to Micah's apartment. As expected, Rafe was a silent companion, so Alex filled in the emptiness with chatter.

"What kind of food do you like? They have everything. I figured we could order in and then if you want, you could shower. By the time you'd be finished the food will be there."

"I'm p-pretty easy."

Alex chuckled. "Oh yeah? Good to know." He shot a look at Rafe who'd turned bright red.

Mentally kicking himself, Alex recognized his personality wasn't making it easier for Rafe. "Don't mind me."

"It's f-fine," said Rafe, who took a deep breath before he spoke. "I'm j-just not used to th-this."

"Used to what?" Alex was curious. The guy was hot, shy and smart. A killer combination in Alex's book.

Rafe made a motion of frustration in the air with his hand. "In c-case you haven't guessed, I'm n-not very good with people." He glanced at Alex before returning to a study of the sidewalk beneath their feet as they walked. "M-most of the time I pr-prefer animals."

Aww, damn, that was sad. "Leave everything to Nurse Alex; put yourself in my caring hands."

They'd reached Micah's building and entered the luxurious lobby. After Lucky greeted the doorman, they headed to the elevators. Alex began to appreciate not having to listen to banal chatter simply to fill air space. It made what they talked about more important somehow.

Finally inside the apartment, he unhooked Lucky from her

leash and she wandered off. Rafe still stood by the front door.

"Come on inside."

"M-Micah won't mind me in his apartment?"

Alex laughed. "He doesn't care; his bark is worse than his bite. You're Josh's friend, which makes you his friend now as well." He tossed the keys on the kitchen countertop. "Go on. Have a seat and I'll get us some beer. Then we can decide what to order."

Rafe set his gym bag down by the door and slid onto one of the stools set up at the breakfast bar. Alex placed a beer in front of Rafe and tipped his own bottle. "Cheers."

After a long swallow that drained half the bottle he wiped his mouth. To his surprise, Rafe had also drunk about half the beer and was eyeing the rest as if he couldn't wait to drink the other half.

"Go on, man, finish it. You look like you need it."

With a grateful smile Rafe nodded and drank it down. Alex silently handed him another one. Everyone had one of those days, where you always had to have one more beer, for whatever reason. Alex knew that better than most, and he also knew how to pass the beers and be a willing, listening ear.

This second beer, Rafe sipped a little more slowly. "Yeah. I saw over fifteen animals today." He traced the lip of the bottle, his gaze fixated on his moving finger. "I also r-ran a f-few miles for the first time in a while and it m-must've caught up with me. Guess you could call me a lightweight." He took another deep swallow and stretched out, his slightly lopsided grin totally endearing.

There were words Alex could call Rafe Hazelton but lightweight wasn't one of them. Attractive as sin, caring to a fault; those were the first words that popped into Alex's mind. Unfortunately, the man might as well have Happily Ever After written across his face, and Alex had long since given up on fairytale endings.

Surprisingly though, Rafe's stutter had lessened. Alex put it down to Rafe becoming more comfortable with him, or maybe it was the beer. Whatever it was, Alex was all for it, since a relaxed Rafe was a fun and easy-going Rafe. And if all the man needed was a few beers to do the relaxing, that was fine too.

"So what should we get for dinner? How about the go-to Chinese?"

Rafe made a face. "Too greasy. Sushi?" he asked hopefully.

Alex could've cared less. He was so thrilled to have company he'd happily chew on some seaweed. "Sure." He picked up the iPad on the counter and logged on to the delivery service he had an account with. At least twenty Japanese restaurants popped up.

"Here, pick whatever you like, then go right through the bedroom and you can shower and change." He handed the tablet to Rafe and watched him choose, his tongue poking out his cheek as he made his selection.

"'Kay, here." Rafe put the iPad down and got up. He walked over to his bag, picked it up and pushed up his glasses to rub his eyes. "Damn, I'm tired."

Alex watched him drag across the floor. "Why don't you stay here tonight?"

Rafe stopped in his tracks. "I d-don't th-think that would be a g-good idea."

Damn. The stutter was back, which to Alex meant Rafe was all nervous again.

"I only thought it would be easier for you, you know, since it's right down the block from your clinic. This way you wouldn't have to go back on the subway. There's an extra bedroom and bathroom, so we wouldn't disturb each other in the morning. I have to leave by six."

Rafe stared at him, wide-eyed. "Six in the morning?"

Alex chuckled. "Yeah. Surgeries are early in the morning so the team needs to get there to prep."

"I'll think about it." Rafe disappeared into the bedroom and Alex placed their food order. Realizing that he hadn't given Rafe any towels, Alex took some from the hall closet and went into the spare bedroom. The shower was running and the bathroom door was left open, so Alex called out to Rafe.

"Hey, I've got towels for you."

No answer. Rafe probably couldn't hear him over the water, and Alex decided to leave them on the toilet seat. The minute he walked into the steamy bathroom, the water stopped and the shower door opened. Before Alex could leave, Rafe walked out and froze when he saw Alex.

"I was bringing you some towels," mumbled Alex as he averted his eyes. *Shit.* Rafe's shyness would make this a supremely uncomfortable moment, so Alex didn't say another word; he turned his back and returned to the kitchen. There was no need for him to be nervous. He downed the rest of his beer and chucked the empties in the recycling bin, taking out two fresh, cold ones for them both.

The buzzer sounded and the doorman announced the arrival of the delivery man. By the time Rafe walked back in, bringing with him a cool rainwater scent, Alex had finished setting out the sushi on two plates. They sat together at the breakfast bar and began to eat.

Alex fumbled with the chopsticks, finally tossing them to the side in favor of the little plastic fork. "Stupid things. I never could learn how to use them."

"It's a skill that t-takes time to develop." Rafe chewed slowly and swallowed. Alex watched the movement of his throat.

"So you're calling me unskilled, huh?" Alex popped a spicy salmon roll in his mouth. Whew, that baby was hot. He chased it down with cold beer. He noticed that Rafe too was making a nice inroad on his third beer. "I think that insult deserves a challenge. Lemme think."

Rafe seemed unperturbed and continued to eat. He finished his rolls and wiped his hands then drank down the rest of his beer. "It wasn't an insult. Merely a st-statement of fact." To Alex's surprise, a small grin flickered on Rafe's lips. Plate in hand Rafe stood, and with the dog at his heels, went into the kitchen.

This was more like it. Alex was glad to see a sense of humor shine through Rafe's nervous demeanor. An idea popped into his head. "I got it." He slapped his knee and jumped up. Lucky began to bark and Alex could hear Rafe shushing her.

Alex swung around the breakfast bar and came upon Rafe who squatted next to the dog. The vision of Rafe beneath him on his knees caused Alex's cock to harden painfully. The man was all too enticing, all the more so because Alex knew Rafe was completely unaware of his looks.

"Do you bowl or play pool?"

Rafe stroked Lucky's ears. "N-no. I don't know h-how to do either of those things."

"So what?" answered Alex, promptly. "Not knowing how to do something never stopped me before."

"Y-yeah." Rafe spoke more to the dog than to Alex. "I'm not you though." He lifted his gaze to Alex.

There was vulnerability in those golden-brown eyes gazing at him; they spoke of past hurts and heartaches, and dreams gone unrecognized. Alex remembered another pair of eyes gazing at him long ago with that same sense of exposure, mixed with sadness. Only those eyes were blue, like his.

"I'll teach you. It's no big deal. That's what friends are for."

CHAPTER FOUR

The next afternoon, Rafe was still contemplating what Alex had said to him as he worked on extracting a nail wedged into a dog's paw.

Friends? Did Alex Stern, big, good-looking and incredibly sexy, consider him a friend? He must've been drunk. Rafe was not the kind of man who had friends like that.

"Good boy." He patted the dog, after cleaning the wound and putting in a few stitches. "I'll give you some antibiotics to give him to prevent infection and Jake here will wrap the p-paw up nicely."

The anxious owner nodded, his frightened gaze on his dog. "He'll be fine though, right, Doctor?" He twisted his fingers together. "I brought him in as soon as it happened."

Giving the man his most trustworthy smile, Rafe nodded. "He'll be good as n-new in a few days. Make sure he stays off the paw as much as possible." Rafe figured the man would carry the thirty-pound spaniel everywhere now. He gave his tech Jake the instructions and left the examination room.

Patty was talking to the rabbit, whom she'd named Nibbles, as she filed away the afternoon's charts. He laughed, watching the rabbit hop after her like a little puppy. The bells over the door chimed and a woman and her young daughter walked in.

"Hello." The woman smiled at him. "We were wondering if you had any kittens to adopt. We lost our cat a few months ago and Maggie here is ready for a new friend."

The little girl was cute; all red curls and big blue eyes. "I miss Buttons but I also miss having a kitty." Her attention was distracted by the sight of Patty holding Nibbles up for a kiss. "Ooh, Mommy, look. It's a bunny." She ran over to Patty. "Can I pet him, please."

"I didn't know rabbits made house pets." The mother watched as Patty held Nibbles in her lap and talked to Maggie.

"They make excellent apartment p-pets. They make no sound, can be litter-box tr-trained and are very loving." Rafe left the woman to squat down next to Patty and Maggie.

"Here, let him sniff you. Rabbits can nip if they get scared."

At that, Maggie drew back, blue eyes round with fear. "I don't wanna get bit."

Rafe beckoned. "Here t-take my hand." She put her little hand in his and he held their two hands together to the rabbit's twitching nose. "Sometimes they're afraid, so they b-bite out of fear. Take it slow with them and they'll lick you."

"Like people right? Sometimes they're kinda mean at first but then you know them and they aren't mean at all."

Out of the mouths of babes.

Together they held hands to the rabbit and he sniffed them, then head butted their clasped hands. Maggie laughed with delight.

"He likes me. And he's soft."

Her mother had come closer to stand behind her. "Maybe you'd rather have a bunny than a new kitty, Maggie?"

The little girl contemplated her mother's words as she stroked the rabbit's ears. When she stopped, Nibbles pushed at her hand, reminding Maggie of her job to keep petting him.

"Oh, yes, Mommy. Buttons was the best and I miss him. I don't want another kitty." Maggie rubbed her eyes with her little fist. "And the bunny likes me already." She touched his head. "No one else has a bunny."

"Would you hold him a few days? I need to talk to her father and he's away on business."

"Of course." Patty smiled. "Nibbles will stay here until you can come for him."

"Don't give him to anyone else." Maggie kissed the rabbit's head.

Rafe stood. "Congratulations." They made arrangements to call in a day or so and left, Maggie chattering excitedly about the rabbit.

He and Patty went over the next day's appointments, as the rabbit hopped around his feet.

The bells tinkled again and Jenny came through the door. "Hi. How's it look?" She greeted Patty, then put her dinner in the small refrigerator behind the reception desk.

"Pretty slow today. Hopefully you'll have a quiet night. How's Bill?"

"Good, thanks. What's going on with you?"

It was the same question all the time. Stop asking already, he wanted to tell her, but didn't want to hurt her feelings. Jenny was constantly on his back to find someone. She'd even tried signing him up for a gay on-line dating service but he refused even a free trial membership.

"Nothing much. Went for a good run yesterday so I feel more human again. I need to make sure I keep it up." Rafe didn't feel like telling her about his evening with Alex. Not that there was anything to tell. Alex was probably bored and needed someone to hang out with and Rafe was available. He was the type of guy who was nice when you saw him, but since he was nice to everyone, Rafe didn't take it past face value.

He was certain as soon as he left the apartment last night, Alex was on to bigger and better things, with someone more fun than Rafe. It was the kind of man Alex Stern was, life of the party, probably the most popular kid in school. A guy like himself wouldn't even be on Alex's radar if not for their tenuous connection through Josh.

Rafe remembered those kids from home. They'd always talk about the movies they'd seen together or whose house they were going to hang out at on the weekend. He'd spent his childhood on the sidelines and to his chagrin, he'd allowed himself to exist that way as an adult, using the animals as a shield against developing relationships.

Jenny planted herself in front of him and glared. "You are not going to spend another summer shuttling between your apartment and this clinic, doing nothing else. I won't let you. You live in New York City, for God's sake. Take advantage of what there is out there." Her face softened. "You're a young, good-looking guy with a successful business. Any man would be lucky to have you. I don't know why you don't see your self-worth."

He shrugged. "I have to work to make sure I can keep up the payments on the clinic. I have a loan for this place, you know that."

"I know. But we're busy here. People in this neighborhood treat their pets like their children. There's no shortage of customers." Jenny glanced over her shoulder and sighed. "And speaking of customers, I'd better get to the first patient before she howls the place down." She placed a gentle hand on his arm. "Promise me you'll think about what I said. Put yourself out there a little. It's not so scary."

It was scary as shit. Rafe gave her a faint smile but said nothing. Instead, he chose to do what he always did; changed into his running clothes and headed out the door to the park, where he could spend an hour losing himself inside his own head. Only now, what was in his head was the smiling face of Alex Stern.

Sleep eluded Rafe for much of that night. Though he'd suffered from mild insomnia through college and veterinary school, he hadn't been subjected to it lately, especially once he'd started running. Usually he was so tired he'd fall asleep on the sofa and drag himself off to bed at some point in the night.

But now at the ungodly hour of 4:30 a.m., Rafe looked out of his windows at the rooftops of the darkened city stretching out before him and thought about what Jenny had said. Was he merely going through the motions of life? He'd never learned to fit in, with his stutter and his disinterest in sports; both of which made him weird and different in his town. And though his parents never did anything to help him and frankly discouraged him at almost every turn, he couldn't let that bond collapse. He was there for the funeral when his father died and still sent his mother money once a month, despite never receiving a thank you from her.

Certainly by now, at over thirty years old he should be free from those tormented years of his youth. He could count on Jenny as a friend and Josh as well. Alex said he wanted to be friends, but Rafe would hold off on that, knowing what people say and actually do were almost always two different things.

He made himself some coffee. Perhaps Jenny was right, he mused, as the thought of another endless summer with nothing to do but work lay before him like a scorched wasteland. Sipping his hot coffee, Rafe shuffled through the mail that tended to pile up during the week. He came across a flyer for a gym opening up by the office. They boasted every state of the art piece of equipment and a running track that opened at five thirty in the morning.

Rafe checked his watch. Maybe this was it. A small step to be sure, but he could join the gym and it would be a place where he could run no matter the weather. Everyone would be so into their workouts he wouldn't have to talk much.

Without stopping to overanalyze it, Rafe packed a bag with workout clothes, showered and dressed in half an hour flat. The subway gods were in his favor and he was rocketing along to the Upper West Side in record time. For it only being 6 a.m., the streets were pretty crowded, but this was New York after all.

Rafe found the gym and took a few deep breaths before entering. A scruffy-faced, good-looking young man with a friendly smile sat at the front desk.

"Morning. How can I help you?"

Now that he was here Rafe hesitated. Then he thought of what Jenny had said; that he was a great guy and he deserved some happiness.

"I-I'd like to sign up." He blew out a sigh.

"Awesome." The guy took out a clipboard. "Fill this out and I'll get someone to show you around." He reached for the phone and spoke with someone. His gaze landed on Rafe's workout bag. "I see you came prepared to start right away. That's great."

A big, muscular guy walked through the door marked Employees Only. Normally Rafe would be intimidated by a man like that but he argued with himself that he had to start somewhere and he wasn't going to leave until he joined the gym.

"Hey, I'm Max. You're looking to join us?"

Rafe swallowed and nodded. "Y-yes." He ruthlessly thrust aside his fear. *Now or never.* "I want to join. I run and I'm looking for a track and maybe to use the equipment as well."

"Great. We have a great track here. Let's take a tour and we can talk while we walk." Max held the door open for Rafe and they passed through. Max chatted with him as they passed by the locker rooms, which were sparkling clean.

"We've only been here about a month so we aren't that busy now. Hopefully we'll get more people from the neighborhood." He indicated the bathroom. "There are showers in there, as well as a sauna and steam."

Rafe peeked inside and saw a few men sitting and relaxing on the cedar benches. "L-looks great."

"Do you live around here?" Max picked up a towel and slung it over his shoulder.

"N-no, I live in Brooklyn but my clinic is a few blocks away." Rafe hefted his gym bag on his shoulder as he followed Max out of the locker room and into the main part of the gym.

"Are you a doctor?"

"Veterinarian." Rafe scanned the floor, noting the equipment and the guys using it. He was happy to see this wasn't a gym for the overly muscle-bound or body-builder type. Everyone looked pretty average and seemed to be concentrating on their workouts. "I figured it would be g-good to come here before I opened my office or after work."

Max nodded. "Yeah. I live in Queens, but I bartend around

here at night and on the weekends."

Rafe didn't know what to say so he merely listened.

"So do you think you're interested in joining after seeing everything? You get a free personal training session when you sign up." Max had led him back to the front.

"Yeah, it looks great." For the first time in a while, Rafe was excited. This was breaking out of his routine as far as he was concerned. Plus, it would give him a place to go to, rather than sit at home all night, wondering what Alex was doing.

Or who, Rafe thought bitterly. The guy probably had people falling all over him. Rafe had spent years protecting his heart from hurt; he didn't need to expose himself to a man like Alex Stern.

He filled out all the credit card information and got his ID card. Excitement bubbled through his veins for the first time since he signed the loan agreement on his practice. Jenny was right. He was tired of being on the outside looking in.

The guy at the front desk waved goodbye to Rafe. His phone buzzed with an unfamiliar number.

Hey. It's Max from the gym. Here's the name and address of my bar. Stop by if you ever want a drink.

Rafe looked at the name. Cueballs. Huh. Interesting name. He saved the contact information, as he walked to his office. Patty arrived moments after he opened and the phones began ringing.

Before he looked up it was lunch time; his stomach growled and Rafe realized he hadn't even had his morning bagel.

Patty walked in. "Rafe, you've been working nonstop. Come have some lunch."

He pushed back the scrub cap from his forehead. "It's like every dog decided to eat something bad and throw up overnight."

Patty gave him a sympathetic smile. "Well, come on. I ordered you a salad from that place you like."

Rafe was touched. "Thank you, Patty. That was really sweet."

He joined her at the table behind the reception desk, grateful for the lull in patients. Patty told him it was hers and her boyfriend's one year anniversary and how when they first started dating she didn't really like him. Rafe listened carefully, interested in hearing the dynamics of a real relationship.

The overhead bells jingled and Rafe sighed. He was tired from lack of sleep and seeing so many animals this morning. He wished he could afford to hire another person, but he couldn't right now. He was lucky he could take on Jenny to keep the clinic open at night.

"Sit here for a few minutes and take a breather. You haven't been off your feet all morning and you look exhausted."

Rafe nodded and didn't even bother to see who'd come in and what animal they'd brought with them. A sauna and steam at the gym was sounding mighty good right about now.

"Hi. I'm here to see Rafe, if he has the time."

Like déjà vu. It was Alex again.

CHAPTER FIVE

Alex had nothing to do today except sleep. He'd been on surgery teams for three days straight and was tired to the core. Yet having a dog meant he couldn't stay in bed, so there he was, at seven thirty in the morning, out with Lucky walking the streets. He figured taking her to the park was beneficial to both of them, as she got her fresh air and a chance to meet other dogs and he got the exercise needed to kick-start his body for the day.

On the way back to the apartment he passed by the veterinary clinic Rafe owned. Alex was impressed at the business the man managed; it always seemed to be pretty busy the times he passed by.

A vision of the shy man flashed through his mind and not for the first time, Alex wondered what Rafe's story was. Something about that man sparked Alex's interest more than any other man he'd met in a long time and it wasn't only because of his pretty eyes and tight, lean body.

Alex narrowed his eyes in thought as he allowed Lucky to pull him down the block toward home. It was more than the physical that intrigued Alex. A cute face and a hot body wasn't enough to keep him interested, not in the long run at least. What he remembered was Rafe's endearingly shy smile and the slight, nervous stutter when he talked. The caring, gentle nature he exhibited with the animals reflected how he treated people. Alex was sure he'd never met a man like Rafe Hazelton and didn't know quite what to make of him. He'd been hanging out with Micah for so long, he wasn't used to nice and sweet.

On his way back home, he passed by the new gym that opened last month, Reps. It looked like a low key kind of place and he made a mental note to check it out when he didn't have the dog with him. It might do him good to join and get him out of his rut. He looked down at Lucky and she stared up at him with bright, eager eyes.

"Okay girl, let's go home and have some breakfast."

She barked and jumped up on him as they took off down the street. By the time they reached Micah and Josh's apartment, they were both winded and ready for a drink. Alex filled her bowl with fresh cold water and made himself a hot coffee.

Sipping his coffee on the sofa, he checked his phone and glanced again at the picture of Micah and Josh on the beach, their faces alight with happiness. Alex was thrilled for his best friend. With his giving heart and calm presence, Josh proved to be everything Micah had been looking for all his life.

People often wondered why he and Micah had never become lovers but it never occurred to Alex to think of the man as anything but his friend. There were some people who were simply meant to be your family, your blood, and you loved them as such. Those were the people who never disappointed you.

He understood Micah and was happy to be a shoulder to lean on when Micah's fucked-up life became too much for him to bear alone. And Alex knew Micah was so deep in his own darkness, he'd never notice Alex had his own demons to wrestle. Sometimes it paid to have a selfish friend. Alex had no desire to dig deep within and expose himself. He was happy to bury his feelings like Lucky would a bone.

His phone buzzed and he winced when he saw the name flash on the screen. *Fuck.* Every once in a while he'd get the odd call from home, Alex assumed, to check and see if he was still alive. The last time he and his parents talked, it was pretty obvious neither they, nor him, had anything left to say that wouldn't result in either tears or hurtful words that could never be taken back or forgotten.

"Alexander?"

His heart skipped a beat. "Father." After all this time he would have been less shocked if the Governor had called him, rather than his father. "What's wrong?"

"It's your mother."

An icy tendril of dread curled around Alex's spine. "Is she ill?" Though she'd withdrawn after Seth's death, Alex remembered his mother as carefree and happy, so unlike his stern and cold father.

"She's well, but very upset still. You know it will be fifteen years since Seth passed away."

Pain sliced through him. "Yes." Alex spoke through clenched teeth. "I'm aware of his date of death, like I remember our birthday. I miss him every day."

"So does your mother. So much so, she can barely get out of bed some days."

"Is she seeing a doctor?"

"I have the problem under control. You haven't made it easier you know, with your behavior."

Of course his father would find a way to blame his mother's problem on him. "How so? I haven't seen either of you in quite a while, if you recall."

"It's time for you to put aside this foolish career; no son of mine should be a failed medical student, prancing around as a nurse. I can pull some strings and get you back into medical school. Of course you'll probably have to repeat your first year—"

Alex began to laugh. "Have you finally gone insane? Because for you to call me up out of the blue and insult me must mean you've lost your fucking mind."

Even through the phone he heard his father's hiss of indrawn breath. "Now see here. You obviously could've been a doctor. Your brother would have wanted—"

"Don't tell me what he would've wanted. No one knew him

better than I did." He thought he had dried up inside years ago; sobbed all the tears out and drained every last bit of pain from his heart. But the wetness dripping down his face told another story.

"I was his father."

"He was my brother, my twin. The other beat of my heart." Alex choked. "He knew I loved him. I always loved him."

"Seth wouldn't have wanted you to be estranged from the family."

That at least was true. His brother was the peacemaker in the family, always intervening in the loud and almost violent clashes Alex consistently had with their father. The two of them would often talk late into the night about everything; it was to Seth Alex first revealed he was gay. And Seth had his own fears which Alex tried, but in the end couldn't help him with, no matter that he would've traded his own life to be able to change that.

"Seth would've wanted me to be happy. Not to follow some preconceived plan you set up for us before we were born and knew who we were." Alex closed his eyes and could hear his brother's voice as if he sat next to him, urging him, guiding him, always in Alex's soul. "Seth always told me to follow my heart."

"And you think wandering aimlessly through life, sleeping with men you meet in bars is what he meant?"

"I'm not aimless. I have a wonderful job, friends, a very fulfilling life. It's a pity you can't see it as such, in this day and age." He pictured his father as he last remembered him, blue eyes like his and Seth's, prematurely gray hair and a tall commanding presence.

"A wonderful job? You're a nurse. You were supposed to be a doctor, a surgeon like me."

"That was never my dream; you knew that. It was yours. I forced myself to be what you wanted but I wasn't Seth. I wasn't the one you wanted; I never was. I tried and thought maybe if I went to medical school like Seth was going to . . ." What the hell was he doing? As much as he didn't want to, Alex couldn't help but seek his father's approval, even after all these years. "You should see how well the patients respond to me. The doctors all want me. I'm on the top surgical team at the hospital."

"But not as a doctor. As a nurse."

Alex pictured his mouth thinned to a tight line, spitting out those words as if they were pieces of rotten fruit.

"You might as well wear a sign that says you're gay."

"Oh, we don't wear signs anymore, don't you know? We all wear buttons now. Pink, sparkly rainbow buttons. With purple unicorns. It's how we gays identify each other in a crowd."

"You and that smart-ass mouth of yours always got you into trouble from when you were a child. This isn't what I worked so hard for all my life. You, a nurse and gay, never to have a home or a family. And Seth—"

"Don't." Alex rasped out, unable to keep the pain out of his voice. "Stop throwing him in my face. I know I could never measure up to him. Don't mention his name to me ever again." He clicked off and threw the phone to the opposite side of the sofa. Lucky jumped up and put her muzzle in his lap, as if sensing his upset. Alex stroked her soft fur, his heart slowly settling down, but still broken beyond repair.

Unable to face getting up and doing anything productive anymore, he pulled the blanket down from the back of the sofa and wrapped himself up in its soft warmth. For the rest of the morning it was just him and Lucky, who, sensing his sadness, barely left his side. Now he knew why Micah was so attached to her. She'd become his friend, in whose willing ear he whispered all his private pain. There was no judgment in her adoring eyes, only simple trust and love.

Funny how in the end, Micah was the one who had it all; the love of a wonderful man and this sweet dog. Alex, the one everyone loved and who loved everyone, had nothing; no one to turn to for solace when he needed to be held.

As the light shifted through the apartment, Alex realized it was time to take Lucky out for a walk. He grabbed one of the little bags of treats he'd made for Lucky for their walks and a bagel for himself, and they left the apartment. The sun beamed down, surprisingly warm for this early in June and Alex, after finishing the bagel, decided he deserved some ice cream.

There was a frozen yogurt truck parked on the corner. He ordered one for himself and on the spur of the moment, he ordered an extra one, figuring he'd stop in on Rafe and surprise him.

Who wouldn't like a surprise fro-yo in the middle of the day?

Juggling the bag with both his and Rafe's yogurt, and Lucky's leash, Alex slipped his sunglasses over his eyes and headed down the block toward Rafe's clinic. He held the door open to allow a man with a meowing cat in a carrier to exit.

He immediately spotted Rafe behind the reception desk eating a salad. Perfect timing for dessert. The curve of Rafe's back accentuated the breadth of his shoulders and the sun hit the chestnut waves of his hair, burnishing it gold. But Alex looked beyond the purely physical, sensing both tension and exhaustion radiating off Rafe's body.

Damn, he looks worn out. Poor guy.

"Can I help you, sir?" The receptionist approached him with a smile and an eye for Lucky.

"I'm here to see Rafe, if he has a moment."

Before the woman had a chance to respond, Rafe's head snapped up and he spun around on his chair.

"A-Alex? Wh-what are you doing here?"

CHAPTER SIX

With a critical eye, Rafe studied Alex and frowned. Though they hadn't spent much time together, Rafe prided himself on seeing beyond the face most people presented to the world; perhaps it stemmed from spending so much of his life with animals. They didn't have the capacity to speak and tell him where their pain was, what hurt inside.

Over the years he learned to look for signs, those little indications that pointed to what dangers hid inside. There might be a ripple of the skin, a tensing of the muscles or that certain pinched look about the eyes that spoke of an inner turmoil not easily discovered by the naked eye. When animals hurt, they often hid away to suffer in silence, fearful of exposure.

People were different. Some people's faces mirrored their every emotion; they couldn't hide their pain and their hearts were an open book. Alex wore his dark, aviator sunglasses like a shield. Rafe's eyes couldn't penetrate their blackness to see into those blue, blue depths, but from the tight lines around Alex's mouth and the white knuckled grasp of Lucky's leash, Alex's emotions were clearly visible to Rafe, if no one else.

"Hey, I was in the neighborhood and brought you a treat."

It was then Rafe noticed the white bag in Alex's hand.

"You brought me something?" Rafe couldn't fathom it.

"Yep." Alex held up the bag. "I wanted a fro-yo and since you're right near here and it's lunch time, why not?" He looked over his shoulder. "You're not busy are you? Otherwise this is gonna melt."

Rafe caught Patty's delighted smile and gave her a weak grin. "Um, I d-don't think s-so, right, P-Patty?"

Shit. Why was he stumbling and stuttering worse than ever? He shouldn't be nervous around Alex. He'd already had a serious discussion with his head about the stupid feelings he had for Alex. Feelings Rafe knew would never be reciprocated; after all, Alex had never given him any indication he was interested in a relationship with anyone, never mind Rafe.

And, Rafe continued to argue with himself, he was an over-thirty-year-old man; too old for silly schoolboy crushes, especially one that had lasted almost a year. He and Alex would be friends, and friends hung out and had dinners and stopped by to say hello at work.

"Of course not, Rafe. Go on. You can relax in your office for a while." Patty smiled, suspiciously wide and bright, and Rafe knew what she was thinking. He planned to set her straight later on, after Alex had left.

"Come on back, Alex. You can bring Lucky. I have some treats in my office."

True to form, Lucky barked at the word treats. She was a far cry from the scraggly stray Josh had found tied to a trash can one cold night over a year ago. Rafe noted her shiny coat and bright eyes and was happy to see Alex had been taking good care of her.

They sat down at the small round table he'd set up in the corner of his office. There was a plastic treat container shaped like a fire hydrant on his desk and Rafe gave Lucky two and a chew stick to occupy herself with. She settled down in the corner, gnawing the stick with obvious pleasure.

In the meantime, Alex had taken out the two containers of frozen yogurt, napkins and bright pink spoons and set one before Rafe and the other in front of him, yet he made no move to open the lid. Rafe sat quietly, observing the tense line of Alex's jaw. He'd learned over the years a person will talk when they want and no sooner.

But Alex didn't speak. He removed his sunglasses, took the top off the container and began to eat. Rafe, used to silence, followed suit and soon the two of them had finished their yogurt and sat with the empty Styrofoam containers in front of them. Still, Alex said nothing and now stared into his empty dish, his jaw flexing so tight Rafe expected to hear teeth cracking. Even for him, the quiet was unnerving.

"Alex, w-why did you c-come here?" Rafe swallowed down his nerves. "I m-mean it obviously wasn't to t-talk."

Watching Alex's fingers toy with the plastic spoon, Rafe imagined those strong, sure hands moving over his body, touching him, grasping him. His mouth dried and he grabbed a water bottle from his desk and took a long drink. He couldn't remember the last time he had an erotic fantasy, especially in the middle of the day.

Alex's fingers stilled from playing with the spoon. "Did you ever wonder why things happen sometimes and if they hadn't, how different your life might have turned out?"

The conversation was not what Rafe had anticipated. This was a side he'd never seen of the free-spirited, happy-go-lucky Alex Stern. In fact, Rafe never imagined Alex as anything but lighthearted; always quick with the jokes and smiles. Maybe he'd been too quick to judge the man. Perhaps the smile was a mask to hide the true man underneath.

Rafe thought for a few moments, choosing his words carefully, not only because he wanted to minimize the stuttering, but because he wanted Alex to know how seriously Rafe took his question. "*If only* may be the two saddest words in the English language, you know? We all question fate sometimes, imagining how we might be happier if only we didn't do that act that led to something bad happening. Or how much happier we'd be, if only we were rich or thin."

Alex sighed and lifted his gaze from the study of his empty yogurt cup and Rafe was struck dumb by the vacant and devastated look in his eyes, their usual bright blue dimmed to an almost muddy gray. Red streaked the normally bright white, almost as if he'd been crying. Rafe wondered what a man like Alex Stern, a man who Rafe couldn't remember ever seeing without a smile on his face, could have to regret? He seemed like the man who had everything.

Rafe couldn't help himself. "W-what do you have to regret? You have friends, a gr-great job." A bitter laugh escaped. "Y-you have everyth-thing."

And Rafe meanwhile continued to fumble his words, tongue-tied and embarrassed. What was it about this man that made him feel like such an idiot? For years now, he'd gotten his stuttering under control, or so he thought. As soon as Alex Stern entered his life however, Rafe unraveled.

A sad smile touched Alex's lips even as a muscle jumped in the smoothness of his cheek. "No one has everything. Some are better at pretending than others."

"Is that what you do? Pr-pretend?"

Alex countered, "Don't we all?"

That comment caught Rafe up short. Instead of answering right away, he busied himself with taking away the empty cups and spoons and tossing them into the trash. Lucky thumped her tail as he walked by, giving him a side-eyed look. He knelt down and scratched her ears and she licked his hand.

Familiar peace settled through Rafe as he continued to pet Lucky. "N-no. I don't pretend. I know who I am and what people think of me. I've always known."

He didn't dare look at Alex; he knew what he'd see. Rafe had been aware of those pitying looks for most of his life. It had stopped bothering him in college and later on, as he mastered his speech impediment, it became a virtual nonissue.

To his shock, Alex knelt down next to him and also stroked Lucky. Not trusting himself to meet Alex's gaze, Rafe kept his eyes lowered, concentrating on Lucky. He should've known, however, that Alex wouldn't be satisfied with the answer Rafe had given him.

"Hey, look at me."

Rafe waited a heartbeat then met Alex's unsmiling face. It was a face that, surprisingly to him, showed strength and compassion, instead of the usual careless laughter. There was no pity in his beautiful eyes but rather an understanding, somehow, of what Rafe felt inside.

Unfortunately for Rafe, what he felt inside chose at that moment to send sparks singing up and down his spine, flooding his long-neglected libido with desire. Angry that he exposed himself so openly, Rafe blinked furiously, hoping Alex wouldn't notice his longing, or smell the heat coming off his body.

"I see a great guy; friendly, concerned with his job, the animals he takes care of and the people in his life."

Rafe swallowed hard. Of course. The superficial stuff. What you might say about anyone you've met a few times. But then again, what could he expect, when he rarely allowed himself to get close to anyone. The problem was he didn't know how. He grew up surrounded by so much silence, people often forgot he was even there.

Taking the time to get to know someone beyond the hello smiles and how's it going took effort; a give and take. Rafe had never had a problem giving. The issue was finding someone who wanted to take what he was offering. Alex seemed real and honest, like he actually gave a damn.

And though he'd been burned before, Rafe still clung to the belief that people were inherently good. That kindness existed without an ultimate expectation of payback.

"Yeah, that's me. Everyone's friend, right?" His laugh sounded shaky even to him, the nearness of Alex overwhelming and so desirable.

"There's nothing wrong with being a good person."

"N-nice guys finish last, h-haven't you heard?" Rafe stood and reached for a tissue to clean his glasses.

"I think that old adage has worn out its welcome, don't you? I never saw the appeal of anyone being an arrogant fuck." Alex stood as well and stretched. Rafe eyed the defined muscles in Alex's back, and imagined how those strong arms would feel wrapped around him. His blood beat a bit faster and hotter and he quickly sat down behind his desk to hide his arousal. What Alex said puzzled him.

"Can I ask y-you a qu-question?" God damn, would he ever stop stuttering around this man. Rafe vowed to redouble his breathing exercises starting that night.

"Sure."

Lucky shook herself, the tags around her neck jingling. Alex snapped her leash back on, preparing to leave.

"How are you friends with someone like Micah? I mean not to insult him, but even you admitted he was not always the nicest person."

Alex hesitated then shrugged. "The Micah you've met, the man who's snappish and short-tempered isn't who he really is. I've known him for almost fifteen years and Micah is a much more complicated person than you could possibly know from the few times you've met him."

"I g-guess it all goes back to sh-showing the w-world who you really are."

"Do any of us do that?"

Round and round they went again, back to the beginning of this conversation and Rafe realized Alex was very good at dodging questions he didn't want to answer.

"Well," Rafe pushed back the hair off his forehead, "I have to get back to work. Th-thanks for stopping by. And thanks for the frozen yogurt." He opened the door to his office.

"No problem."

Rafe held the door open and Alex passed by him with Lucky on her leash. Before he walked any further down the hall, Alex stopped.

"What're you doing tonight, after work?"

Rafe was taken aback. Suddenly the world was in an alternate universe, where guys like Alex wanted to spend time with guys like him.

"Um. I j-just joined the new gym up the b-block. I was going to go there and run." There. He made it through with hardly any stumbling.

Alex's eyes brightened. "Cool. I passed by there this morning and thought about joining. How about I pick you up when you get off work and we go together?"

They were walking down the hallway when a thought struck Rafe. "You must miss Micah a lot, huh?" That had to be the reason Alex was hanging out with him.

"Well, I mean we talk still, 'cause he has to check on his baby here." He glanced down at Lucky who had her eye on a dog sitting in the waiting room. "And to tell you the truth, I'd started easing myself out of his life, once Josh came into the picture. No one likes to be a third wheel, you know?"

In the half hour they'd shared together, the haunted look had disappeared from Alex's eyes and he'd reverted back to his playful, happy nature.

"Yeah, I know what you mean."

"Besides, you owe me." Alex leaned on the reception desk.

"I owe you?"

"Yeah." Alex cocked a blond brow and a jolt of lust surged through Rafe.

I'd like to kiss him. Just one time to know what he tastes like.

"You insulted my hand to mouth coordination. For that you must pay a penalty of my choosing."

Pretending disgust, Rafe turned his back on Alex, even as his pulse raced. "If I m-must."

"Great. I'll see you at five thirty then. That's when you get off, right?"

Rafe nodded.

"Bring your A-game. Prepare to bow to my inherent greatness." With a wink and a smile, Alex left, sucking all the life out of the room.

"Wow, he's gorgeous."

Rafe hadn't realized Patty stood next to him. "Pretty much."

"Do you like him?"

"He's nice. We're friendly."

"That's not what I asked, Rafe." She grinned at him. "You do like him, don't you?"

"Who's my next patient? Is it the cat or the dog?"

Exasperated, since she knew she'd get nothing further from him, Patty pointed to the woman with her little dog. "It's Peaches. She's got the runs."

Charming. "Okay," he sighed. "Bring her in and I'll get the rubber gloves."

CHAPTER SEVEN

"You're going where, tonight? And with who?" Even over the phone and from three thousand miles away, Alex could hear the shock in Micah's voice.

"Whom, Micah. I know you're a doctor and didn't take many English courses in college, but try not to sound illiterate." Alex lay on the sofa watching *The Food Network* and tossing a ball for Lucky.

A heavy sigh escaped in his ear. "You know they say that absence makes the heart grow fonder, but not in your case."

"Micah, Micah. You know you love me." Alex proceeded to make kissy noises into the phone. The show ended and he realized he'd be late for meeting Rafe if he didn't haul his ass up and out of the apartment. "Listen, I have to go."

"Why? It's not like you have a hot date or anything?" Micah laughed.

A small dart of annoyance shot through him. "Why? Is that so impossible for you to imagine?"

"Yeah, it is. You've never been serious about anything, except your job, and if Josh and marriage has taught me anything, it's that a relationship is hard work."

Micah's words stung more than Alex thought possible. Did people really think he was that shallow? "Fuck you."

"Jesus, what's got your balls in a knot?"

Alex could hear someone in the background and then Josh

came on the phone. "Alex, how's it going?"

Irritated, Alex didn't bother to hide the annoyance in his voice. "I'm fine but tell your husband he's getting on my nerves."

"What did he do now?"

Josh was a good guy and not for the first time Alex wondered how the easy-going man put up with Micah. "Nothing different than usual."

"Talk to me, come on." Josh's soft voice coaxed Alex's bad temper down a notch.

"Do you think I have no depth, that I'm shallow?" It was imperative for Alex to hear what Josh thought of him. Josh was nice, and hadn't known Alex for years, so he didn't have any long-standing, preconceived opinions of him.

"What brought this on?" asked Josh.

"Your husband couldn't believe I might have a date," Alex huffed. Even he could hear the petulant tone in his own voice. Christ, he sounded like a high school kid.

"You have a date?" Josh's voice rose in excitement. "Who is it?"

"It's not a date; Rafe and I, we've been hanging out lately, but I'm asking what *if* I had a date? Could you believe it or is it so preposterous?"

"Of course it's not, and Micah doesn't think so either. Nothing would make us happier than to see you fall in love."

Whoa. "Uh, no one mentioned love. I'm only talking about a date."

Josh, however, was now on autopilot and had marriage on the brain. "It's time for you to meet someone who'll see you for the wonderful man you are. You've never fooled me, you know. Rafe is a wonderful guy, and very lonely. I don't know why I didn't think of the two of you before. You're perfect together."

That's the problem with some people. Once they were in love they thought they had to match everyone else up in their world. "You're watching *The Bachelor* again, aren't you? Your grandmothers have you hooked on that show."

"There's nothing wrong with finding love. You have to open

your heart up to accept it, that's all."

Time to shut this conversation down. "Look, I have to meet Rafe in a few minutes." He checked his watch. "Crap, I'm late. I'll talk to you guys tomorrow. Don't worry, Lucky's doing great." He clicked off and immediately sent a text to Rafe.

Hey. Sorry. Running late. Be there in a few.

He got a text back in a few minutes.

I left already. Figured you got busy and forgot.

That stung. Granted he was fifteen minutes late, but Rafe should've called him to find out where he was. Alex grabbed a tee shirt, shorts, and shoved his keys and wallet in his pocket then headed out the door. Why would Rafe think he'd forgotten? They made plans and Alex always remembered his plans.

The sidewalks were crowded with people leaving work, but he dodged around everyone, and made it to the gym less than ten minutes after leaving the apartment. Alex remembered he wasn't yet a member and spent twenty minutes filling out the requisite paperwork to sign up. He headed to the locker rooms to change and stowed everything away, except for his phone. Figuring Rafe was already running and wouldn't see or hear his text, Alex decided to get in his own workout and warmed up by running on the treadmill for about half an hour, then did some lifting.

The gym was surprisingly empty; only a few women on the treadmill and one other guy in the weight room with him. Maybe it was because the gym was so new. Alex enjoyed having the space almost to himself, and not having to wait for a machine was a bonus.

His body humming pleasantly with the increased endorphins from his activity, Alex re-entered the locker room, intending to take a shower. He rounded the corner and picked up a towel. When he turned around he came face to face with a very hot and sweaty Rafe.

God damn. The man's shirt was damp, his skin pink and glowing from his exertion. His reddish-brown hair was plastered in wet curls to his head, and his chest heaved from his run.

No man had ever looked as desirable to Alex and he couldn't help himself.

Alex slid his hand around the nape of Rafe's neck, his fingers sliding through the curling tendrils of Rafe's hair, as he pulled the man into his chest. Rafe tipped his head back, his eyes dark and wide as they searched Alex's face.

"What are you doing?" Rafe licked his lips and another bolt of want shot through Alex as he followed the trail of Rafe's pink tongue.

"Damned if I know," Alex muttered, then lowered his mouth to Rafe's. Soft and warm, Alex couldn't remember ever feeling lips so velvety plush and full against his own. Rafe gave a muffled squeak, then melted into Alex's arms, returning the kiss with an intensity that surprised then excited Alex. Uncaring that they were out in the open area of the locker room where anyone could walk in on them, Alex sucked on Rafe's plump lower lip, before sliding his tongue into the warm, accepting cavern of Rafe's mouth, where it met with the hesitant, then increasingly strong thrust of Rafe's tongue. Alex sighed with longing from the firestorm exploding in his bloodstream.

The unexpected hunger surging through him threw Alex off balance, but he couldn't control the need to feel Rafe beneath him. Alex shoved Rafe backward up against the wall, covering Rafe's body with his own. Through the fog of lust swirling in his brain, Alex pushed up against the hard thrust of Rafe's erection, rubbing against the thin material of Rafe's shorts. Rafe groaned, his hot breath gusting past Alex's ear.

Thank God he wants this, wants me too. Alex took Rafe's face between his hands and teased his nose up against Rafe's before gently kissing his mouth, not bothering to question the unexpected tenderness stealing through him. He trailed his fingers along the line of Rafe's upper lip, tracing the sweet curve of his cheeks, before finally cradling Rafe's jaw with the palm of his hand and planting tiny kisses on Rafe's cheeks and trembling lips. Rafe moaned and molded his body up against Alex's, burying his face in the nape of Alex's neck. Alex was surprised to feel Rafe's body shaking in his arms and pulled him to his chest, soaking up his warmth.

They stayed like that, simply hugging, before Rafe took a deep breath and pushed away from Alex, his brown eyes sparkling with golden lights.

"Wh-what was th-that?"

Alex hated hearing Rafe sound so nervous and unsure, as if he questioned Alex's motives.

"That was me, kissing you." Alex nuzzled Rafe's neck now, inhaling the man's warm, soft scent. No matter they were both sweaty from their workouts, Alex could have stayed like that for hours; holding Rafe, feeling the play of his long corded muscles beneath his fingers, tasting the saltiness of Rafe's skin on his lips.

"Why?"

"Are you serious?" Alex grabbed Rafe's hand, half dragging him into the bathroom where they faced a full wall of mirrors. "Look at you." He placed his hands on Rafe's hips, aching to slide his arms around Rafe's waist and hold him close again.

But Rafe remained unyielding, his face creased in confusion. "I don't understand."

Alex pushed aside the hair at Rafe's nape and pressed his mouth against the soft skin there. Rafe trembled but Alex held him firm, continuing to nibble and nip at Rafe's neck.

"You're gorgeous." Alex kissed Rafe's shoulder. "Sexy." He kissed Rafe again, this time yanking him tight against him, wanting Rafe to feel the heaviness of Alex's cock against his ass.

"Do you feel that, baby? That's because of you. That's all you need to know." Alex flexed his hips, thrusting against Rafe, loving the heavy-lidded, glazed look that entered Rafe's eyes.

Sounds of people entering the locker room filtered through to where he and Rafe stood, and with regret, Alex pressed a final kiss to Rafe's head, and stepped away from him. Immediately, he missed the heat of Rafe's warm and yielding body.

Rafe shot him a troubled look from beneath lowered lashes and without a word, snagged a towel from the pile on the bench and entered the showers. From the corner of his eye, Alex watched as Rafe touched his lips with the tips of his fingers, his head bowed as if a great weight rested on his shoulders.

I didn't do anything wrong. At least he thought he didn't. He'd sensed an attraction between him and Rafe for a while now, sparks zinging between the two of them whenever they were together. Alex had simply made the first move, since he knew Rafe, shy as he was, wouldn't do it.

Always one to act on his impulses, Alex hadn't stopped to think whether Rafe would welcome his kisses and touches. Did he come on too strong, or read Rafe completely wrong? Maybe he only wanted to be friends and not friends with benefits.

Alex grabbed a towel of his own and entered a shower stall where he quickly washed away the sweat of his workout, hoping Rafe wouldn't leave before they had a chance to talk. With the towel barely holding up around his waist, Alex sped back into the locker room where his breath caught in his throat at the sight of Rafe sitting on the bench in front of the row of lockers. Like Alex, he wore only a towel draped around his slim hips and Alex noted his sinewy frame and the lean muscles of his arms. His chest was covered in swirls of light brown hair and Alex could just make out the rosy nubs of his nipples poking through.

"Hey."

At the sound of Alex's voice Rafe looked up to meet his gaze. A gnaw of anxiety grew within Alex at the doubt in Rafe's eyes.

"Hi." Rafe answered, licking his lips.

Alex cock hardened watching Rafe's tongue and he tore his gaze away before he did something stupid like kiss Rafe again, or rip off the man's towel and drop to his knees to swallow him down.

Fuck.

"Uh, so anyway, we're still on for dinner, right?" Alex secured his towel around his waist and nodded to the guy who walked by, who had spotted him earlier in the weight room.

"I-I d-don't know." Rafe fiddled with his lock, turning the dial until it sprang open. He pulled open the locker door and removed his gym bag. Without looking at Alex, he pulled his shirt over his head.

"Seriously?" It was suddenly imperative for Alex to look Rafe in the eye and have a heart to heart with him about what might be happening between the two of them. "Come on, man, don't be like that. It's only a dinner."

"Only a d-dinner, only a kiss. N-nothing is ever serious and imp-portant to you, is it?" Rafe's furious whisper hurt more than Alex ever imagined. Certainly more than the teasing words from Micah several hours earlier which had angered Alex.

"That's not true. I only meant that we aren't deciding world peace or anything. We're two friends, having a burger and maybe hanging out."

"It's all changed now though. You don't kiss all your friends." Rafe bit his full lower lip and shot Alex a side-eyed glance. "Well, maybe you do, but I don't."

"I don't either. You should know that by now."

"I d-don't know anything about you, really, other than you're fr-friends with M-Micah and Josh and wh-where you work." After some hesitation, Rafe slipped on his boxers and pulled on his jeans, buttoning them up.

"Not much to know. I'm a pretty simple person." Though sad to see Rafe's body covered once again, it allowed Alex to concentrate more on their conversation. "Do you want me to say I'm sorry for kissing you?" Alex glanced around and dropped his voice as more people began entering the locker room. "Would that make you feel better?" He didn't feel sorry, not in the least. In fact, Alex wanted nothing more than to keep kissing Rafe's pink, full lips and feel his skin ripple beneath his fingers.

Rafe slid around on the bench so they faced each other. "I w-want you to be truthful with m-me. I'm n-not the k-kind of guy s-someone l-like you goes for."

A cold chill wrapped around Alex's heart. "Someone like me? What do you mean?" He dropped his towel and stood stark naked as he opened his locker. When he turned around he saw Rafe's wide-eyed gaze, his cheeks stained red.

"Oh yeah. This. This is me. I stand naked in a locker room

with my cock hanging out. If that embarrasses you, I'll say I'm sorry for that." He slipped on a tee shirt that said "Nurses do it with Care."

"I m-meant everyone likes you. You're fun and good-looking. Always happy. Nothing bothers you." Rafe fiddled with the straps of his gym bag. "I'm too quiet, shy even. The one who overanalyzes everything. We're polar opposites."

That's what comes from playing your part too well. Sometimes the people you wish could see the real you believed the façade. Alex had hoped Rafe was different, but that was the thing about walls. You do such a good job building them so strong and tall no one can breach them, even if you want them to tumble and fall. You don't know how to create that chink in the armor you live inside.

"Right. I'm the good times guy. But that has nothing to do with me kissing you. Or wanting to kiss you again." He reached for Rafe, but the man drew back with a shake of his head.

"I d-don't believe in h-hooking up for the sake of sex. I can g-get that with my h-hand. I don't understand how you can separate the two. And as for us? I'm sure I'm not your t-type."

It had been so long since Alex had met a man who didn't simply want to get laid, he was at a loss to answer at first. He needed that white-hot blast of sensation to sear away the sticky mess of emotions that cluttered up his mind. When life became too much, Alex knew finding some random guy could make him forget, wipe away all the problems he couldn't face. At least for a little while, before the mind games came back to the playground of his mind, remaining one step ahead in the never-ending game of catch me if you can.

Sex for the sake of having sex. It had always worked before; why did Rafe have to make it so difficult?

"I don't know that I even have a type, like you say. But I enjoy spending time with you. Don't you miss the companionship, the touching?" He'd liked kissing Rafe, and Alex knew he'd like to be touched in return.

Rafe shrugged and averted his eyes. "You don't m-miss

wh-what you never had, right? M-my parents were undemonstrative, and I d-didn't really have m-many friends gr-growing up."

"What about boyfriends, sex?" Now Alex's curiosity was peaked. "You had to have had some experience. You're a great kisser."

Rafe's cheeks grew pink and he ducked his head. "Um. There's been a few." He glanced around at the other men at their lockers in various stages of undress and his eyes met Alex's in a mute appeal before skittering away to stare at the floor.

The guy was fucking adorable. "Come on." Alex swiftly finished dressing. "Let's continue this with a big burger and fries. I'm starving." He hefted his gym bag over his shoulder.

"That kind of defeats the purpose of our workouts, don't you think?" Rafe chuckled as he laced up his sneakers then grabbed his bag and brushed by Alex on his way out the door.

Alex inhaled the fresh soapy scent of Rafe and already missed their raw and sweaty embrace from before. "I figured we've already worked off our calories and can enjoy ourselves tonight." He peered at Rafe through his wet hair and gave a winning smile. "Please?"

Shaking his head, Rafe laughed and gave him a crooked smile. "You're imp-possible."

The taste and feel of Rafe's soft and yielding mouth remained on Alex's tongue; Rafe's warm scent rested inside his body, beating through his veins. Alex wanted to hear more about Rafe's childhood and maybe understand more about the man who'd wormed his way under Alex's skin like no one ever had before. It hurt Alex to think Rafe only knew him as a man without a serious side; someone who Rafe thought would screw him and simply walk away. If it was true, Alex had only himself to blame, as he played his part too well. He couldn't be mad at Rafe, if those were the only signals he was sending out.

It would be best to keep his distance like he always did. But even as he thought that, Alex wanted nothing more than to curl his fingers into Rafe's shirt and tug him close, and listen to the soft, needy sounds Rafe made as Alex kissed him. Time and time again, Alex had joked with Micah and told him how he had no desire for a relationship or a steady man in his life. Aside from Micah, who came as close to being a brother as Alex had allowed, he'd loved only one person in his life and Seth had died, leaving Alex bereft, broken and almost unable to go on.

"I've been called worse. Let's go then." He breezed past Rafe and out into the early evening of the city, leaving Rafe to hurry after him. If Rafe thought Alex was a player, who was he to disappoint?

CHAPTER EIGHT

The cool June evening air failed to register against Rafe's heated cheeks as he trailed behind Alex. The unexpected kiss they'd shared earlier set his body buzzing with a combination of wonder, desire, fear and longing. Even as he hurried to keep pace with Alex's angry strides, Rafe struggled to keep from grabbing onto the man's arm, forcing him to stop and continue the conversation they'd started in the gym in the middle of the street.

But Rafe had made a mistake; a stupid one that had hurt Alex. He could tell by the brittleness of Alex's smile and how his blue eyes, which only moments before had been filled with unexpected sweetness, shuttered down, becoming distant and cold. He'd done exactly what he'd accused others of doing to him: judging a person based on a preconceived idea, without any basis in fact. That was foolish and inconsiderate beyond belief, considering how he'd suffered all his life from people making snap judgments about him, simply because of his stutter and his shyness.

Shame burned through him and Rafe knew it would never be right again between the two of them unless he apologized and cleared the air. He, more than anyone else, should realize people aren't always who they show to the world.

"Hey, wait up. C-come on."

His strides slowed a bit, but Alex didn't speak or turn his head to look Rafe's way.

Rafe reached Alex's side and touched his arm lightly. "Alex, I'm sorry."

Alex faced him then, startling Rafe with the blaze of emotion in his normally laughing blue eyes. "You keep saying I am a type, and I have a type. Why don't you tell me what that is? For someone who claims he barely knows me, you seem to have me all figured out." He gestured impatiently to the pub they stood in front of. "Let's go here. They have good burgers."

Following Alex silently, Rafe practiced his breathing, desperate to not stutter any more in front of Alex when he spoke. By the time they'd been seated in a large wood paneled booth, he thought he had himself under control.

But Alex had his own agenda it seemed and that didn't include talking, at least not right away. The menu hid his face, and even though he'd said he wanted a burger, he seemed to be reading every damn word, cover to cover and memorizing it.

Rafe was used to dealing with animals and knew his patience would be rewarded eventually, if he took the time and didn't press for answers. Like the pets he treated, Alex tended to turn all growly and defensive when he was upset or annoyed.

"I thought you wanted a burger."

A few beats of silence passed. "I'm picking out my toppings."

The petulance in Alex's voice made Rafe smile. "I like mushrooms, myself."

"Hmm."

The waiter approached and Rafe ordered a burger with sautéed mushrooms and beer battered fries, and a Brooklyn lager.

"And for you, sir?" The waiter stood with his pad and pen poised for Alex to give his order.

Finally, Alex lowered the menu. "I'll have the same and a Corona."

The minute the waiter disappeared, Alex took out his phone and Rafe grew annoyed.

"You can be m-mad at me b-but that's rude."

One thing Rafe hadn't counted on from Alex was silence. In all their past encounters, Alex had been boisterous, lively and the one to try and make everyone happy. Rafe likened him to a big Golden Retriever puppy, bouncing from person to person, happy and loving everyone, expecting to be loved in return.

Without a word, Alex slipped the phone back into his pants and braced his elbows on the table, cradling his chin in his hands. "Sorry."

Truthfully, Alex didn't sound sorry at all. He sounded sullen and Rafe winced, knowing he was the cause of Alex's upset. The blue eyes staring back at him were clouded with pain. For Alex to be this unhappy with Rafe's comment that he wasn't his type, had Rafe wondering what really was going on inside of Alex that he didn't want people to know about.

It was what drew Rafe to study to be a veterinarian; an instinctual cognizance of the internal feelings of the animal, since it couldn't speak and tell anyone what was wrong. It was up to him, as the doctor, to ferret out the diagnosis and information necessary to relieve whatever pain the animal was feeling.

The longer the two of them sat in this booth staring at each other without speaking, the more Rafe became convinced that Alex was suffering. He'd bet his life there was a side to Alex he'd never shown anyone, not even his best friend Micah, and Rafe itched to discover the Alex Stern nobody knew. Like a wounded animal, Alex became extra protective of himself, retreating when he was hurt, becoming snappish even when those around him might only want to help and alleviate his pain.

Through his years of practice and experience, Rafe had learned to help and comfort, to step in when his expertise was needed, and step away when there was no hope left at all. What Alex didn't know was that Rafe always held out hope for life, and though he might give the appearance of a man ruled by quiet and calm, in truth he was tenacious as a bulldog and refused to accept defeat.

So Rafe allowed Alex to sit in his moody silence until their beers came and they both took long, bracing swallows.

"Can I speak now?"

Alex shrugged. "Suit yourself." That offhand comment led Rafe to believe Alex didn't expect much from people or life in general. Perhaps he too had been disappointed by the people who should have always been there for him and weren't.

"All my life I've been told I was different and that kids wouldn't like me because of my stutter. When I realized I was gay, I knew my struggle only increased ten-fold. It made me retreat even more."

Alex traced the lip of his beer bottle with his finger. "Yeah. I can understand that to an extent."

"That's my point. You can understand it to an extent, but not really. I'm not saying this in a spiteful way." It was so important to Rafe to make Alex understand where he was coming from. "You're a big, good-looking man with a great personality. Everywhere you go, you make friends so easily; people gravitate to you naturally. It's a gift, if you think about it."

"I have many gifts," said Alex with a wink and smiled for the first time since they sat down. Rafe wasn't fooled.

"You're deflecting," he stated, and like Rafe knew he would, Alex stopped smiling, his mouth thinning to a tight line. "Don't get angry with me."

"I'm not. I'm only wondering when you decided to appoint yourself as my therapist."

Rafe pinned Alex with a stare and a raised brow. "When someone sticks their tongue down my throat, it's a signal to me that maybe we've gone beyond a handshake and a 'Hi, how are you.'"

Alex stared at him for a moment, then his eyes creased with amusement and he started to laugh. He didn't stop, even when the waiter arrived with their food.

Rafe folded his arms and glared. "I'm not finished. You make friends easily but it's all on the surface, isn't it? I bet people don't ever really get to know the real you, do they?"

Once again, Alex stopped laughing, only this time it seemed he'd had enough. "I don't have to listen to this shit." He looked around for the waiter. "I'll get my food to go."

"That's what you always do, don't you. Instead of talking about things, you make a joke or run away. It's easier to run away."

As Rafe spoke, Alex's face grew dark with anger. Now that he'd started talking, Rafe couldn't stop; the words spilled like water rushing from a dam.

"I know what it's like. My reason is obvious. I spent almost my whole life hiding behind a wall of silence. But what reason do you have to play the class clown all the time? People would like you no matter what."

For a moment Alex stared at him, then smiled a real smile, the first all night. It kindled a glow in his deep blue eyes.

"Do you realize something?" He leaned forward and Rafe swore he could feel the warmth radiating from Alex's body across the table.

Caught up in the moment, Rafe couldn't look away. The sounds of the pub faded in the background, including the music, which unfortunately had gone from '80s retro to modern day rap. "Wha-what?" His mouth tasted dry even with the beer he'd drunk.

"You barely stuttered, not at all until now."

Alex's large warm palm slid over his own hand and gave it a squeeze. "That's great isn't it? You must be getting more comfortable with me." A wide grin broke across his face. "Guess that tongue down the throat action worked for something."

Stunned, Rafe sat back in the booth. Amazing how he hadn't noticed. Over the years Rafe's stuttering had been less of a problem when he became familiar with a person and more comfortable in their presence.

"Yeah." Rafe gulped down his beer. Getting drunk might help as well. He never drank that much but he knew it would loosen his inhibitions and being with Alex meant learning to do the unexpected, didn't it? He gulped down the rest of his beer.

"Maybe we ought to try it again later?" Alex's fingers tickled his palm. "You know, in an effort to populate a scientific study as to the effect of deep tongue kissing on stuttering."

"You're crazy," said Rafe, laughing weakly as desire raced through him. The mere thought of kissing Alex again made him hard. Flustered, he pulled his hand away from Alex and began to eat his burger.

"You wound me to the core." Alex pressed his hand to his heart. "I do this as a sacrifice and a man of science."

Unable to respond, Rafe chewed his burger and watched as Alex began to eat his own food. The tension between them dissipated and while Rafe hadn't gotten the answer to his own questions about Alex, maybe the two of them were on their way, working toward some kind of friendship.

A fresh beer appeared in front of him and he gave Alex a questioningly look.

The man shrugged. "Beer is like potato chips. Nobody can have just one." He took a long drink and then attacked his fries with gusto.

As he continued to stare at Alex, a pang of longing hit Rafe and a slow, steady ache beat in his veins. Desire ignited his blood and he wanted this man with a fierce passion he didn't know existed inside him. Rafe wanted Alex much more than the little flutter of attraction he thought he'd had for Josh last year and more than the only relationship he'd ever had, back in college.

Alex was an enigma; he seemed to have closed himself off from relationships and perhaps most friends, except those he'd trusted for years. Was Rafe wrong to assume Alex wouldn't be interested in a relationship and only wanted sex? Not that there was anything wrong with that, but Rafe had never been able to separate head from heart, thus his solitary state.

Would Alex ever even be able to fall in love? Neither one of them had won any prizes in the relationship game. He'd never had one that was real and he'd guess Alex hadn't either. In that respect, Rafe realized with a start, the two of them were more similar than they realized.

All these thoughts running through his mind confused him, so he drank more of his second beer. He'd never really been in love and hadn't had much experience because of his stutter and shyness, and it appeared Alex wasn't exactly king of the relationships himself. Rafe didn't need Alex to confirm that for him; it was obvious. His lighthearted approach to life and constant joking were the smokescreen he surrounded himself with to prevent people from coming too close and finding out who he really was.

They'd both finished their food and sat comfortably in the large booth; Rafe picked at the label of the beer bottle and Alex hummed softly. The music had mellowed to '70s R&B and Rafe idly listened to The Main Ingredient sing "Everybody Plays the Fool." He smiled to himself, wondering if that was a roundabout answer to the thoughts running through his mind.

He went to take another swig of his second beer, but found it empty. He squinted into the bottle, peering down its amber depths. Alex nudged his leg.

"Hmm?" Blinking, Rafe rubbed his eyes and peered at Alex across the booth.

"I see you're not a heavy drinker."

Rafe laughed and it turned into a yawn. "Uhh, yeah. I d-don't go out that much, so . . ." He shrugged and reached for his glass of water.

"Maybe you should come back with me to the apartment. I don't think you should go home on the train, alone and buzzed."

Wide-eyed and with his thoughts whirling, Rafe's heartbeat ratcheted up. "Uhh, I d-don't th-think that's a great idea." He gulped his water down.

The waiter appeared with the check and before Rafe could say anything, Alex slapped down his credit card and gave it right back to the waiter without even looking at the total.

"Why not? Do you think I'm going to take advantage of you?"

Rafe gaped at Alex in disbelief. The waiter returned and Alex signed the check and slid out of the booth. Rafe hurried after him, out the door and onto the sidewalk, not paying that much attention to his surroundings, when he heard his name being called.

"Rafe, Rafe."

Shit. Jenny. What is she doing here?

Alex stopped and Rafe almost barreled right into his back. As it was, Alex had to grab Rafe by his arms to keep him from bouncing onto his back. The funny thing was, Alex didn't let him go, but rather tucked his arm around Rafe in a gentle, protective gesture. The night air was temperate, yet an unfamiliar heat of a different kind rose within Rafe, flooding his body with a now familiar ache of want that always seemed present when he was near Alex. He relaxed into Alex's arm, and felt the man tighten his hold around him.

"Are you all right, Rafe? You look kind of out of it."

Jenny faced him, concern etched on her face.

His face burned and he knew he must be blushing bright red. Unable to remove himself from Alex's strong hold, Rafe adjusted his glasses and gave a weak laugh. "Ah, yeah. Hi, Jen. I'm fine, we, Alex and I, h-had some dinner."

He could see her gaze shifting from Alex's face to the arm he'd slung around Rafe, holding him tight. A small smile flickered over her lips.

"I see. Aren't you going to introduce me?"

"Oh, yeah." Rafe blinked up at Alex, who gave him a wink.

"I'm Alex, a good friend of Rafe's."

Being that she was a great judge of character, Rafe watched her face with anxious anticipation.

"Rafe never mentioned you before."

Alex loosened his hold on Rafe to lean over and whisper loud enough for Rafe to hear, "He wants to keep me all to himself. He's not a sharer."

Jenny's eyes grew wide. "Are you two dating?" She rounded on Rafe and shot him an evil look. "How could you not tell me? Me of all people." She threw her hands up in the air. "Ughhh. Men. Gay or straight you all suck at giving information."

Rafe managed to pull free of Alex's embrace. "We're not dating. We're friends, friendly really. We don't know each other that well."

Confused, Jenny looked at him then to Alex, who stood scowling. "Seems one of you needs to get your story straight. Maybe you should come back to the office, Rafe." She patted him on the arm. "I can make you some coffee and you can crash on the sofa there if you want."

"But—" Alex tried to protest, but Jenny, in full mama bear protective mode, cut him off.

"No problem for me, Alex. I'll take it from here. Nice to meet you." With a tug on his arm, Jenny tried to pull him with her down the block. Rafe planted his feet on the sidewalk and stopped. "What's wrong? Let's go." Jenny pulled at him again, but he remained steadfast.

"Uh, I'm going with Alex, Jenny." He might be buzzed but he wasn't about to let Jenny decide what he should do with his life. He wasn't her child; he hadn't been anyone's child in forever.

They locked gazes and she smiled.

"Okay, honey. Have fun."

With careful steps, he walked back to Alex, whose smile beamed bright as Rafe drew close. He put his arm back around Rafe and they began to walk in the direction of Micah's apartment.

"I'm glad you came back," murmured Alex in Rafe's ear. "We don't have to rush anything."

So many things ran through Rafe's mind, as he and Alex walked through the darkened streets. For Alex, bringing home a man was probably nothing new, nothing special, but for Rafe, he hadn't gone home with a man in years. Alex would be an amazing lover, of that Rafe had no doubt. His body clenched in anticipation of the night ahead.

Rafe was willing to see where this would lead, if anywhere. Was he right in thinking that Alex was willing to take it one step further?

CHAPTER NINE

Unable to believe his good luck, Alex welcomed back Rafe with a small hug, which allowed him to keep an arm draped casually around the man's shoulders. Though Alex had the distinct feeling Rafe's friend Jenny didn't trust him, in all honesty, Alex's plans for Rafe that evening had no ulterior motive. He couldn't allow, in good conscience, a slightly inebriated Rafe to travel home alone on the subway.

Of course it didn't mean he wouldn't try to sneak in a few kisses before putting the man to bed. Alex wasn't stupid. He knew Rafe was chock full of inhibitions and self-doubt, and if being a little buzzed helped him to discover his sexual side, who was Alex to deny them both the pleasure of a night of exploration and sin?

Besides, walking down the street, with his arm around Rafe's sweetly yielding body was nice, he thought. Rafe sighed and Alex tightened his arm around his shoulders. This stroll through a summer evening in the city with a man he truly liked as a person could almost make Alex believe a place existed where he'd be happy with himself and his own life.

He leaned over to whisper how glad he was that Rafe had decided to come back with him, and lost himself in the man's intoxicating scent of heated skin and the gym's earthy shower gel. Without thinking, he buried his lips in Rafe's soft wavy hair.

"Wha-What're you doing?" Rafe muttered.

"Nothing." Alex kissed Rafe's head, unable to tear himself away from the unexpected hunger of being close to this man.

"Feels like something."

"Does it feel good?" Alex attempted to keep his voice neutral; but he couldn't help the small smile that broke across his face.

"Um, yeah." Rafe glanced up at him, his red-rimmed eyes a bit hazy behind his black-framed glasses. "Why are you smiling?"

"No reason. Let's get you home and into bed."

Rafe stopped short this time, and glared at Alex. "I'm n-not sl-sleeping with you."

"I don't recall asking you," answered Alex, trying not to laugh at the crestfallen expression Rafe tried to cover up with a frown.

"Oh." Rafe said quietly, embarrassment written all over him. "Yeah, right."

They turned the corner and the large apartment building reared up before them in the dark. It was quite late then and few people were about, mainly those who walked their dogs before turning in for the night. Without any hesitation, Alex pulled Rafe to his chest, and placed his hands on either side of the man's face to gaze into the startled expression in his eyes.

"That doesn't mean I don't want you. I do. Not tonight though, when you've had too much to drink."

Something that looked like disappointment flashed across Rafe's face. "I'm not drunk. Maybe I'm not stone cold sober but I'm getting more annoyed by the minute with everyone, both you and Jenny deciding what's best for me. I'm not a child." He reached up and before Alex could say a word, Rafe grabbed him around the neck. "And right now what I think is best for me is kissing you goodnight." He slammed his mouth down on Alex in a bruising, harsh kiss.

Holy shit, this was the last thing Alex expected coming from Rafe. Instant electricity sparked through Alex. "Oh God, baby, what are you doing to me," he groaned, even as his hands slid around Rafe's waist to yank the man closer. Rafe's hard body molding to Alex contrasted with the softness of his full, hot mouth and Alex lit up like fireworks with sensation after sensation exploding through him. Alex glided his hands up Rafe's back, feeling the wiry muscles flex under his hands, then he stopped and held onto Rafe, wanting to wear him over his skin like his favorite old tee shirt from his college days.

Way too soon for Alex's taste, Rafe pulled away and his mouth gleamed wet in the moonlight, his lips swollen and dark. "L-letting you know I'm finished with w-waiting for everyone to make decisions for me. Goodnight."

Still reeling from the shock of the spectacular kiss, Alex hardly registered that Rafe had hailed a cab and left him standing on the sidewalk, aching and alone. He blinked in the darkness, staring openmouthed at the cab's taillights as they receded up the block.

"Shit," he muttered as he waited a moment to steady his wobbly legs. What the hell had gotten into Rafe? Alex chuckled as his body cooled down sufficiently for him to walk without pain or embarrassment. The guy had gone from zero to sixty without a moment's notice and it turned Alex on like he hadn't been in years.

He entered the apartment building and greeted the doorman on his way upstairs. Lucky's tags jingled as he opened the door and he braced himself for thirty pounds worth of puppy love.

"Hey girl." He knelt down in the hallway to receive her greeting. "Did you miss me? Let me pee and then we'll go for a walk."

The dog danced around his legs and he gave her a treat from the bowl on the kitchen counter on his way to the bathroom. After relieving himself and brushing his teeth to get rid of the dank taste of the beer, he snapped on Lucky's leash and they left the building for their last walk of the night.

Alex allowed the dog to take the lead. As they meandered down the block, he received an incoming call. Hoping it was

Rafe, he hit the button. "Hello?"

"Hey, what's up?"

Not Rafe, but Micah. Disappointment shot through him. "Oh, hi."

"Christ, who died? You sound so upset."

"No. I thought you were someone else, that's all." Alex pulled out a plastic baggie and cleaned up after Lucky.

"Your mysterious boyfriend?"

"Fuck off, Micah. Did you call for a reason?"

Micah's tone softened. "You know I'm kidding, right?"

Alex, however, was in no mood for jokes. He was tired, frustrated and horny as hell. "What happened? Josh told you to be nice to me?"

"Alex, come on. I'm sorry. You know I love you and I wish you the best. If you've met someone—"

"I haven't," Alex bit out, frustrated because he could still taste Rafe's sweetness on his tongue and scared because he wanted Rafe back, wanted more of him.

"All right." Micah exhaled. "I'm calling to ask a favor. Could you stop by Silver Trees and check on Ruth and Ethel for us? We've been able to Skype with them every night, but I'd feel a little better if someone was to physically go there and see them in person. I know it's a lot to ask—"

"I'm happy to stop by and visit with them. You know I love those ladies."

"Thanks. I owe you one."

Alex shook his head even knowing Micah couldn't see. He and Lucky turned back up the street and walked back into the building. "No, you don't. I'm here for you. Always have been, always will be."

The silence was so deep on the other end Alex looked down at the phone to make sure they hadn't been cut off. When Micah finally spoke his voice sounded troubled.

"I know I've been a lousy friend all these years; selfish and most of the time a bastard. But you know you're my family, right? And I'm always here for you, no matter what. It hasn't changed."

Alex didn't answer right away; he let Lucky inside and took off her leash before he sat down on the sofa.

"You have Josh now and I understand priorities shift and things change. I don't want to be your second husband, Micah. Josh shouldn't have to worry about my feelings."

"That's bullshit. Josh loves you. You're very special to both of us. And I know lately you've been going through some personal stuff. You don't have to talk about it now, but we will when I come home."

That's what Micah thought. For fifteen years Alex had kept his life to himself. Micah getting married and becoming the Happy Homemaker wasn't going to change Alex's mindset. By the time Micah came home, he'd become so wrapped up in his life and his grandmother, he'll have forgotten all about this conversation.

Alex would make sure of it.

"Micah. I promise to go visit the ladies tomorrow. But now I have to go to sleep since I have surgery in the morning."

"Hmm. All right. Tell them we love them."

"I will."

"And Alex? I love you. You know that, right?" Micah's anxious voice did give Alex pause.

"I know. And I love you too."

He ended the conversation and sighed, leaning his head back against the back of the sofa, staring at the blank slate of the ceiling. There was a niggle of guilt in his chest that he'd never confided anything to Micah, his closest friend. But, Alex justified to himself, Micah was newly married, worried about his grandmother and getting his own life together. He didn't need the added responsibility of dealing with Alex's own fucked-up guilt and self-doubt.

Best to leave his problems behind and be Happy Alex, Smiling Alex. The Alex everyone knew and loved, and who didn't exist.

Checking his watch, he saw it had been some time since

Rafe had left in the cab, and he wanted to make sure the man had gotten home okay. Without stopping to think too hard as to why it made a difference to him whether Rafe made it home, when he'd never cared about any other man before, Alex dialed and waited impatiently for Rafe to answer.

"Alex? W-what's wrong?"

God he sounded all sleep rough and sexy. Alex bit his lip and steadied his breathing. "I wanted to make sure you got home all right."

"Yeah." Rafe let out a huge yawn and Alex heard the sheets rustle. "I got in about ten minutes ago and I didn't even bother to brush my teeth. I fell right into b-bed."

Alex got up and crossed the living room to his bedroom. An evil thought crossed his mind but he needed to be in bed to effectuate it.

"You did, huh? Did you bother to get undressed?" A vision of Rafe's tightly muscled lean body flashed in Alex's mind and he wiggled out of his own pants and lay down on the bed.

"Uhh, yeah?"

"I'm in bed too. All alone."

"Come on, Alex. I wasn't going to sleep with you tonight. You know that."

Sighing into the phone Alex hated to admit Rafe was right. "I know. But it's fun to tease you."

"Goodnight, Alex."

"Night, Rafe."

He clicked off and tossed the phone to the foot of the bed. Looking down at his stiff cock, he figured it wasn't fair to waste a raging hard-on and reaching over to the night table he un-snapped the bottle of lubricant and finished himself off. It didn't take more than a few minutes and several dirty thoughts about Rafe to send him spurting across his chest with a deep sigh.

He grabbed some tissues and wiped himself off, then rolled on his side and fell into a deep dreamless sleep. For once.

"Good afternoon, sir, what can I get for you?"

Damn, that British accent was sexy as hell. Alex idly glanced at the good-looking salesman at Sinfully Rich, the new high-end chocolate shop that opened down the block from Micah's apartment.

"I'd like two half pound boxes of chocolates, please."

"Certainly." The salesman, whose name was Tristan, Alex noted from his name tag, picked up two gold boxes. "These are our assorted, handmade chocolates. We make them every morning." He gave Alex an inviting smile, and Alex felt his piercing blue eyes assessing him.

Funny how normally Alex would be in full-on flirt mode right about now, maybe asking for free tastes, with a wink and a heated glance. Instead, anxious to stop by Rafe's clinic, Alex checked his watch hoping to catch him before he left for the day. The text he'd sent earlier didn't show as having been read, nor did Rafe answer him so Alex remained unsure.

"Can I also have a box of chocolate truffles?"

"Of course. Do you want those wrapped?" The salesman took a pair of tongs and slipped half a dozen truffles into a box.

"No, they're for me."

"Splendid. It's always nice to treat yourself." The salesman smiled back at him, wide and bright. "I'll slip in a few extra." He winked. "On the house, of course."

"Thanks." Careful to avoid responding to the man's obvious signals of interest, Alex handed over his credit card and scrawled his signature on the receipt.

"I put my card in the bag in case you're ever in need of chocolate again." Tristan smoothed his hair back. "I'm more than happy to give you personal service for all your sinfully rich needs."

Whoa. Was he ever that blatant in his flirting? Alex took the bag and left the store, hurrying along the street. Hopeful Rafe was waiting for him, Alex quickened his steps. The surgeries he assisted in this morning, instead of tiring him, had energized him; they'd had good outcomes and the patients' families were there to help and lend support.

Alex wondered if he were ever ill, if his parents would even show up; the last time he knew his mother was in a hospital was when Seth was sick. His father of course lived in the hospital.

If he'd become a doctor like his parents wanted, could they overlook the fact that he was gay? He doubted it. Both his mother and father lived in a world of black and white, right and wrong. Their narrow-mindedness and inability to color outside the lines, as Alex saw it, was part of the reason he'd always clashed with them. Early on in his childhood Alex recalled feeling different that the others around him, yet they only wanted him to conform and fit in, not express his differences and spread his wings to fly.

It was easier to discard the son they never loved as much, than change their beliefs and suffer through the embarrassment of a gay child.

Their last talk still played in his mind.

"You don't have to live this way, Alexander. You have the choice." *Always impeccable in a suit and tie even at home, his father stood by the fireplace, a tumbler of scotch in hand. "If you cared about the family, instead of only about yourself and your needs, you'd see what this was doing to us, especially your mother. She'd barely been able to get out of bed since your brother passed. Now your news has sent her into a tailspin I don't know how she'll recover from."*

"But if I was straight and still going to medical school she would be fine, right?"

All his father had to do was brush off Alex's answer and tell him he was wrong. That they could work it out somehow. But it wasn't meant to be.

"But you're not and you aren't, correct?" The piercing blue gaze raked Alex. "You've been a disappointment to us on so many levels." As if it pained him to look at Alex, his father turned away.

Alex sat clutching his own drink, hopeful the glass wouldn't shatter to pieces in his hand, like his heart already had in his chest. "I've always tried to do my best."

His father raised that hawk-like gaze from its study of the fire to meet Alex's. "Obviously, your best isn't good enough. It never was."

Alex reached the door to Rafe's clinic and vowed to put his parents out of his mind. When he pushed open the door, the waiting room was surprisingly crowded with people and their pets. No wonder Rafe didn't contact him, he'd been busy with his own problems. The receptionist had a harried look on her face, a far cry from the smile the day before.

Alex recognized Jenny, the woman he met last night. She gave him a brief glance with raised eyebrows, and beckoned him over.

"We're swamped right now. At least six dogs and three feral cats have been poisoned and Rafe has been going nonstop since eight thirty this morning. It even made the news this afternoon; I came by early to lend a hand, and called in a few friends to help. I'm waiting for them to call me back." She pulled on the elastic of her ponytail to tighten it. "Thank God we haven't lost any animals, although I heard from one owner that a dog in his building died."

Fear stabbed through Alex's heart. If anything happened to Lucky, he might as well kill himself. Micah would never forgive Alex if anything happened to his beloved dog. "Holy shit that's awful." He set the bag with the chocolates down on the counter. "Is there anything I can do to help?"

Her eyes softened with relief. "He needs to take a break. Can you force him to leave, even if it's only for a little while, like to eat something? He won't listen to me."

"Leave it to me." Alex patted her on the shoulder. "I'll drag him out of here. Bodily, if I have to."

Jenny shot him a funny look. "You really like him, huh?"

Startled, Alex thought for a moment then smiled back at her. "Yeah. I kinda do."

"He's a very special guy and I love him to death. Rafe needs more real friends in his life."

Alex squirmed a bit under her scrutiny. "I consider him a friend."

"Good." She gestured to the back. "He's free right now. Take him somewhere, anywhere, for at least an hour or two. It's been hell here."

A thought popped into his head. "I know exactly where to take him."

CHAPTER TEN

"Where are you t-taking me?" Rafe protested as Alex literally pushed him out of the clinic. Jenny was of no help to him as she stood holding the door open for them as they left. "They need me."

"You're about to drop where you stand and Jenny told me you've barely stopped all day." The firm grip Alex had on his arm allowed him to lean a little more on the man than he normally would have. Three beers the night before and the craziness of the day had Rafe almost trembling from exhaustion. "They need you able to stand. You'll be back, don't worry. I'm only taking you for a short visit."

"A visit?" He slanted a look at Alex who continued to walk with him in tow. "W-where to?"

"Did anyone ever tell you you're cute in those glasses?" Alex squeezed his arm.

Rafe rolled his eyes. "Oh, shut up." But he smiled as he said it, and his heart did a happy jig in his chest.

They walked up 85th street toward Central Park. Rafe hadn't been outside all day and took in deep, cleansing breaths of the fresh air. The smell of disinfectant and sick animals had taken up residence in his skin and he couldn't wait to take a shower later and wash it all away. For now, it was nice to walk with Alex and feel the warmth of the late afternoon sun beat down upon his face. They stopped at the corner, waiting for the light to change.

His eyes fluttered closed.

"Am I that boring that you'd fall asleep on me?"

Alex's amused voice jerked Rafe out of his somnambulant state. "Sorry," he mumbled, his face flaming hot.

"Hey, it's fine. I was teasing. You can use me as your pillow anytime, but I'd prefer it if we were both lying down, preferably naked and in a bed."

That was the thing with Alex. He joked around so much, Rafe couldn't be sure when or if he was ever serious. It was why he'd decided to leave last night, before the tension that had built up between them as the night had progressed exploded into something uncontrollable. Something Rafe would regret. Because once Alex touched him, Rafe knew he'd be finished; he'd never be able to slow down, nor want Alex to stop. Even now, Rafe could barely admit to himself the true cause for his sleepless night—the vivid memory of the kiss they'd shared in the locker room. Rafe kept replaying it over and over in his mind.

He thought they'd begun to open up to each other last night at dinner. There'd been moments when Rafe believed he'd seen beneath Alex's mask, but couldn't be sure. And while his body responded to Alex's touch, he didn't have the experience or the desire to play the game as cavalierly as Alex did. Rafe couldn't imagine hopping from bed to bed and man to man with aplomb. So he did what he did best and withdrew, but Alex, tenacious as a terrier, kept coming back, though Rafe didn't understand why.

What if Alex was really attracted to him? the devil on his shoulder argued. Why assume the worst about the man? In all the time they spent together, Alex had never talked about other men or behaved like a player. Was it possible his own insecurity caused him to assume the worst about Alex, unjustly?

Those thoughts whirling through his head, Rafe barely noticed they'd stopped.

He glanced up and found himself in front of the assisted living facility where both Micah's and Josh's grandmothers lived. He'd only met them a few times, but they both seemed like very sweet ladies.

"Uhh, Alex. Wh-why am I here?"

Alex had already passed through the automatic sliding doors, leaving Rafe to hurry and play catch-up with him.

"W-wait." Rafe placed himself between Alex and the elevator doors. "Answer m-me."

"Micah asked if I would check up on them and I thought maybe you could use a change of scenery." He reached around Rafe and punched the up button. "You've met them before."

"It's n-nice you offered to visit them. You have a great s-sense of family; it m-must be nice to be so close."

The doors slid open and Rafe continued to talk as they walked down the hallway. "Neither of m-my parents liked sp-speaking to me, since I stuttered so much. We usually ate our dinners in fr-front of the television, where my father would yell at the evening news and complain about how b-bad his life was." The suffocating loneliness of his childhood returned and Rafe recalled the nights he lay in bed with only his books and his dogs for comfort.

The man at his side never had the problems Rafe faced growing up; Alex wouldn't know what it meant to be rejected by the people who were supposed to love him. He'd grown up, most likely surrounded by adoring parents and a wide circle of friends.

Alex's jaw clenched tight but he said nothing, except, "Here's Ethel's apartment." He knocked and waited. It only took a moment or two before the door opened and a smiling young woman peered out at them.

"Yes?" Her voice had the lovely lilt of one of the Caribbean islands.

"I'm Alex, a friend of Ethel's and Ruth's grandsons." Before he could continue, Ethel's voice rang out from further within the apartment.

"Lilli, who is it? Is that Alex I hear? Come inside."

"Come on." Alex breezed in with Rafe next to him. "Hello, ladies. Look who I brought to visit."

Ethel stood in the center of her spacious living room, while

Ruth sat on the sofa. Rafe remembered this place as a homey, beautifully decorated apartment with mementos of her life surrounding her. In its pride of place on her buffet table was the large wedding photo of Micah and Josh.

"Oh, Rafe, so lovely to see you again." She turned to Ruth. "Ruthie, look who came to pay us a visit. Micah's dear friend, Alex, and their other friend, Rafe."

Ruth's faded blue eyes stared at him and he could see how hard she tried to place him in her memory.

"You probably don't remember me; it's been a while since we met." There was little he could say to make Ruth feel better. At least she looked well.

"How about me, Ruth? Have you forgotten how we danced at the wedding?" Alex leaned over to kiss her cheek. A swell of relief ran through Rafe as he watched Ruth's lips curve in a smile.

"Alex, yes, of course I haven't. You were the most handsome man at the wedding next to Micah and dear Josh."

"Some might say even better looking, if truth be told." They all laughed and Rafe marveled at how effortlessly Alex fit in wherever he went. Alex knew what to say to make himself and everyone comfortable.

"So, Rafe dear." Ethel's sharp-eyed gaze studied him. "Tell us a little about yourself. We haven't had a chance to talk to you much, for all the times we've met."

To Rafe's embarrassment, his throat closed up and though he desperately tried to relax, from past experience it was clear he wouldn't be able to speak without stuttering horribly. In mute appeal he turned to Alex who by some stroke of luck caught his eye, saw his panic and took control.

"Ethel, Ruth, look what I brought you." He lifted the gold bag in his hand and the women's avid attention switched from Rafe to Alex. "I know it's your favorite."

"Is that chocolate?" Ethel gasped, clapping her hands. "Oh, I haven't had a good piece of chocolate in what seems like forever."

"I got each of you a box, but don't eat it all at once." Alex handed Ruth and Ethel their boxes and gave each an indulgent smile as they kissed his cheek.

"You are the most darling man. But very naughty for not telling anyone you were dating." Ethel patted Alex's cheek as she turned and gave Rafe a wink. "I'm so happy you two are together. You make such a lovely couple; and so handsome." She took a bite of her chocolate. "Oh, isn't it delicious, Ruthie?"

Ruth couldn't answer as her mouth was full. But her eyes gleamed bright as she nodded and held the box out for Lilli to take a piece.

"Ethel, we aren't dating; merely good friends. I brought Rafe along because he had a rough day and needed a break."

Rafe finally got his tongue to work. "That's right." He swallowed hard. "We're only friends."

"*Only* friends can become more if you let it happen. Now, the way I see it you two don't need to be hanging around with two old ladies. Alex, make your report to Micah and Josh now that you've seen us. Go and have some dinner you two and enjoy the night."

Before Rafe or Alex could say anything, Ethel had the door open and hustled them out into the hallway. When Alex opened his mouth to protest, she shut the door firmly in their faces.

Dumbfounded, Rafe could only stare at Alex, who braced his hand on the door, shoulders shaking with silent laughter.

"D-did they just throw us out?"

"Mmmph." Alex choked a bit, struggling to regain control. "That Ethel is something else. But she's right about something." He began walking, swinging the small box of chocolate he'd bought for himself.

"What?"

"We should get something to eat, you especially."

"I'm fine. I'm only going to stay another hour at the clinic then head on home." Rafe caught up to Alex as he waited for the elevator.

"Have dinner with me," wheedled Alex. He widened his

eyes and pouted. "I'm lonely."

Rafe's brows raised in skepticism. "You? I highly doubt that."

"Why?" Alex's brow furrowed. "You don't think I get lonely?"

Yes, he thought, *I know you get lonely and I'm beginning to see through those walls, Alex, I want you to tell me why. There's something holding you back and it's killing you, I can see. Trust me with your secrets.*

"Yeah. I think you get lonely. I know I do and it sucks."

The elevator reached the main floor and they exited and walked out of the building, heading back toward the clinic and Micah's apartment.

"Well then." In a gesture Rafe was quickly coming to learn was commonplace for Alex, he draped his arm around Rafe's shoulder and pulled him close. "We can both use the company. I want to have dinner with you."

Alex, Rafe noticed, was a very sensory person. Demonstrative by nature, he constantly held Rafe's hand or squeezed his arm whenever they were together. And Rafe discovered he enjoyed the heavy warmth of Alex's arm around him as they walked together.

"Please?" Alex faced him as they stood and waited for the light. "I can't bear another night alone in that apartment."

The honesty in Alex's eyes stunned Rafe into silence, but he nodded. After revealing his vulnerability, Rafe didn't have the heart to say no to Alex.

A delighted smile crossed Alex's face. "Really? Great. What do you want to get?"

They passed by restaurants of every nationality and by mutual consent decided hero sandwiches were the easiest way to go. Within fifteen minutes they were back at the apartment and Rafe held the bags while Alex unlocked the door. Lucky jumped on them, tail wagging furiously, and together they laughed at her antics.

While Alex took care of Lucky, Rafe took the sandwiches

into the kitchen. He imagined having a real relationship with a man, one where they would come home at night and have dinner, then talk about their day. He took down the plates from the cabinets and set them on the counter. Still half daydreaming, he almost jumped out of his skin when Alex's arms slid around his waist.

"Shh. It's only me. You looked so tired and sad I figured you could use a hug right now."

Rafe's heart began beating in a frenzied pace as he struggled with this unexpected turn of events. Was all this a ploy to get him into bed?

Alex buried his face in the space between Rafe's shoulder and neck and sucked the sensitive skin there.

"What're you doing?" Rafe knew his voice sounded weak and breathy with desire. That was what Alex did to him: set him on edge until in reality Rafe may have been standing with his feet firmly on the floor, but he might as well have been teetering on a tightrope, suspended hundreds of feet in the air with no cushion beneath him to save him if he fell.

At the touch of Alex's lips to his neck, all sense of reason fled his brain and he couldn't have cared less. He moaned, tired of holding his emotions in check. He wished he could live life like Alex did, uncaring of what others thought and said about him.

"Let me make you feel good."

Rafe recalled his favorite quote from Muhammed Ali: "Don't count your days, make your days count."

Rafe was tired of not counting, of not leaving a mark anywhere or with anyone. Alex swept through his life like a tornado, clearing away everything in its path, making way for a clean, fresh start. Maybe it was time for him to make that new beginning, make this his springtime. A rebirth.

Without waiting for him to answer, Alex backed him up against the counter and caged him between his muscular arms. Rafe shuddered remembering their explosive kiss at the gym, and by the way Alex's eyes darkened and his breathing increased, Rafe suspected he was thinking the same thing but wasn't sure and the old insecurity kicked in.

"Why?" Rafe managed to gasp, even as Alex nuzzled against his neck, his very warm and eager tongue licking a fiery path up Rafe's throat. "Why me?"

"Why not? You've been driving me crazy all week." With a tender touch, Alex brushed the hair off Rafe's forehead and rested his hand on Rafe's cheek. "Your mouth, your smile; everything about you calls to me. And now, when you've been giving yourself all day long?" He brushed his lips against Rafe's and Rafe swayed toward him, unable to stop the almost giddy sense of hope and desire that curled in his stomach. "It's time someone who cares about you, gives you some attention and affection."

His breath catching in his throat, Rafe's hand curled into Alex's chest, bunching up the soft cotton of his shirt. Alex's lips, hot and gentle, searched for Rafe's, and when they finally touched, Rafe placed his hands on Alex's face to hold him in place, afraid Alex might stop, might be a figment in his mind and float away. Alex pressed firm, searching kisses on Rafe's trembling mouth, sliding his tongue over Rafe's lips before slipping inside Rafe's mouth. One of Alex's hands splayed across Rafe's chest and the other rested on his hip, his thumb drawing circles over the exposed skin between Rafe's shirt and jeans.

Their bodies swayed together, standing in that confined space, yet Rafe's heart had never been so free. Alex kissed him gently, the sweetness of his lips creating an ache in Rafe's chest. A languorous sense of well-being stole over Rafe and he gripped the cool edge of the countertop to prevent from melting into a puddle of happiness. A wellspring of emotion, of wanting to be loved, broke free, like sparkling bright water spraying from a fountain.

To his shock, Alex sank down on his knees and with a knowing smile, unzipped Rafe's jeans and tugged them down to his ankles. The evidence of Rafe's excitement bulged out from his boxers. He'd never been so hard in all his life, and from the sight of Alex's flared nostrils and hungry gaze, it wouldn't take long before he'd come.

"God, you're beautiful." Alex hooked his fingers into the waistband of Rafe's boxers and pulled them down, exposing his swollen cock to the naked air. "I bet you taste delicious too," he said and took Rafe's cock into his mouth. "Ummm," he hummed around the thickness of Rafe's cock.

"Oh God," Rafe cried out, bucking against the incredible wet heat of Alex's mouth. The pad of Alex's tongue swirled over the sensitive head of his cock and probed the tiny slit, sending shivers of desire curling around Rafe's spine. Alex flattened his tongue and dragged it up the hard ridge on the underside of Rafe's cock, mumbling, "so fucking sweet," sending Rafe into a tailspin. All he could do was hold on to the counter and whimper, even as he thrust his hips forward.

"Umm," Alex lapped at the thick crown of Rafe's cock and reached down with a hand to fondle his sac. "I knew you'd be like this, your cock all pretty, waiting for my mouth and you all hot and squirmy. Tell me baby, do you ache for me—" he curled his hand around Rafe's cock and cupped his balls, "—like I ache for you?"

Heat suffused Rafe's body at Alex's frank sex talk, but he wasn't surprised by it. The man could charm the stripe off a skunk with his silver tongue. Prickles of awareness raced up and down his skin thinking of Alex's tongue and how badly he wanted to feel it on his cock again. There'd never been anyone who'd cared what he felt or needed before; sex had been something he'd sought for necessity, when the loneliness and solitude proved too much to bear, and he wanted someone to touch his body.

"Yeah, I do," he murmured. "So damn much." He reached out and stroked Alex's hair, then gave it a little tug, bringing Alex's mouth down harder on his cock.

With wide, bright eyes, Alex slanted a heated look up at him. "You want it hard? Don't be afraid to tell me." That magical tongue swept across the head of Rafe's cock and Alex's mouth opened wider, taking Rafe in even deeper.

"Yes," Rafe hissed, as lust, hunger and a sense of power

poured over him at the sight of Alex on his knees, that full mouth wrapped around his cock. A tingling began in his balls and his heart rate kicked up a notch. "Fuck, Alex. Yes." His hands braced onto the countertop and he began to thrust harder into Alex's beautiful mouth, watching Alex's eyes roll back in his head then close in ecstasy.

That was all the impetus Rafe needed. "Alex," he sobbed as the heat and rush of his orgasm swept through him, stealing his breath, rendering him almost blind with desire. Rafe's legs sagged and his elbows caught on the edge of counter, preventing him from falling to the floor. To his credit, Alex took everything Rafe gave, never once hesitating, even licking his lips after pulling his mouth off Rafe's cock.

Alex patted Rafe's thigh with affection, giving his hip and the sensitive skin of his abdomen several gentle kisses, before standing and pulling up Rafe's boxers and pants. There was a softer look to Alex's face and Rafe, still breathless and shaking, slipped his arms around Alex's waist. Their foreheads touched and Rafe closed his eyes, soaking in the closeness and heat of Alex.

Their breaths mingled and Alex tipped his head to the side to kiss him, and Rafe could taste his own slightly salty essence on Alex's lips. An ache rose within him to give this man release and comfort of his own. With trembling hands Rafe reached for Alex's waistband, but Alex waylaid his plan and instead laced their fingers together.

He began humming a tune in Rafe's ear and started to sway in place, his eyes closed and a soft smile on his lips. "Dance with me," he whispered, holding Rafe close as they moved together, his mouth resting by Rafe's ear as he continued to hum what Rafe recognized as "(I've had) The Time of My Life," from *Dirty Dancing*.

Stunned by the romantic gesture, Rafe allowed himself to fall into the moment and closed his own eyes, slipping away into a sensual whirlpool of desire as they rocked together. It was the single most passionate moment of his life. "Alex," he murmured. "What's come over you?"

"I think you did, if I recall."

Rafe opened his eyes and caught the tail end of Alex's grin before their eyes met. The intensity of Alex's gaze robbed Rafe of all ability to breathe and he gasped to draw in air.

"Hasn't anyone ever done anything for you because you're special?"

This was a dream come true for Rafe, standing flushed and shaking in the arms of a man like Alex, the sweet words pouring over him like wine. Like he did everything else, Alex touched him with a sureness borne of confidence, his fingers skimming over Rafe's jaw, the pad of his thumb tracing the outline of Rafe's mouth.

Breaking out of his fog of lust, Rafe recalled how he wished to push himself past his boundaries, and licked Alex's thumb, circling the finger with his tongue. He swiped only once before Alex growled and pressed him hard up against the kitchen counter, the incredible hardness of his erection resting firm and strong against Rafe's stomach.

"I won't lie and say I don't want to fuck you. But you need to be sure of it all if we're to take it to the next step."

"Sure of what?" It was hard to make life choices with Alex's cock throbbing between them like a fucking laser sword. "I, I want you t-too," said Rafe, the blazing heat from Alex's eyes scorching his blood and making it almost impossible to think about anything other than having this amazing man as a lover.

Alex kissed him then, his hand sliding behind Rafe's neck to hold him tight, his fingers tangling in Rafe's hair. "I'm not boyfriend material; I won't be sharing my feelings, calling you to say hi during the day with silly jokes or buying you roses and champagne." He rubbed his cheek against Rafe's. "But I will make sure your needs are well taken care of and you always go to work with a smile on your face." He kissed him again and whispered, "I won't share you with anyone, and I'm yours for as long as you want me."

Though it wasn't the declaration Rafe had hoped to hear, he

realized it was Alex at his most honest, and Rafe could appreciate it.

"You needn't worry about me falling in love with you, Alex. I know that would be futile." Before he could continue, his phone rang. He took the phone out of his pocket.

"Hey, Jenny." Rafe listened for a moment while Alex busied himself in the kitchen. "Okay. I'm on my way." He slid the phone back into his pocket and turned to Alex. "Rain ch-check on the sandwiches, I'm afraid. Sh-she's swamped again and can't reach our back-up p-person as they're on vacation." He buttoned his pants and zipped himself up. "I have to go back."

Without a word, Alex slipped the sandwich back into the paper bag and handed it to Rafe, his eyes dark with understanding. "I'll talk to you soon."

For a moment Rafe thought Alex might kiss him goodbye, but when the moment dragged out with nothing happening, he blinked and gave an uncertain smile. "Uh, well, okay. I'll see you."

Rafe hurried from the apartment back to the clinic, wondering what in the world he'd agreed to and why. But for the first time he had something to look forward to, even if he didn't know when or even if it would actually happen.

CHAPTER ELEVEN

The apartment stood silent after Rafe left, the only sound coming from Lucky's jingling tags as she scratched herself. An unfamiliar sense of loss and loneliness stole through Alex, which he attributed to the abrupt end of his playtime with Rafe.

"Damn that guy can kiss," Alex said out loud and received only an answering yip from Lucky, who sat at his feet, with a hopeful expression on her face. Unable to resist her, Alex pulled out several pieces of roast beef and her avid eyes tracked him as he placed them in a plate on the floor for her.

He did this all on autopilot, his head still in the amazing kiss from before. Rafe might be quiet and shy on the outside, but the sweet smile and wide brown eyes hid a depth of untapped heat Alex couldn't wait to unleash. One taste of that man's mouth wasn't nearly enough to satisfy him, Alex was only now beginning to understand, and he cursed himself for not suggesting Rafe return here to the apartment after he finished his shift.

He ate his sandwich then flopped on the sofa with his truffles and Lucky. He took out the box and ate one, then decided they were too rich and put the box on the table for another time. Lucky nosed around for a bit, then lay down with a chew toy and together they watched some television. By eleven o'clock, he was half dozing, his mind occupied with kissing and sucking Rafe off. Alex had been happy to give the guy a blowjob; Rafe had been so overworked and stressed, it relaxed him immediately. What Alex hadn't planned was the dancing together in the kitchen. He hoped Rafe didn't get any romantic ideas from that gesture.

It wasn't one he'd ever done before and he couldn't imagine a repeat performance in the future.

Unable to remember with any clarity what he'd seen on the television for the past three hours, Alex decided it was time to take Lucky out for one last walk then go to bed. He didn't have a surgery scheduled for tomorrow although the rest of the week was busy.

"Let's go, girl." He heaved himself off the sofa and with Lucky dancing around his feet, snapped her leash on and took her outside. They strolled around and Alex fought the pull to walk past Rafe's clinic. It didn't make sense wanting to see Rafe again when the man had only left him several hours before, but he shook off the feelings and deliberately turned his back on the corner where he'd make the turn to the clinic and walked back to the apartment.

He texted Micah then, letting him know how Lucky was doing and sending him a picture of her. He received an immediate response.

Thanks. How'd your date go?

Annoyance tightened Alex's chest as he swiftly answered.

I said it wasn't a date. I'm going to bed. Night.

He heard an answering ping a minute later but chose to ignore it, and continued on back into the apartment. Lucky made straight for her pillow and he went into the second bedroom he'd been using, stripped and went to bed. Although he fell asleep moments after his head hit the pillow, it was a restless, troubled sleep, as both Seth and Rafe were on his mind.

He awoke, groggy and disoriented. When he checked the time the digital clock glowed 3:30 a.m. About to fall back asleep, he heard an unusual noise in the living room that had him instantly awake and out of bed. Alex made it to the living room when he smelled something horrible and heard terrible gagging noises.

"Lucky? Lucky, girl where are you?" He searched around the living room and found her lying down next to the sofa, whining, covered in her own excrement.

Panic seized his heart and uncaring as to where he stepped, he rushed over to her. The poor dog raised her head a little off the ground then lay down again, and whined. It was then Alex noticed the box of truffles he'd left on the coffee table was knocked over and empty. Seven of the rich chocolate balls had been eaten.

His first thought was, *Micah is going to kill me.* His second, more rational thought was to get her some help. At this time of night Rafe's clinic would be closed, but not trusting anyone else, he didn't give it a second thought and dialed Rafe's cell phone. It rang and rang with no answer.

"Where the fuck can he be?" Alex screamed as Lucky threw up again. Alex was almost incoherent with fright when his phone vibrated and Rafe's name flashed on the screen. Relief swamped through him as he answered, not greeting the man but immediately pouring out the story.

"Oh God, Rafe, it's Lucky. She's vomiting and there's diarrhea all over the apartment. Help me, please." He never begged so hard in his life. Not since Seth died and he'd asked God to take him and not his brother.

"Alex. Calm down. What happened?"

He quickly relayed the situation to Rafe; how he suspected Lucky ate seven of his dark chocolate truffles.

"Shit. She's probably poisoned herself. Okay, do you have any hydrogen peroxide?"

"How the fuck should I know?" Alex snapped. "It's not my apartment."

"And yelling at me isn't going to help Lucky, is it?" Rafe shot back.

"I'm sorry," whispered Alex. "You have no idea how scared I am."

"I know, I know," soothed Rafe. "I'm coming now. I have the peroxide. I'll hop in a cab and be there as fast as I can."

"Thank you," Alex choked out.

He hung up and went to sit with Lucky who by now couldn't lift her head. She kept whining and crying and he felt so fucking helpless as all he could do was stroke her head and wipe her muzzle with a wet dishcloth. He had no idea how much time passed before he heard knocking at the door.

"Thank God." Alex carefully placed Lucky's head on the pillow he'd brought out to make her as comfortable as possible, then raced to the front door and pulled it open so hard it banged against the wall. Rafe stood there with a black bag, his face grim.

"Where is she?"

"Over here." Alex pulled him by the arm to where the dog lay. Hovering anxiously, he watched as Rafe prepared a syringe of hydrogen peroxide and squirted it into her mouth, stroking her throat in order to get her to swallow. Alex watched as Rafe assisted Lucky to her feet and walked her into the bathroom. After about fifteen minutes, she began to vomit in earnest and Rafe stayed with her until she finished. He then picked her up in his arms and placed her in the tub, where he washed her with warm water and shampoo.

Meanwhile, Alex gathered cleaning supplies and cleaned up the mess and by the time Rafe emerged from the bathroom, his shirt wet but with a towel-dried Lucky, the place had been restored to normal, although it might take a while for the smell to go down. Luckily, there weren't any rugs that had gotten ruined.

Rafe placed her in her dog bed and she closed her eyes, worn out from her ordeal. Never having seen Rafe at work, Alex marveled at the veterinarian's ability to remain calm in the face of all the turmoil. He, on the other hand, was a mess; his heart pounded and his hands refused to stop shaking.

"Alex, are you all right?"

He glanced up to see Rafe standing by his side, a concerned look on his face.

"No." He sank to the ground and covered his face with his hands. "What if she dies? It'll be all my fault. It's always my fault." He couldn't stop shaking, barely registering Rafe's arms around him, picking him up and leading him to the bathroom.

"Come on, let's get you cleaned up."

"But Lucky—"

"Is going to be fine. You called me right away and she threw everything up. Tomorrow you'll bring her in for a check-up but there shouldn't be any lasting effects." With a practiced calm Alex registered as his method of operation, Rafe stripped Alex and turned on the warm water. "Get clean and I'11bring you fresh clothes." He pushed Alex in the shower.

Alex let the heated water spill over him and slowly washed off the mess of the evening. When he finished, he saw Rafe had left him clean sweats and a tee shirt folded up on the vanity. Hoping the man hadn't left, Alex quickly dried off and got dressed, not bothering to dry his hair before hurrying into the living room. To his relief, Rafe sat on the sofa, his head back on the cushions, an exhausted look on his face.

"Rafe."

The man's eyes opened and he gazed at him.

"Do you feel better?"

"No, no I don't." The guilt and the fear coupled with the shaking made it hard for him to breathe. "What if she isn't going to be fine? Micah will never forgive me. He's all I have; my only friend. He'll hate me." He sank down next to Rafe and grabbed his shoulders. "I didn't know she'd eat the chocolates. You know how I love her; I'd never do anything to hurt her."

"Shh." Rafe's arms came around him, but the cold fear remained. He couldn't stop shaking; it seemed like years since he'd been warm. "It's going to be fine. Lucky's going to be okay, I promise."

"Are you sure?" He pulled Rafe close by his tee shirt, fisting the cotton in his hands. "You're not saying that to make me feel better, are you?"

Warm golden sparks kindled in Rafe's eyes and he leaned his forehead in to touch Alex's. "Yes, I'm sure and no, I'm not." His breath blew past Alex's face, warm and with a hint of something spicy, as if he'd sucked a cinnamon candy recently. "She needs to rest now, and I'm thinking so do you."

At Rafe's attempt to stand, Alex forestalled him by taking him in his arms. "Don't, please," he begged, unashamed at the pleading tone in his voice. "Don't leave me here all alone."

This apartment may be like a second home to Alex, but a second home presupposed a first; which didn't exist. The place he called home wasn't much to brag about. His apartment was merely a place to sleep and dress before work; since his parents no longer welcomed him at their house, he'd bounced around from apartment to apartment, but mostly staying with Micah. Once Micah and Josh began living together, Alex had withdrawn on his own, and spent more time at clubs and his neighborhood bars.

Not his apartment, though, never there. If he did he'd have to face those white walls of condemnation where he'd see not only his parents' faces staring back at him, accusing him of all his failures in his life, but also his brother's gentle eyes and sad smile, giving him absolution and forgiveness.

So now, with Lucky having seemingly made it through the worst of her trauma and the night still looming ahead of him silent and habitually lonely, Alex broke apart in Rafe's arms.

"Stay with me? Please? I need you." Those words, never before said to anyone, cost him everything. He focused on Rafe's face, falling into the man's gentle eyes. He should've known though, that Rafe, being the open and honest person he was, would want the truth.

"Why?"

One simple word but it held meaning and if he had the ability to express himself correctly, so much promise.

To his shock Alex wanted to tell him.

"To chase away the loneliness and shadows. To help me pretend I'm not such a fuck-up, like my—like so many people think." He stumbled, almost revealing more of himself to Rafe than he'd ever thought about before. "Please?" He fisted the damp cotton of Rafe's shirt. "Please stay and hold me tonight."

They sat in the darkened, hushed room, and with each

passing moment, Alex's hopes died. Then Rafe stood and held out his hand.

"Come on. Let's go to bed."

Slightly shocked at Rafe's decision to stay, Alex nevertheless scrambled to his feet to join Rafe. They headed to the bedroom, where Rafe squeezed his shoulder and whispered. "Y-you get into bed. I need to t-take a quick shower."

Alex nodded and slid into bed, hugging the pillow, listening to the comforting sounds of another person in the apartment with him. As Rafe said, he was quick and was back in the bedroom within five minutes. He came out with only a towel slung around his waist and brought with him the humid air from the heat of the shower and the fresh scent of toothpaste.

Alex raised his head from the pillow. "You brushed your teeth? Did you use my toothbrush?"

Rafe knelt by the side of the bed. "You had your mouth on my cock this afternoon." His lips curved in a teasing smile. "Does it bother you if I used your toothbrush?"

Hmm. Point taken.

And because it was a night of surprises and firsts, Rafe dropped his towel and slid into the bed next to Alex. "I-I think we should pick up where we 1-left off this afternoon, except for one thing."

Alex shifted to give Rafe room and slid around to face Rafe. "What's that?"

Rafe took Alex's face between his hands and kissed him until he lost all capacity to breathe or remember his name.

"It's time for me to take care of you."

CHAPTER TWELVE

The one thing Rafe hadn't counted on was Alex's vulnerability. Like every living creature, Rafe realized, even the strong, when pushed to their limits, can fall apart and shatter. And Rafe recognized he was witnessing Alex shattering before his eyes.

"Shh." He stroked Alex's back with the same caressing touch he'd use on any frightened, sick creature he needed to calm. "It's going to be fine." What Alex had said earlier—"It's always my fault"—revealed the extent of his internalization of some long-standing pain, a side of him he never allowed the world to see. Not even his best friend Micah.

Rafe pressed his lips to Alex's damp blond curls and let his heart settle to its normal steady beat. For as much as Alex was at his most broken, Rafe himself was treading unchartered waters tonight. Even though he had feelings for this man, it was never Rafe's plan to be here with Alex in his bed.

But plans be damned along with the consequences that went along with them. Rafe could no more leave Alex tonight than he could stop his heart from beating. And he knew the time had come to take that plunge and open himself up to someone, even knowing that there was no potential for a relationship or future. Alex was worth the inevitable hurt and heartache that would come when he left Rafe.

"You're in some kind of pain and I don't like seeing that. It hurts my heart." Rafe swept his fingertips across Alex's cheek, reveling in the scratchy stubble, melting a little as Alex rubbed up against his hand like an animal seeking to be petted. "Let me make you feel good."

Like a great golden cat, Alex lay beneath him, his strongly muscled body smooth and beautiful. And Alex held his hand then kissed it and whispered low so Rafe almost missed his words.

"Make me feel, Rafe. It's been so long. Make me feel."

His heart tumbled in a lazy somersault in his chest at Alex's shocking admission. Unable to hold back any longer, Rafe took Alex's mouth in a harsh kiss, pouring out the years of want and need he'd never before had the chance or ability to pursue. Alex moaned, his body hardening in Rafe's arms. Their tongues met and swept against each other, twisting and twining in a desperate dance, as Rafe slid his hand through Alex's silky hair, anchoring Alex's mouth hard against his own.

Rafe's cock thrust upward and he flexed his hips welcoming the corresponding push of Alex's erection against his thigh, even as their mouths tore at each other. His arms tightened around Alex as he deepened his kiss, giving into all the hunger he'd held in for this man for so long. Their breaths mingled and Rafe felt dizzy, faint with the rush of not only being possessed by Alex, but of possessing him as well; it was time to claim Alex as his own.

They broke apart, gasping, as the soft morning light broke through the blinds, sending stripes of pale color across the bed.

"Please, Rafe." Alex whispered, his eyes wet and dark with hunger. "Please."

Desire ran through Rafe's bloodstream like a flame on a trail of oil, traveling down his spine to rest in his groin. "Do you have—"

"In the drawer next to the bed," Alex broke in, anticipating his question.

With a gentle brush of lips Rafe kissed Alex's cheek, leaving him for a moment to find the condoms and lubricant. Sensing

Alex's need, Rafe nevertheless held Alex's gaze as he took the tube, hesitating, wanting to make sure he was reading the man correctly.

When Alex nodded, Rafe took control. He squeezed some of the cool gel and brushed up against Alex's hole. Alex jerked and groaned, the walls echoing with the sound of his pleadings. He slid a finger partly inside, and found himself gripped by the tight heat. He slid all the way in, then added a second finger, and twisted, stroked and curled them up and around his gland until Alex, writhing and gasping beneath him, began to piston himself on Rafe's fingers.

"More," he begged, wrapping his legs around Rafe's waist. "I want you, now."

Rafe rolled the condom onto his aching cock, and slicked it up with the lube, hoping he could control himself and not ex-plode when he entered Alex's body. He'd planned to go slow, but at the first push inside Alex, he couldn't help himself. It had been so long and he'd wanted this man so much he sank into the tightness and the heat, feeling Alex open then grip him, drawing him deep inside.

"Oh, God, yesss," he hissed through gritted teeth, pushing further and harder until his balls rested against Alex's ass. It was a position Rafe never thought he'd find himself in, his cock bur-ied inside Alex, the man's legs wrapped around his waist, his arms reaching out to be held. There for Rafe to hold, heal and love.

"Oh, baby," Alex moaned, as Rafe began to move, slowly at first then with increasing intensity and strength until the bed was banging against the wall and their bodies grew slick with sweat.

"Oh God," Alex sobbed, his legs gripping Rafe around the waist. "Rafe," he called out as he thrashed his head back and forth on the pillow. "Rafe, please."

His hand still slick with the lube, Rafe grasped Alex's rigid cock and began to pump him from the base to its thick head, watching the play of emotions across Alex's face, and bracing himself with his other hand to keep sliding in and out of Alex. One, two, three more strokes, and Alex froze and cried out, shaking beneath him. His cock erupted all over Rafe's hand, shooting streams across his stomach and chest.

"Fuck," Rafe breathed, in awe of the sight of this beautiful man coming undone in his hands. He had little time to enjoy the sight as Alex opened his eyes and with a smile that blazed stronger by the moment, began to urge Rafe on.

"Harder, baby," Alex pushed his hips up, meeting Rafe's downward thrusts. "Need you. Want you hard." They rocked together and Rafe held onto Alex's shoulders, his fingers gripping into the heavy muscle as Alex heaved up to meet his strokes.

"Alex," Rafe cried out, "Alex." His hoarse cries rang out amid the sound of their sweat soaked bodies coming together. He sensed the impending ache and tingling of orgasm barreling down upon him, his hips pounding into Alex as his life at that moment centered on the point where their bodies joined. Rafe choked on his cry of release, his body jerking and trembling even as he came harder than he ever did in his life. His vision blurred and Rafe swore he saw stars before his eyes. Alex's passage gripped him hard as his cock throbbed and pulsed, emptying into the condom. Breathing hard, he collapsed on top of Alex. After a minute when Rafe tried to move, Alex held him firm against his chest with a heavy arm.

"Don't, not yet. Lie here with me."

Surprised by the unexpected tenderness, Rafe lay still, Alex's thumping heart beating fast alongside his own. Sudden tears rushed to Rafe's eyes and ashamed of his emotional state, Rafe burrowed his head in Alex's neck. To Rafe's shock, Alex put his arms around him and held him close, as if sensing his need for comfort.

Finally Rafe lifted his head, stared down into Alex's face and gave him a hesitant smile. "Hi." He licked his lips, suddenly nervous to talk, even though he still lay naked and breathless in Alex's arms. "How do you feel?"

Once again, with that surprising tenderness, Alex smoothed

his hand across Rafe's cheek. "I feel fucking amazing, thanks to you." He cupped Rafe's cheek, and the frozen part of Rafe's heart, the one he'd buried long ago behind that stone wall of hurt and shame began to melt in the warmth of Alex's smile. "I never would've guessed it."

"Guessed what?" Rafe shifted and slid out of Alex. He removed the condom and threw it away, returning to the bed and Alex's welcoming arms.

"You." Alex studied his face and Rafe knew he blushed red, from the heat in his cheeks.

"What do you mean, me?" He wanted to look anywhere but at Alex, but he was trapped and couldn't move.

"You're so calm and quiet on the job." Alex's voice turned teasing. "Who knew you'd be a tiger in the bedroom."

"I—I . . ." Rafe faltered, having no way to express the way he felt, how deep his emotions ran at their coupling. Words as usual failed him, and he didn't want to embarrass himself so he merely brushed the back of his hand against Alex's cheek.

Alex didn't have that problem and grinned, pulling Rafe back into the circle of his arms. "You don't have to say anything." He kissed him and they lazily explored each other's mouths, as Rafe's heart bloomed in his chest.

Alex's mouth kissed a heated trail along Rafe's chin and down his neck, while his hands busily explored Rafe's ass, massaging each cheek. A gasp escaped Rafe at the delicate touch of Alex's finger.

"I like knowing something about you no one else does." Alex brought his finger to his mouth and wet it, Rafe watching his action with heavy-lidded eyes. A wicked grin teased Alex's lips as he took that same finger and slowly sank it inside Rafe to the base.

Rafe moaned, allowing the incredible sensation of Alex's finger moving inside him to awaken his hunger. And like the man himself, teasing, taunting and wicked, yet so intuitive and understanding, Alex added another finger, instinctively knowing where Rafe craved the twist and the pressure. He brushed up against Rafe's prostate, curling his fingers to glide them over the knot of tissue and Rafe surged up against Alex's hand, pushing his fingers deeper and harder.

"You like that, right baby? You like it hard and strong, huh?" Alex continued to twist and brush his fingers against Rafe's sweet spot, driving him insane with pleasure. "I like it when you're all hot and bothered."

Rafe continued to hump against his hand while Alex whispered dirty thoughts in his ear, setting his body on fire. "You should always be naked and sweaty in my bed. That's how you like it, don't you?"

With one final drag and twist of Alex's fingers, Rafe splintered apart, coming in an aching burst of release, his orgasm smaller but no less intense with his cock trapped against Alex's firm stomach, and Alex's hand buried in his ass. It was raw, hot and sexy, like Alex himself.

When he came back to life, Alex gave him a funny smile and got up to go to the bathroom. Replete, his body sated and loose from this unexpected night, Rafe could hear the water running. Several minutes passed before Alex came back, towel in hand, and climbed into bed with him.

"I looked in on Lucky and she was still sleeping. How about I clean you up now, tiger?"

Rafe glanced down seeing evidence of his last bout of lovemaking with Alex sprayed on his stomach and chest and ducked his head in embarrassment over revealing so much in the early morning light. "Uh, yeah. Sh-sure." Uninhibited joy was something Rafe hadn't allowed himself to feel since college, since the days when he and Kyle had been together and he'd thought his world was perfect and would last forever.

At least this time he knew enough ahead of time to make the choice with his eyes wide open. And Alex was sweetly loving, kissing Rafe's chest as he wiped him up, then tossing the wash cloth over the side of the bed, taking him in his arms again only this time to hold him close.

"Why don't we catch some sleep for a few hours? I know

I'm beat but you must be wrung out."

Rafe could hardly keep his eyes open and without thinking lay his head on Alex's shoulder, breathing in his scent of sweat and heat and coconut shampoo. "Hmm, that sounds like a plan, at least for a few hours." Happier than he'd been in years, he closed his eyes and drifted, snuggling into the curve of Alex's arms.

Rafe blinked his eyes, struggling to re-enter wakefulness and glanced over at the clock to see 7:30 a.m. Hmm. Not too much sleep but well worth it, as he took a peek at Alex's broad, naked back. He itched to smooth his hands across that expanse of warm flesh, but knowing where that would lead, he regretfully held back and slid quietly out of bed.

He first went to the living room where he checked on Lucky and saw to his relief the dog looked well; her eyes were bright and her nose was cold and wet to the touch.

"You did a number on us last night didn't you, girl?" He fondled her ears and she thumped her plumy tail and whined. "No more chocolate for you, okay?" He kissed her head and she laid her head down, content to rest after her traumatic night.

Thank God she seemed to come through the problem with no lasting damage. He'd have Alex bring her in so he could check up on her vitals and give her a clean bill of health. One last pat and Rafe knew he needed to shower and dress to get to the clinic. Crossing the living room as silently as possible so as not to wake Alex, he went into the bathroom.

Soaping himself and running his hands over his body, Rafe marveled at a human being's ability to adjust and experience happiness no matter how many times they'd been knocked down in the past. He'd grown up with cold and withdrawn parents, yet he still had the capacity to love not only the animals he took care of but people as well. Rafe thought he'd loved Kyle and maybe he even had, but his inexperience and feelings of unworthiness and shame over his stutter always left a question in his mind as to whether there was even a relationship at all.

The sex he'd experienced before tonight had for the most part been unremarkable; in the beginning there was always the hot rush of release and initial excitement that something might click, but it never went any further than that. Hooking up with Kyle, getting sucked in by his wide, friendly smile and whispered promises in the dark had tied him up into knots.

He'd made an easy victim, falling so hard and fast. Looking back on it now, he couldn't say he regretted the relationship, or whatever it was that they had. It taught him about himself. He learned his own self-worth and that he was a survivor. So for that, at least, he could thank the man who broke his heart, wherever he may be now.

Rafe rinsed himself off and washed his hair. Holding his head under the rush of water from the showerhead, he replayed the night's events in his mind, his body hardening at the remembrance of Alex's hands and lips on his body.

With a sigh of regret, Rafe turned off the water and wrapped himself in a towel. He decided not to bother shaving. He'd already used Alex's toothbrush and didn't want to freak the guy out and use his razor too. The feelings Alex had wrung from him last night, the gutting release and unfettered ecstasy, were like nothing he'd ever imagined possible. It blazed through him like a backdraft, searing and obliterating everything in its path.

Rafe gazed in the mirror and the truth washed over him like a pail of icy water. He could easily, so damn easily as a matter of fact, fall in love with Alex. That sobering thought dismayed him and spurred him into action.

"No, no. Never. Not going to happen." Rafe towel dried his hair roughly. "Get it out of your head. He needed someone last night. I could've been anyone last night. All I was, was a convenient bed partner."

Armed with his good intentions, Rafe took a dry towel, tied it around his waist, and opened the bathroom door to get his clothes from the bedroom.

When he saw Alex wasn't in bed, Rafe surmised he'd gone

into the living room to check on Lucky. He dropped the towel, about to get dressed but at the sound of loud, angry voices, he pulled up his sweats and ran out bare chested to the living room.

Micah and Alex stood face to face, arguing. At this point, neither one had noticed him; they continued to point at one another and yell.

"How could you have been so irresponsible, Alex? God damn you, Lucky could've died."

"But she didn't. She was taken care of and you can see she's fine."

"And so what then? You think my dog's okay so you pick up some trick and bring him back to my home to fuck him?"

Maybe he'd made a noise; he didn't know. But he began to shake as both Alex and Micah spun around to stare at him.

"Holy shit, Alex." Micah's gaze raked him from head to feet.

Rafe realized what he must look like; shirtless and barefoot, his hair still damp. "H-hi, M-Micah," he said weakly.

Even more wild-eyed than before, Micah spun back around to face Alex, who stood scowling right back at him. "Rafe? You're screwing Rafe? What the fuck is wrong with you, Alex?"

Humiliated, Rafe couldn't remain in the same room with the battling best friends. He raced back to the bedroom and slammed the door behind him taking deep breaths, knowing he couldn't speak, should anyone want to ask him what happened.

But no one came.

CHAPTER
THIRTEEN

At the sight of Rafe's stricken, white face, Alex strode over to his best friend and stood nose to nose with him, unintimidated by Micah's dark and angry expression.

"First of all, I didn't almost kill Lucky. Yes, she ate chocolate but I left it out by accident. And as soon as I saw she was in distress I called Rafe, her veterinarian, in case the California sun fried your brain and you forgot who that man is." By this point, Alex was less and less inclined to be nice to Micah, and decided to let it all come out.

"I almost wanted to kill myself because the thought of something happening to your dog would have upset you. And yet when you come in, all you can think of is who I might be sleeping with? I'm beginning to realize maybe what people have been saying to me for years is true; that I get nothing from you as a friend. It's been all take and no give, with me doing all the giving." He folded his arms and glared at Micah, ignoring Josh who'd come in to stand like a sober soldier at Micah's side.

"Alex," Josh broke in. "Thank you for taking such quick action to help Lucky and when Rafe comes back out here I'll say the same thing to him."

"I didn't do anything except get her the help she needed, which you knew I would do. Rafe did everything." He shot Micah an evil stare. "For you to call him a common trick I fucked is way beyond the pale, even for you, Micah." Alex watched

Micah wince, perversely glad his words had wounded his best friend, as Micah's earlier words had hurt him. "I guess that old saying of a leopard not able to change his spots is true. You're still that same bastard you always were. You'll never change."

Knowing Rafe must be embarrassed and hiding out in the bedroom, Alex was halfway across the living room before he turned around to face his two friends, who hadn't moved. "Oh, and you're welcome, for living here and taking care of every-thing while you went on your honeymoon. Don't worry, I'll be out of your hair as soon as I can."

"Alex, please—" Josh implored, but Alex was in no mood to placate his best friend's husband, no matter how nice he was. This had nothing to do with Josh, it was between him and Micah.

"Forget it, both of you. I think the time has come for me to put some space between us and give you the chance to start your life together. I said from the beginning you don't need a third wheel and I meant it." He locked eyes with Micah. "Maybe I need to see about working on another surgical team as well."

Micah paled and Alex knew that hit his friend hard. They'd worked together for years and Alex knew Micah counted on him for surgeries.

"Please, Alex. Don't do anything rash." Once again it was Josh who spoke, not Micah, who stood sphinxlike and mute.

"We all do what we have to do."

Without another word, he hastened into the bedroom to find Rafe so they could both get dressed and leave. He owed Rafe an apology for Micah's behavior, since he knew Micah wouldn't do it himself, and Alex wanted to prolong his time with Rafe. He entered the bedroom to find Rafe fully dressed and sitting on the edge of the bed, staring at the floor.

"Hey. Give me a minute to get my stuff together and we can go catch some breakfast before you hit the clinic." He began to stuff his things in a duffle bag and in record speed, was packed and ready to leave. His attempts at conversation were met with monosyllabic responses in a flat, tired voice. Alex didn't think much of it, chalking Rafe's quiet demeanor to lack of sleep.

Grinning to himself, Alex pictured a repeat performance of last night, and couldn't wait to curl up next to Rafe tonight.

"Ready?" He placed a hand on Rafe's shoulder and leaned in for a kiss, but Rafe pulled back. "What's wrong?"

Twin slashes of color stained Rafe's cheeks. "I know last n-night was simply a one-off; neither of us pl-planned it. You don't have to pretend for me."

"Uh, I have no idea what you're talking about. I thought we had a great time."

Rafe nodded. "We did, but it d-doesn't mean it's going to happen again. Sometimes time and circumstances throw people together. You were in distress and needed comfort."

"So last night was a pity fuck for you?"

Rafe's color rose higher but Alex didn't care at this point. First the fight with Micah and now Rafe was telling him the only reason they had sex was because Rafe felt sorry for him.

"You don't understand."

"Oh, I understand everything." Alone again. Now he didn't even have Micah to hang out with, or Rafe for that matter. He was really fucking alone.

"No, you don't."

The sharpness of Rafe's voice surprised Alex. "Fine," he said, irritation clouding his voice. "Why don't you explain it to me then."

Rafe's gaze kept flickering to the door and Alex knew he was probably nervous that Josh or more likely Micah would come in and interrupt them.

"Don't worry. Micah is steering clear of me for now, and I of him. He won't bother us."

Visibly relaxing, Rafe studied his clasped hands as he spoke. "I'm not expecting any grand words of passion or love; that would be silly and delusional on my part. We had a great night and I wanted you to know I really enjoyed it." He swallowed and Alex couldn't look at Rafe's mouth without thinking how soft those lips felt against his own.

"I did too," he whispered. "So what's the problem?"

Frustrated, Rafe clenched his fists. "I'm not a casual person. I take things seriously and to heart; maybe too much, some people say. But I can't imagine only one time with you is going to be enough, yet I don't have the right to hold you to more. You've already told me you aren't boyfriend material, that we aren't together." Rafe pressed his lips together in a tight line and blinked, refusing to lift his focus off the floor.

It hit Alex like a punch to his gut that Rafe didn't want to stop sleeping together, he wanted to know what to expect. The truth was, Alex had no idea; he'd never been in this position before. So he spoke from his heart, hoping what he said made sense.

"I also told you I won't share you if we're sleeping together. I think we're friends and that's more important than anything; at least for me. No matter what physical relationship we have together, it's nice to know you have my back and I have yours."

"You do?" Rafe's honest eyes held a question Alex surmised was the product of a long ago hurt. One, he vowed, Rafe would tell him about.

"Baby, I've got your back and your front and every piece of you in between. I may be a crazy, fucked-up jigsaw puzzle, scattered all over the place, but the important pieces, my heart and my brain, haven't been lost yet." Alex took Rafe's hand and pulled him up to his chest. "We're friends. I take care of my friends." His lips curved in a wicked grin. "Some better than others." Now he kissed Rafe, slow and sweet, the ache of their past passion building in his blood. With great difficulty he broke the kiss, the dazed expression in Rafe's eyes telling him Rafe was as affected by the kiss as he was.

"We can be friends and still have a physical relationship, as long as we know the friendship is always the most important part." Alex hefted the strap of his bag to his shoulder and looked around to make sure he hadn't left anything important.

"I agree. I-I'm glad we're friends." Rafe smiled at him.

"Me too. Let's go so we can grab some coffee and a bagel before you have to start work."

Rafe fell into step with him as they left the bedroom. "No surgeries for you today?"

Alex checked his watch, "I agreed to fill in for some colleagues this afternoon, so we can have coffee together before I go back to my apartment and drop my bag off."

"Where do you live, anyway? I've never heard you mention."

His apartment could be anywhere, for all the time he spent in that space. There was nothing personal there, except for the pictures of him and Seth and him and Micah. "Downtown."

Rafe said nothing else as they entered the living room, where Josh and Micah were both sitting on the floor next to Lucky. Alex made straight for the door, but Rafe, being the kind and caring person that made him such a good vet, of course had to check on Lucky.

Alex chose to remain in the hallway and watched Rafe squat down to give Lucky a brief, yet thorough check-up. From what Alex could see, she was alert and happy, basically sitting in Micah's lap.

"You'll want to bring her by sometime today so I can look her over. I need to be certain she's okay." Rafe stood and wiped off his hands with the paper towel Josh handed to him. Lucky slowly got up from Micah's lap and walked over to Alex and he bent down to pet her.

"I'm sorry, sweetie." She licked his face and he scratched behind her ears, a favorite place of hers.

"I'm sorry too, Alex," Josh said.

He gave Lucky one final pat and stood. "You have nothing to be sorry for."

"I don't want you and Micah to argue about this." Josh glanced over his shoulder back at Micah who pretended to look through the mail. "I know he'd be crushed if anything happened to your friendship, as would I."

Alex picked up his duffle bag. Rafe had come to stand by his side. "You know Josh, a year ago I would've let it slide and laughed it off as 'Micah being Micah.' But I'm not willing to do that anymore. Some people have to figure out that the world doesn't revolve around them. Other people count and simply because they don't flail around, snarling and screaming doesn't mean their hearts and their heads aren't just as engaged."

"You know Micah loves you. You're brothers."

Pain shot through him and before he could stop himself he blurted out, "No. I had a brother but he died." He remembered the date. Fifteen years ago today he lost Seth. How fitting; both men gone with the summer wind.

Shit. He hadn't meant to say anything. Maybe Micah was too busy and hadn't heard.

Micah dropped the pile of mail he'd been holding and stormed over to where they all stood frozen in the hallway. The envelopes, magazines and department store circulars skittered across the floor, creating a crazy patterned carpet. His eyes flashed dark with a dangerous emotion Alex had never seen before.

He'd heard.

"Fucking hell, Alex. What are you talking about? You never said you had a brother. I've known you for all these years and you never said a word? What's wrong with you?"

Rafe squeezed his arm, as if to let him know he stood by him. Grateful for his presence Alex hefted the bag on his shoulder and spoke directly to Josh. "Welcome back. I'm sure we'll talk soon." He turned on his heel and left, shutting the door in Micah's shocked and angry face.

It didn't give him the sense of satisfaction he'd anticipated, Alex mused as he and Rafe rode down in the elevator. Instead there was the shaky awareness that for the first time in years he'd exposed himself and let his secrets out into the wild.

They exited the building to a bright and sunny day. The air blew crisp and fresh with the scent of earth and sun. It was springtime in New York City and it was glorious, if you were of a mindset to enjoy. Alex was not, and saw no beauty in the bounty, nor allowed himself pleasure in the richness of the cerulean blue of the sky or the bright green tender leaves of the newly planted flowers in the flower boxes outside the windows of the brownstones.

"So let's go get that coffee, huh?" Alex faced Rafe with a smile, which abruptly faded at the concern etched across Rafe's brow.

"You've known Micah for all these years and you never told him you had a brother?"

"It never came up." But even Alex heard how lame he sounded and from the incredulous look Rafe gave him, Alex knew he didn't fool the man. "I'd rather not talk about it." Pasting a grin on his face, Alex began to walk down the block toward the busy avenue, where they could have their coffee. Rafe would be halfway to his clinic and he could take the subway back to his apartment. Alex had taken only four or five steps before realizing Rafe remained standing where they were, feet planted solidly on the ground, with an intransigent look on his face.

Probably not the right time to tell him he looked adorable, but Alex didn't want to get into a personal, uncomfortable discussion right there, especially on a busy street.

"You're cute when you're annoyed." He pecked a kiss to Rafe's lips, but Rafe didn't soften toward him or kiss him back. Alex sighed and brushed the hair off his forehead. "What's the matter?" Where Micah was normally only interested in the world according to Micah, never questioning if Alex abruptly switched topics or steered their conversations back toward whatever Micah might be interested in, Rafe was attuned to the world around him. He cared about people's feelings and was a sensitive soul, but nobody's fool.

"I don't understand you," said Rafe shaking his head. "How can you have b-been friends with Micah half your life yet he doesn't know you have—had—a brother?" Rafe walked by his side, looking everywhere but at Alex.

Had a brother. Such a small change of letters makes such a seismic shift in reality. Cold seeped through him though the sun's rays beat warm against his back. A choking sensation caught Alex in the throat; he couldn't talk about Seth. He wouldn't.

"Alex?" Rafe stopped walking and led him off to stand by a

lamppost papered with flyers advertising a neighborhood stoop sale, a Man with a Van and someone's poor lost kitty named Tiger. They faced each other but Alex found he couldn't maintain eye contact with Rafe and he read more about Tiger the missing cat. He couldn't lie to Rafe's soft eyes, and to his own astonishment, he didn't want to.

What he didn't count on was Rafe's stubborn insistence in continuing conversations Alex so obviously wished to end.

"Okay, Alex. I see you don't want to talk about this right now and I can respect that. You're hurting, aren't you?" Now Rafe moved closer to him, so close Alex could hear him breathing. "I'm hurting for you. All my life I wished I had a sibling; either a brother or a sister to talk to, since my parents barely spoke to me. To find out you lost your brother—" Rafe wiped at his eyes, "—it's ripping me apart, imagining your pain."

"My twin. Fraternal but so close we might as well have been identical." Though he whispered it, he knew Rafe heard him, over the sounds of honking cabs, over the roar of exhaust from the buses and the far-off wail of a fire engine. "I—I can't right now. Please."

Never. Alex never begged, but here he was, on an increasingly busy street corner, laying his most painful and private secrets bare, pleading with Rafe once more. This was different and important; Micah was someone he was a friend to; it was a one-sided relationship. Rafe was a man he'd been learning to share a friendship with. They could forge a relationship together if Alex was willing to take it one step further and open his heart.

CHAPTER FOURTEEN

The clinic may not have been as busy as it was the day before but Rafe welcomed any distraction, as his mind was a hamster wheel of activity, constantly in motion and spinning around and around with no end. Once he finished up with the last animal, a cat suffering from severe hairballs, Rafe collapsed in a chair. Jenny was in the back examining room with a little girl and her hamster who'd gotten scratched by the family cat. Without needing to ask, Patty handed him a cup of coffee, which he took with a grateful smile.

"Thank you." He sipped the steaming hazelnut blend and let the warmth spill through his body. Rafe imagined he could feel it entering his bloodstream, giving him energy. *Last night had really kicked my butt,* his lips smiled around the rim of his coffee cup. *In more ways than one.* The memory of Alex's teasing fingers inside him brought him to a place he'd only read about in books and laughed off as being unreal.

Nothing unreal about how his body responded, he chuckled to himself, as even now a rush of lust flooded through him. The reality of Alex was so much better than any fantasy he'd dreamed about for the past year. The feel of Alex's hot passage gripping him as Rafe drove himself inside, and Alex's cries of passion that Rafe still couldn't believe he'd wrung from Alex's gasping lips, all were inconceivable only a month ago. Rafe had never come so hard in his life. All that was secondary though, to

Alex's startling revelation about a twin brother and his absolute wretchedness over his death. Rafe hated having to leave Alex today, but made a promise to himself to visit him tonight. Alex had been so kind to him lately and even before last night's incredible physical experience, Rafe believed they'd become true friends.

No one can ever have enough friends, and Rafe certainly couldn't say he had too many. There was no one from his childhood he kept in contact with and he was Facebook friends with a few people from college and veterinary school, but only through his membership in several alumni associations. Amazing to think eight years of his life had gone by without a single person making enough of an impact that he'd want to keep in contact with them.

Several years ago, Kyle had sent him a message about getting together "for old-times sake." He lived in California now and said he'd be in town on business, and gave Rafe his hotel and phone number. Rafe knew what he wanted and vowed not to be taken in again. Curiosity won out and when he looked at Kyle's profile and saw the smiling man with his arm around his wife and a young child in her arms, Rafe was disgusted. Angry at the subterfuge Kyle was committing on his unsuspecting wife, Rafe deleted the message and never responded.

Alex was a whole different type of person. His big-as-the-sky personality and open, friendly nature made him a natural magnet for people. This darker side of him, the one Rafe had seen this morning, was unexpected and jarring. If a man like Alex wasn't really happy, what hope was there for someone like himself?

But how well did he know the real Alex? Alex could simply be the teasing, fun-loving man everyone knew him to be. Or, as Rafe was beginning to suspect, did Alex hide behind his jokes to deflect people from digging too deep and discover what was hiding beneath years of pain?

Rafe tossed his empty cup in the trash and rubbed his eyes. They were gritty and achy and there was nothing more he'd have liked than to crash into his bed and sleep, but he owed it to Alex to be there for him tonight as a friend. He pulled out his phone and texted him.

Hey, let's hang out tonight and watch a movie. My treat for dinner.

He waited a few minutes for an answer but nothing came. Perhaps he was still at the hospital, but looking at his watch, Rafe didn't believe that to be true. Surgeries ended much earlier in the day, even he knew that. After a moment's hesitation, he called Alex directly.

The phone went straight to voicemail. Shit. One thing he knew about Alex was he was always on his phone. The perk of being the social creature he was, Alex was always receiving texts from someone or making plans for the evening. If he cut himself off from his friends, he was hurting worse than Rafe realized.

"Patty, remember we needed to do a reverse look-up on a patient one time when we only had their cell phone?"

"Sure, why?" She swiveled around in her chair.

Ignoring her question, he responded with one of his own. "Can you look up this number for me?" He watched her take down the number then find the website and after a few minutes, he had Alex's address near Union Square.

"Thanks." Re-energized, he jumped out of his seat and stuffed his phone back in his pocket. Jenny was leading the little girl and her mother out, lecturing her how she needed to keep the cage away from the cat.

"But Princess wanted to be friends with Herbie. I didn't think she'd hurt him."

Jenny smiled at them. "I know, but cats see hamsters as bigger mice and don't know better. I'm sure Princess didn't mean to hurt him, but better to be safe, for Herbie's sake. From now on, keep him in his cage whenever Princess is nearby."

Good luck with that, Rafe thought. As soon as the mother and daughter left, he took Jenny aside. "Listen, I'm going to take off now."

"I know." Her eyes twinkled at him. "Hot date?"

His face heated at her teasing. Damn the blushing. "No, I,

um, I want to go check on Alex. He had a fight with his best friend and he was really upset the last time I saw him."

"Those are the two guys who came in this afternoon with the shepherd mix, right?"

He nodded. Micah and Josh had brought Lucky in earlier and she checked out fine. He told them to watch her carefully and make sure she stayed hydrated. Micah was in a dark and angry mood, and Rafe stayed as far away from him as possible. Josh pulled him aside when Micah went to pay for the visit.

"He's so hurt and angry at Alex. Micah can't believe Alex never told him he had a brother. And the worst part is I don't know how to make it better. I never thought they'd split apart, but this has me worried for their friendship."

Rafe strengthened his resolve to be there for Alex, no matter what. "Yeah. Alex and Micah have been friends for years and they're at a rough patch. I want to be there for him."

Perceptive as ever, Jenny slipped an arm around him and gave him a hug. "You're a good friend and he's lucky to have you."

Rafe shrugged. "I haven't done anything yet, but I'm going to do my best."

He left the clinic, his mind busy with what he was going to say to Alex as he got on the subway to go downtown to Union Square. First thing was to practice his breathing again. He was determined to conquer his stutter in front of Alex, no matter that the man still set him on edge each time they met.

By the time the train pulled into the 14th Street station, Rafe was in control. He checked the address on his phone and hurried the few, short blocks to Alex's apartment building, which surprisingly was a walk-up with no doorman. He'd always imagined Alex in a luxury building. Once again the man surprised him.

When he pressed the button with Alex's apartment number, there was no answer. He waited a few minutes and tried again, with no luck. Damn. He watched as a good-looking man approached the building carrying several bags from the supermarket in one hand and a dog on a leash in the other. Even though he knew it was wrong, Rafe pulled out his phone and began to speak in a loud voice.

"Hey Alex, yeah I'm downstairs. I've been buzzing you, man."

The man smiled at him and the dog jumped on Rafe's legs.

"Oh, I'm so sorry, he gets excited with new people." He scolded the dog. "Jamison, down boy."

The dog, a large mixed breed, faced his owner with his tongue lolling out and barked. The man rolled his eyes and hushed him. "Jamie, shh. You're impossible."

Rafe laughed. "It's okay. I'm a v-vet. I'm used to d-dogs." Shit. Again with the stutter. He breathed deeply. "Can I get the door for you? I'm here to see a fr-friend, Alex Stern." He figured if he gave Alex's name the man would trust him. This new, devious part of his nature surprised him, but then again he'd changed quite a bit since becoming friends with Alex. And Rafe would do whatever was necessary for his friend.

"That would be great, thanks. Would you mind holding his leash while I open the door?"

"Sure." Rafe held onto the dog, while the man opened the outer door with his key, and held the door open with his foot to allow the man to pick up his bags then, still holding the dog, Rafe followed him inside. The door slammed behind him.

"I can take him now, thanks." The man gave him a friendly smile. "Alex is on the third floor. There's no elevator I'm afraid."

"That's okay." He turned to go.

"Hey."

Rafe turned back at the man's voice. "Yes?"

"I'm Marcus, Marc. Nice to meet you."

"Oh. Same here. I'm Rafe."

"Alex is a lucky guy."

Rafe's face flamed. "We're, um, friends, that's all."

"Yeah?" Marc cocked his head. "Well, I know for a fact Alex isn't home since I just left him in the supermarket. Should I be worried about letting you in? Are you some crazy stalker?" His eyes danced in amusement at Rafe's obvious shock.

Before Rafe could stammer out his excuse, the door slammed behind him.

"Rafe? What are you doing here?"

Alex hadn't shaved and his hair looked as though he'd spent the day running his hands through his curls. His tee shirt stretched over his broad shoulders and his shorts hung on his hips, showcasing his flat abdomen. Rafe, remembering how all that wonderfully smooth muscled skin felt beneath his hands and mouth last night, stared dumbly at Alex for a moment.

"Uh," he stammered then remembered why he was here. Not to get laid, but to help a friend. "Can we talk?"

A guarded look shuttered Alex's face. "Sure. Follow me." He headed up the stairs. "See you later, Marc." He carried a bag with two six-packs of beer.

Following quickly behind Alex, Rafe gave Marc a good-bye wave. Neither he nor Alex spoke until they entered Alex's apartment.

"You want a beer or water or anything?" Alex tossed his keys in a bowl and headed for the tiny kitchen. "I know I need a drink." He took out two bottles of Corona and without waiting for Rafe's response, gave him one.

Rafe, sitting on the sofa, took the bottle but immediately set it down on the small table next to his elbow. Still standing, Alex had already downed half his bottle and seemed poised on the verge of becoming one with the rest of the six-pack.

"Why are you here?" Alex said bluntly. "And how did you get my address?" Before Rafe had a chance to answer, Alex stormed over to him. "Did Micah give it to you? Did he ask you to come talk to me—"

"No." Rafe cut in. "He didn't ask, no one did. I . . . I f-found it m-myself." He held Alex's angry glare. "I was concerned about you after this m-morning and wanted to m-make sure you were okay," Rafe finished softly, breaking Alex's stare to study the floor. His glasses slid down and he pushed them up the bridge of his nose.

"Oh."

"Remember what we talked about earlier. That we're friends first, above everything else. Well, I'm here to be your friend."

The silence deepened between them, marred only by the outside noises of ambulance sirens from the nearby hospital and screams of children playing in the park.

The sofa shifted and Alex's bulk settled next to him. "We *are* friends. Thank you for reminding me of that. You deserve more from me. I've held everything in for so long because if I let it out I'm afraid I may not be able to stop crying."

Not daring to look at Alex for fear of wanting to kiss him again, Rafe shrugged. "It's okay."

This was the real Alex, Rafe realized. The Alex no one else had ever seen.

"No. I'm sorry I snapped at you. It wasn't nice. And you started stuttering around me again which means you're nervous—I made you nervous which shouldn't be happening."

Embarrassed now, Rafe tried to move away from Alex, but Alex held him back, placing a hand around the nape of his neck. "Don't."

That one word froze Rafe in place. He sat still, Alex's electric touch sending aching jolts of desire through his body. "I, um . . ." He didn't know what to say and licked his lips in nervous consternation.

Alex's thumb caressed his skin in tantalizing circles. "Whatever is going on between Micah and me has nothing to do with you."

"I know, but you're hurting and—umph."

Alex covered Rafe's mouth in a bruising kiss, pushing him back on the sofa until he lay flat beneath the body he'd been ogling only moments before. For a moment he yielded, groaning aloud. Alex took that opportunity to slip his tongue into his mouth and Rafe allowed it until he pushed against Alex's shoulders and, with great reluctance and every working cell in his brain screaming at him, backed away. He swiped his hand across his mouth.

"What was that for?"

Alex smirked. "I thought after last night you'd figured it out." He stood and Rafe backed away.

"I didn't come here to get laid."

Alex stared at him. "You didn't?" His brow furrowed in confusion. "Why not?"

Despite himself, Rafe laughed. "Because I wanted to talk to you."

"Fucking is more fun," sulked Alex. "Talking is overrated."

The man was impossible. "Alex," Rafe shook his finger at him, "there's more to life than sex sometimes."

"Oh the hell there is," groused Alex. "It's one of the necessities of life: air, water, food and hot sex, and not necessarily in that order."

Rafe sighed. "What am I going to do with you?"

Alex grinned and pulled him close. "I can think of several things right now that might be illegal in some states."

This time when Alex kissed him, Rafe didn't stop him. He hazily remembered the promise he'd made to himself to not allow Alex to deflect the conversation away from the fight with Micah and stand firm.

But those were promises made when he was alone, without Alex's warm hands playing over his body like a concert pianist played his instrument. And Alex was an incredibly skilled and gifted musician of love. Alex's smile was gentle as he removed the glasses Rafe knew sat askew on his face, placing them on the table. His large hands caressed Rafe's face, as if he were learning the texture of his skin and shape of his jaw, then almost in desperation, Alex's mouth slanted hungrily over his and Rafe felt the last of his resistance melt away as he fell into that kiss. As if sensing his surrender, Alex cupped Rafe's ass and yanked him hard up against his chest.

"Want you now, baby." Alex pulled Rafe's shirt over his head and threw it in the corner, then buried his face in Rafe's neck, sucking the skin under his jaw, marking him with nips and teasing bites.

"Oh God," he moaned, dizzy with the spiraling desire winding through his veins. Rafe made a halfhearted attempt to speak. "Alex, wait . . ."

"No." With his blue eyes blazing, Alex took off his tee shirt and tossed it over his shoulder, then yanked down his shorts and stepped out of them, revealing the thick bulge of his cock. "I finally have you where I want you; here, alone with me and I'll be damned if I'm going to stop for anything except to put on a condom and get inside you."

From anyone else, those blatant, sexual words might have turned Rafe off but coming from Alex's lips they only made him harder. He'd never been so turned on in all his life and the fact that Alex wanted him so badly was a huge boost to his self-confidence. Shocking himself, Rafe blurted out. "Then do it. Fuck me until I scream the walls down."

Alex's eyes darkened and Rafe swore he heard him growl like a feral animal. "Let's go to bed." He took Rafe by the hand and half dragged, half ran with him across the large room of the studio apartment, to the king-sized bed hidden behind the screen. Rafe found himself tossed onto the bed with Alex standing over him, looking like a fire-breathing lion.

In what felt like slow motion, Rafe fumbled with the buttons of his jeans, only to have his hands brushed aside. "And here I thought you were good with your hands." Alex popped each button, never breaking eye contact. When the last button popped, he reached underneath Rafe's ass, grabbed the top of the jeans and pulled them down. "Houston, we have lift-off." Alex smiled and caressed Rafe's straining cock through his boxers then hooked his fingers on either side of the material and tugged them down and off.

"Gorgeous." Alex licked Rafe's cock from base to tip, then engulfed the head in his mouth.

"Oh fuck," sighed Rafe, the slow roll of ecstasy beating through his entire body. "Oh baby, I can't hold on."

Alex, one step ahead of him, had already taken out the lube and condoms. There was no tenderness now as Alex slid first one then two heavily slicked fingers inside Rafe's hole, twisted them and pumped them in and out several times before removing them.

"I'm so fucking hot for you I won't last." He rolled on the condom. "So I'm going to fuck you hard now, but you see all the rest of these?" Alex held up a strip of condoms and waved them in front of Rafe's face. "By tomorrow morning, we're gonna use these all up." He tossed them aside and flipped Rafe over, smoothing his hands over the mounds of Rafe's ass, kissing each cheek, before separating them.

Rafe tilted his hips as Alex rested his hand on the base of his spine and glanced over his shoulder. Seeing Alex guiding his cock into his hole then push inside him, stretching his passage to accommodate his thickness, Rafe moaned at the pleasure pain. It had been a long time for him and Alex was the biggest man he'd ever had. Alex draped his bulk over Rafe, sliding his hands through Rafe's hair, then down his arms, pinning him to the bed. He didn't stop kissing him, even as he thrust inside Rafe with maddeningly slow, penetrating strokes, rolling his hips, hitting Rafe's sweet spot over and over again until Rafe cried out from the pleasure rocketing through his body.

Rafe raised his ass and pushed back to meet Alex's plunges, reveling in Alex's grunts and sighs even as his own desire rolled through him in wave after wave of splintering pleasure. They rocked together, Alex's thrusts becoming harder, his hands moving more purposefully over Rafe's body. Alex snaked an arm around him, reaching underneath to grasp Rafe's cock.

"Oh God, yes." Rafe drove his cock hard into Alex's slick hand, desperate for the friction he needed to come.

"You like that, huh? You like it hard, baby?" Alex stroked him with long, drawn-out pulls, adding an evil little twist on the head of Rafe's cock that had him whimpering as his balls began to ache and his muscles twitch. The drag and slide of Alex's cock, slamming in and out of his ass, set off a trembling deep within Rafe, a precursor to the orgasm threatening to explode.

"Yesss," Rafe hissed, shoving his cock harder into Alex's

hand, rolling his hips faster and faster. "Now, oh God, Alex, now." With one final wail, Rafe convulsed and came, shooting so hard and strong his vision blurred and his entire body shook with powerful tremors. He clutched the bedsheets in his hands and writhed underneath Alex, gasping and shaking.

"Hold still." Alex splayed himself over Rafe's back, settling himself inside Rafe further than anyone had ever touched him. Warmth filled Rafe, as Alex shouted, plunging deep inside him as he came, causing him to shudder and buck hard up against Alex's hips, which rested flush upon his ass.

"Damn, Tiger." Alex rested his cheek against Rafe's head, his breath drifting past Rafe's ear. "What the fuck are you doing to me?" He kissed Rafe's cheek and pulled out slowly. "Do you hurt?"

"A bit," admitted Rafe, smiling into the pillow before turning over to lie flat on his back, spread-eagled. "But well worth it."

"Glad to be of service," Alex chuckled as he tied off the condom, tossed it in the trash and climbed back into bed. "I wasn't kidding about before, you know." He pulled Rafe into his arms and Rafe didn't even try to resist at this point. His body had the consistency of a wet noodle; it was all he could do to cling to Alex. There'd be time enough for him to speak to Alex later, and find out what hurt him so badly.

"You weren't, huh?" Rafe settled into the circle of Alex's arms enjoying the unexpected tenderness of Alex's embrace. He slanted a look up into Alex's relaxed, smiling face and placed a kiss on his chin before closing his eyes. "Give me some time to recover at least." He wriggled his ass into Alex's groin and laughed at the corresponding jerk of the man's cock against his naked flesh.

"Mmm. I specialize in recovery room services." Alex rolled over, taking Rafe with him. "I have an excellent bedside manner."

Rafe closed his eyes and drifted off to sleep, feeling somehow like he'd won a battle but lost the war.

CHAPTER FIFTEEN

True to his word, Alex made sure not to let Rafe rest much that evening. After their second round of heart thumping, world rocking sex, Rafe lay flat on his back, with his eyes closed and a smile plastered on his face.

"I surrender. Whatever you want, all my worldly goods are yours. Give me a white flag." He shifted then groaned, flopping back against the pillows. "Don't make me move though." His eyelids fluttered then rested still. "God."

It took a moment for Alex to catch his own breath. "You called?" He propped himself up on his elbow and brushed a kiss over Rafe's lips.

"Very funny." Finally opening his eyes, Rafe blinked then squinted up at him. "Where did you put my glasses?"

"I'm keeping them hostage, to make sure you don't run away from me until I'm ready to let you go."

Rafe reached out and brushed his fingers along Alex's jaw. "I'm not going anywhere."

Their eyes held. Alex's heart gave a funny bounce and he found it hard to breathe again. Unwilling to let the mood turn serious, Alex forced himself to grin and get out of bed. "Well, we have to eat. I'm all for ordering takeout and spending the rest of our night here in bed."

He grabbed his iPad and Rafe's glasses and brought both back to the bed. Rafe sat up, his eyes dark and wistful.

"Are you asking me to stay?"

Alex stared at him, gape-mouthed. "Do I honestly need to? I thought it was a given. Besides," he joked, "I always buy my dates at least a dinner."

Rafe froze then turned away, but not before Alex caught the flash of hurt in his soft eyes.

Fuck. "I didn't—"

"It's fine, Alex. You don't owe me any explanations." Rafe slipped out of bed and Alex couldn't stop staring at his long, perfect body with that beautiful ass he was beginning to crave. No fucking way. He'd already screwed things up with Micah, he wasn't about to let this friendship crash and burn before it barely got off the ground.

"No. Please." He raced around to Rafe's side of the bed and pushed him back down, sitting next to him. "Listen to me. I was kidding. You know me, I'm always joking. It's how I deal with all the shit in my life. But I don't want you to think you're not special."

Rafe said nothing, only the hurt in his eyes told Alex he wasn't buying what Alex was saying.

Frustrated, Alex scrubbed his face with his hands. "I'm not used to this, this friends and lovers thing. I joke around so I don't have to think about things too hard. I've never had a relationship before."

"So why me?" Always honest himself, Rafe deserved answers.

"I don't know," said Alex, helplessly. "You—you're different."

And Rafe was. Looking into Rafe's open face, Alex could see a history behind those eyes that spoke of past hurts and shame. Rafe had only briefly talked about his past, in bits and pieces, but Alex knew there was a wealth of stories he'd yet to share.

Grimacing, Rafe stared at the floor. "Yeah. Different."

Horrified that Rafe had taken his words out of context, Alex sat helpless, watching Rafe withdraw into his protective shell. He couldn't let that happen. Not after this amazing evening the two of them had shared. The taste of Rafe was fresh on his tongue and Alex could still hear Rafe's cries of completion, and feel Rafe trembling in his arms.

Alex couldn't remember lovemaking so intense, so personal that he'd wanted to spend the rest of the night wrapped around the man he was with, yet the thought of Rafe leaving now, with the darkness of the evening stretching before him, left Alex bereft and cold.

"You are." Alex grasped Rafe's arm. "So different." He kissed Rafe's lips, feeling them soften beneath his. There was something so sweet and giving about Rafe's kisses, he could drown in them for hours, but Alex had other plans. He slid to his knees between Rafe's legs. "Let me show you." His fingers traveled up Rafe's thighs, through the wiry hair on his legs, then he leaned in to kiss the enticing slant of Rafe's hip bone.

"Alex," breathed Rafe. "You don't have to do this." But even as he protested, Rafe's hands clutched Alex's hair to bring him closer. His breathing grew unsteady as Alex lapped the head of his cock.

With a light push, Alex shoved Rafe backward. "I never do the things I have to do. Only what I want to do. And I want you." He then slid his mouth all the way down the rigid length of Rafe's cock until he could feel the thickness of its head brush the back of his throat. He began the draw and slide, the suckle and licking until Rafe, twisting his hands in the bedsheets, thrashed his head back and forth and let out a plaintive, sobbing cry of release, shooting his warm seed down Alex's throat.

"Alex, Alex." Rafe shuddered and lay back, spent and slicked with sweat. Alex licked his lips and kissed his way up the smooth skin of Rafe's torso until his face hovered over Rafe's.

There were flecks of tears on Rafe's eyelashes and without thinking, Alex leaned over to kiss them away, then continued down to Rafe's full mouth. Their kisses were leisurely and sweet and Alex found that to be more exciting and pleasurable than the hurried mashing together of mouths with men he barely cared about. When Rafe reached up and looped his arms around

Alex's neck to hug him close, a sense of peace rolled through him, like nothing Alex had felt ever before. It was special, it was real and it was only because it was Rafe. At one time, a thought like that would have sent Alex running for the hills, yet tonight it only made him hold Rafe closer, skin to skin, to feel the beating of his heart.

They stayed that way for several minutes, then Alex pulled back to smile into Rafe's eyes. "You, me, this. It's all different, okay?"

Rafe nodded, his eyes wide and open as the sky.

"But different in a good way. A way I want to get to know better. Something we can explore together. You understand what I mean?" Alex rolled onto his side, remaining close enough to feel the heat radiating from Rafe's body.

Rafe shifted till he too was on his side and facing Alex. "Yeah. I do. And that means you too. I want to get to know you too."

Keeping his tone light, Alex shrugged. "Sure. I'm pretty much an open book."

Rafe snorted then scrambled off the bed, picked up his boxers from the floor and slipped them on. "That's a joke. Look how you deflected when I started asking questions." He picked up his jeans and pulled them on. "You get to a certain point and then you shut things down and push me away."

"Are you leaving?" Alex sat up. "Why are you getting dressed?"

Rafe stopped buttoning his jeans and stood still for a moment. "I don't see the point r-really. If you c-can't be honest with m-me, then wh-what are we doing here?"

"Having fun? Enjoying life?" He jumped off the bed to stand in front of Rafe. "Why do we need to analyze everything? Sometimes it's best to let it slide and move forward."

Rafe bit his lip and shook his head. "Yes, we have fun, but there's more to life than that." He then finished buttoning his jeans and walked past Alex to find his shirt. "The way we move forward is to talk, learn about each other. If you're not interested we might as well forget this."

Alex's words obviously didn't have the intended effect. Rafe wasn't Micah, who was so immersed in his own pain he couldn't handle anyone else's.

Rafe cared about people and wouldn't be sloughed off with simple bullshit explanations and pat, self-help phrases.

Rafe saw right through him, and that scared Alex to death. But as he watched Rafe button his shirt, Alex knew he had to make a decision. One that might break him in the end, but if it worked, could bring them both the sweetest of rewards. It meant stripping back his shield, that façade he'd perfected over the years. He wasn't sure if he could do it all, but maybe it was time for that first step.

"You don't believe that though, do you?" Alex joined Rafe in the living room and pulled on his shorts. "You want me to talk." He made a face.

For the first time Rafe laughed. "I think it's safe to say you know how to talk, sometimes too much."

"Hey," he said. "Was that a dig?" He tried to pretend injured pride but Rafe was too damn cute to stay angry with.

"Nope. Merely a statement of fact. Take it as you wish."

Alex caught Rafe's eye. Though they'd just gotten out of bed after a marathon evening, desire slammed back into Alex and he wanted Rafe again.

The naked emotion must've shown on his face but this time Rafe was quick enough to evade Alex's grab and he placed himself behind the sofa.

"Uh uh. I'm only going to fall for that one time." Rafe folded his arms and smirked at Alex.

"Fall for what?" Alex widened his eyes innocently. "I thought we'd sit on the sofa and watch some TV."

Rafe rolled his eyes. "Is that why you tried to grab me?"

"Maybe I wanted to snuggle." Alex huffed.

Rafe burst into laughter. "You're crazy, you know that?" He checked his phone, then stuck it back into his pocket.

"No sexy texts from a cute guy?"

Looking confused, Rafe stared at him. "Now I know you're

certifiable. Who'd send me something like that?"

Alex grinned to himself. *Oh baby, you are so naïve.* Rafe was cute, sexy and sweet; a killer combo. This friends-with-benefits was better than Alex ever imagined.

He quickly retrieved his clothes, picked up his keys and slipped on his flip flops. "Well now that you've killed the mood, why don't we go out and get some dinner."

Rafe chuckled. "I am starving." He nudged Alex with his shoulder. "You gave me a workout."

"The night is young, baby. The night is young." Alex slung his arm around Rafe's neck as they left the apartment. They walked down the block and passed by his neighbor Marcus walking his dog.

"Alex, how's it going?"

He'd never liked the guy, and didn't like the way Marcus's knowing gaze raked over Rafe.

"Have a good evening, Marc."

"Not as good as yours, huh?" Marc grinned at him, while Alex scowled. "Rafe seems like a really nice guy."

"Yeah and we're both hungry so if you'll excuse us . . ."

"I'll bet you are." Marc's laugh followed them down the block and inexplicably put Alex in a black mood.

"I gather you don't like him." Rafe held the door open to the corner pizza place and Alex passed through. "I thought he seemed nice."

"You think everyone's nice because you're nice." Alex pointed to the booth in the corner. "Why don't you grab those seats and I'll order us a pie."

Rafe walked over to the booth and sat down while Alex gave the order. Alex returned with two bottles of water.

"You know," Rafe began, and his words came out deliberately. "I'm not that nice. At least not like you think."

Alex realized Rafe's method of speech, the carefulness of his chosen words, was how he prevented his stuttering. His admiration grew for the man for overcoming the speech impediment, and that protective wave rose up again. Alex wanted to shield

Rafe from hurt and keep him from seeing the ugly side of life.

"Come on. You're the type to always think the best about people, even when they do the wrong thing or act stupid." He opened the bottle of water and took a swig.

"You make me sound like a pushover. I get angry at people if I think they're mean or unjust." Rafe took out napkins from the holder and passed some over to Alex, keeping some for himself. "You've never seen me angry, really."

"Who would you have ever gotten angry with?" Alex almost laughed until he noticed Rafe was truly annoyed. "Rafe?"

"It's not important. It doesn't matter anymore."

Their pizza arrived and they busied themselves with the red pepper flakes and garlic. They each took a steaming slice and waited for it to cool. Alex thought Rafe would speak but he didn't and focused his attention on the pizza.

"Eat me, Rafe." Alex joked as he twitched Rafe's slice of pizza.

For the first time Rafe didn't smile at one of Alex's jokes and instead kept staring at the slice, his jaw tense.

"Hey, what's wrong?"

"Nothing."

But Rafe's voice was clipped and short and as Alex watched Rafe massacre his slice of pizza, he realized the man he thought he knew might have as many secrets as himself.

CHAPTER
SIXTEEN

For Rafe what had begun as an evening full of the promise of passion and uninhibited fun turned dark and laden with memories he'd thought buried for good. Alex seemed to realize something had gone awry and tried his usual jokes and stories to bring him out of his funk, but it didn't work.

By the time they'd finished the pizza, Rafe wanted to go home. He'd yet to make up the sleep from the night before, and this evening's activities with Alex hadn't afforded him any chance to relax. The only thing he looked forward to now was climbing into his bed, wrapping himself up in his comforter and staying there the whole night.

They left the pizza place, and Alex turned back up the block toward his apartment. Rafe put his hand on Alex's arm to hold him.

"Um. I think I'm gonna head home. I'm really beat."

Disappointment flared in Alex's eyes. "Oh. Okay sure."

If Alex had wanted him to stay, he'd have made an effort to dissuade him, but when he so easily accepted Rafe's excuse, Rafe knew he'd made the right decision. Sure they'd had a great time tonight, but like Alex said from the beginning, it was just sex. "Friends with benefits."

So he gave a bright smile and even pecked Alex a kiss goodbye on the lips. "I had fun tonight," he said softly. "Thanks." He walked quickly up the block to the nearest subway station that would take him home to Brooklyn. It took him about fifteen minutes to walk to his train; though it was dark, there were plenty of people out on the street, enjoying a late-evening walk or an ice cream. He used the time to clear his head, even as he eyed the couples walking with their arms lovingly entwined.

The ache of loneliness swelled in his throat and he hurried his steps, anxious to get home. The train was crowded but he welcomed the distraction and within half an hour he was walking up the steps by Grand Army Plaza. Though he'd told Alex he wanted to go home, and he'd looked forward to getting into bed, he now wanted to sit under the stars and look up at the sky.

He found a bench by the arch and looked up at the rearing horses, the stars winking behind the looming, shadowed figurines soaring into the night. His body ached pleasurably from Alex's lovemaking and despite himself he wondered if Alex had gone home, or if he went out in pursuit of another man.

Stop thinking about him, you idiot. You're not a couple. Hanging out with Alex, getting caught up in his "live life to the fullest" personality, pushed Rafe beyond his limits, but it wasn't without risk to his heart.

Rafe got up from the bench and walked the few short blocks to his apartment building. He'd made the smart move to leave Alex tonight. If he'd stayed, Rafe knew he'd allow Alex to take him back to bed and while that would be a marvelous way to spend the evening, Rafe had to put a barrier up to prevent himself from falling in love. He recognized the signs and they were all there in blazing bright colors with flashing lights.

He took his key out, unlocked his door and picked up his mail, not bothering to look at what he knew were either bills or advertisements. Rafe tossed the small bundle on the coffee table and flopped down on his sofa, wincing slightly at the ache in his ass. Why now, he wondered. Why after so many years of being alone, was he craving the company of others?

His phone buzzed and toeing off his shoes, he took it out of his pocket to read the text.

Miss me yet?

Despite his vow not to tie himself into knots over the man, Rafe was happy to get a text from Alex. Maybe his words from the afternoon had sunk in. Biting his lip, Rafe decided to play the game.

Who is this?

Very funny.

Is it Marcus?

What the fuck?

His phone rang.

"Hello?"

"Did that bastard get your number? He's a fucking player, don't fall for his bullshit."

Rafe smiled to himself but answered as nonchalantly as possible. "Alex? Oh, hi. What's up?"

"Oh, hi? What's up?" Alex sputtered. "What's up?"

Rafe fell over on his sofa, laughing. "Alex, I'm the one with the stutter."

"You little shit. You're teasing me."

"Me? I don't know what you mean."

Alex huffed out in an injured tone. "And here I thought you were the nice one."

"What do you want, Alex? I thought you'd be out somewhere." Rafe reached for his mail and began to sift through the inevitable bills. A letter from an attorney's office postmarked Allentown, Pennsylvania, caught his attention.

"Why would I go out? I didn't plan on doing anything tonight; I have surgery tomorrow morning."

When was he going to stop making those snap judgments about Alex that he hated people making about him? "Oh." Rafe slit open the envelope and pulled out a letter.

"I thought we were going to spend the night together." Alex said, sounding like a sulky little boy who'd dropped his ice cream cone on the ground.

Rafe scanned the letter and his heart stopped, then began thudding like a sledgehammer in hard, painful beats. "I'm sorry, I have to go." He ended the call and with precision, placed the phone on the coffee table, on top of a magazine where the front page model's smile gleamed so wide and bright, she must have been staring at a steak dinner.

The phone immediately rang again, but he didn't answer it. He stood, still holding the letter, and walked over to the lamp, as if the brighter light could shed secrets that went beyond the sparse contents.

Dear Mr. Hazelton,

Please first let us offer our condolences to you at your mother's passing. We are the executors of your mother's estate. According to her will, you are the only surviving child and heir. Please contact us at your earliest convenience to facilitate the disposal of her house and transfer of assets.

Very Truly Yours,

J. Frederick McSweeny, Esq.

Dead. His mother was dead and he never knew. Shouldn't he have had a sixth sense that something was wrong? It was his mother, for God's sake. He grew inside her, they'd been connected by their blood.

He was dimly aware in the background of his phone continuing to bleat out a ring. Without even bothering to see who was calling, he shut off the ringer and threw it back on the sofa. Thoughts whirled through his head as he tried to remember the last time he'd talked to her, but it had been at least several years. Even on the holidays she hadn't once bothered to pick up the phone and call him herself. She had however, continued to deposit the checks he sent her.

With all thoughts of sleep driven from his mind, he paced his living room, formulating a plan of action for the next few days. First things first. He'd have to leave early tomorrow as the drive to Allentown would take a couple of hours. He logged on to his computer and made a car rental reservation. With that done, he retrieved his phone and even though it was late, called Jenny, knowing she'd be awake. He put her on speakerphone so he could multitask and pack while they talked.

"What's wrong?" Her anxious voice filled the apartment.

"My mother died and I have to go home for a few days." He carried the phone with him to his bedroom where he opened his closet and pulled out his travel bag. With swift efficiency, he began to pack what he'd need for a trip he estimated shouldn't take longer than three days.

"Oh, Rafe, I'm so sorry." Her sympathetic voice touched him.

"It's fine. You know we hadn't spoken in years. It's almost as if a stranger died. I feel so detached about the whole thing." He stopped his packing for a moment. "Does it make me a bad person that I'm not crying? She was my mother, after all."

"Honey, you've told me only a little about yourself but you could never be a bad person. It sounds like she wasn't the best mom?" Jenny's hesitant question put a faint smile on his lips.

"You could say that."

"Then don't beat yourself up about it. And go and take as much time as you need. I have several friends I can call to fill in shifts for the rest of the week if necessary." Her voice softened. "I'm sorry you have to do this alone. Is there anyone who can go with you?" She hesitated. "What about that guy Alex you've become friendly with. I bet—"

"No." He cut her off and resumed packing, throwing underwear, socks and a few tee shirts in the bag. His suit hung in the closet and he slipped a garment bag around it to hang in the car. "I'm fine on my own."

I always have been.

He zipped up his bag and returned to his computer. "Thanks for finding coverage for me. I gotta go, I have to make a hotel reservation."

"I'm sorry, Rafe. Are you sure you don't want to tell someone else?"

"No. I'll call you when I get there and check in."

He ended the call. There were plenty of hotels in the area and he made a reservation at the one closest to his mother's house. It never occurred to Rafe to stay in his mother's house. The place held nothing but bad memories and Rafe had no desire to spend any more time there than he had to. Knowing he would have a long day tomorrow, he brushed his teeth, stripped down to his boxers and went to bed. He lay quiet, listening to the sounds of traffic from the street below and watching the night shadows play along the walls of his bedroom. It saddened him to think though he tried his damnedest, he couldn't dredge up a single pleasant memory of either his mother or his childhood at all.

He closed his eyes and drifted off to sleep.

At eight o'clock the next morning he was already on the road. He'd checked his GPS and the New Jersey Turnpike was its usual early morning horror show of tractor trailers and car accidents. Since he didn't have to arrive at a specific time, Rafe chose a somewhat more scenic route even with going through Staten Island. He kept the radio loud to drown out the silence in his head and had a large thermos of hot coffee next to him. The miles fell away and even though he hadn't traveled back this way in years, the scenery rose up before him, achingly familiar.

He stopped for gas off the highway, refilled his coffee and picked up something nondescript and nonthreatening to eat. While he waited for his tank to fill up, he checked his phone and saw there were at least half a dozen texts from Alex that started out half-joking, then disintegrated to annoyed, upset and finally a bit angry.

It was really better this way, Rafe thought as he deleted the texts. Because no matter how well they meshed together physically, he and Alex were too different as people. Alex was all bright lights, big city and nights filled with fun, while he was too quiet, uncomfortable in groups and more of a homebody.

With the tank full, he re-entered the highway and continued on. It didn't take long before he rounded the curve and the "Welcome to Pennsylvania" sign greeted him. His stomach tightened and a sour taste rose in his throat. He'd returned home for summers during college, but once he entered veterinary school, Rafe always managed to find himself jobs so he wouldn't have to go home. The last time he was here was close to ten years ago, when his mother left him a message that his father had died, and the date of the funeral, "if he wanted to come."

Now, these ten years later, she'd been buried without a single family member around her. Rafe wondered what made up her DNA to be the way she was; so distant and so cold. He sighed, switched the radio station and sped along the highway, anxious after two hours of driving to reach his destination.

Allentown had never fully recovered from the downturn of the 1980s; even the vast Dorney Park couldn't make up for the thousands of jobs lost when the steel mills closed. There were vast auto dealerships now and he wondered how many cars people could afford to buy. Still the parking lots seemed crowded, so perhaps it was on an upswing. Rafe navigated the new winding highway roads but thanks to his GPS found his hotel quickly and checked in with no hassle. It was a fairly new, mid-range chain hotel, clean and generically pleasing. The young woman at the front desk was certainly perky enough and within minutes he was in his standard room with a queen-sized bed that looked surprisingly inviting.

First things first. He texted Jenny and told her he'd arrived safely. As he knew she would, she called him.

"How are you feeling, honey?"

He smiled. She was such a mother hen. Hopefully she and her husband would have that baby they'd been trying for. "I'm good. A little tired but f-fine."

"Good. I have one of my pals, Derek, filling in today. He's a great guy."

"Sounds good." He yawned and stretched.

"You sound exhausted. Bet you didn't get much sleep last night."

"Mmm. You'd win that bet. I'm going to call the lawyer's office and make an appointment hopefully for this afternoon. Then I'm going to take a nap."

"Perfect. Keep in touch."

"I will. Bye."

Before he got too tired he called the lawyer's office and made an appointment for later that afternoon. He tossed the phone on the bed and went to use the bathroom. The harsh lighting revealed every tired line in his face and he winced. "Damn, man. You look like crap."

From the interior room, he heard his phone ringing and thinking it was the lawyer's office, he nearly tripped over himself racing to get to it before they hung up.

"Hello?" His voice breathed heavily into the phone.

"I'm glad you finally decided to take my call."

Alex. Damn.

"Uh, hi, Alex."

"Hi, Alex?" his voice came through high and incredulous. "I've been trying since last night to get you and all I get is a 'Hi, Alex?' What the hell, Rafe? Where are you?"

Dodging Alex's question, Rafe responded with one of his own. "Don't you have surgery?"

"Stop changing the subject." Frustration poured off his voice. "Rafe, talk to me. What happened? Where are you? I called the clinic and they said you went away for a few days."

"My mother died."

Alex's breath hitched in Rafe's ear and in the background blared the sound of an intercom paging a doctor.

"Damn. I'm sorry. I know it's inadequate—"

"No, it's not. I should feel something, right? She was my mother. But the funny thing is, I don't. Not really. Nothing that makes me overwhelmingly sad and want to cry." Once again, Rafe needed validation. "Does that make me a bad person?"

"No, baby. It doesn't." Alex's voice touched him like a caress and Rafe curled up on his bed, clutching the phone, as the words flowed over him like warm honey. "You couldn't be a bad person if you tried."

"I think you're saying that to get laid." Rafe chuckled but to his surprise, there was no answering laughter.

"I don't give a shit about that right now. You may think you're not grieving but I can hear it in your voice. You lose a piece of yourself when one of your family dies."

"Like you did with your brother?"

Rafe held his breath, hoping Alex would answer him.

"I didn't lose a piece. I lost everything."

The pain in Alex's voice tore at Rafe. How devastated Alex still was, even after all these years. "You're still grieving aren't you?"

"I'll never stop; how can I? It's like losing the other side of myself, the better half. And every once in a while my parents call to remind me how much of a failure I am, compared to him." He sucked in a deep breath. "How did you manage to turn this around to talk about me? Where are you now? You shouldn't be alone."

"I don't mind being alone; I'm used to it. And I went back home to deal with her estate."

"Tell me where you are. I can join you and keep you company."

The longing to see Alex hit Rafe like a fist, but he didn't want to grow too dependent on their friendship. "It's okay. I'm fine. It helped to talk to you."

"You're a stubborn pain in the ass, aren't you."

"I can be." Rafe smiled. "But thank you for offering. It means a lot knowing you're my friend."

"Call me? Let me know how things are going there."

Sounds of activity increased in the background; he heard several voices speaking and Rafe knew Alex needed to get back to work. "Sure. I will."

"Promise me, Rafe. Otherwise I'm going to hunt you down and find you."

Warmth bloomed through his body at the authoritative tone of Alex's voice. "I promise. Now get back to work before they fire you."

"Bye, Rafe."

"Bye."

Something had happened—he and Alex had finally crossed that imaginary line that separated casual acquaintances from intimate friends, and it had nothing to do with sex. This went beyond physical. And though Rafe hadn't had close friends before, he knew enough to understand their friendship had evolved to something special. He had a person he could count on besides Jenny.

The physical ache was there, as was the desire to hold Alex close and be comforted in return. But knowing someone was out there who thought about him filled Rafe with the dawning realization that he could either return to the place of his birth like he left it, shy as a wild deer and afraid to speak out loud, or he could walk in triumphant, as the successful businessman he was, and demand respect from the people who could never be bothered to pay attention to a child who was a little bit different than they were.

For the first time he had people like Alex and Jenny who knew him as he was, flaws and all, and cared for him and about him all the same. It made believing in himself easier when the voices of doubt whispered in his ear.

CHAPTER SEVENTEEN

He was off his game and everyone knew it. Alex tossed his sweat-soaked surgical cap in the trash and braced his hands against the sink. It had been the shittiest week in years and it wasn't over yet. The only bright spot was that Micah had extended his honeymoon, so Alex didn't have to work with him or run into him at the hospital. From the hospital grapevine Alex heard that Micah and Josh had left for the Hamptons and had taken their two grandmothers with them.

He squelched down a throb of pain. He and Micah hadn't spoken since their fight; not a text or a phone call even. This was the longest period they'd gone without talking since their school days. Micah's bewildered, angry face would remain with Alex for a long time; realistically Alex knew he'd been wrong to keep the most important part of his life from the most important person in his life.

How could he explain the reasons why? With a heavy sigh, Alex exited the post-op area and walked down the hallway, lost in his own thoughts. He nearly jumped when he felt a tap on his shoulder.

"What? Oh, hi Laura."

He smiled at the neurosurgeon. Laura Chang was one of the defendants in the discrimination lawsuit last year that had resulted in her and Micah winning a large settlement and them all leaving the hospital they'd worked at. Alex had followed Laura to this hospital; Micah had scaled back on surgeries, preferring to teach now, so Laura was thrilled to have Alex for her team, when he didn't assist Micah.

"Hi, sorry to scare you." She tilted her head, assessing him. "What's wrong? You don't seem like yourself."

Whoever that is anymore. "Lots on my mind."

"Have you heard from the guys? Are they back from California?"

His chest tightened. "Yeah."

When Laura noticed he wasn't forthcoming with any more information, she gave him another one of those sharp-eyed, assessing looks of hers and nodded. "Well, um. Okay. I wanted to let you know the next surgery is cancelled. The patient is spiking a temp."

Alex breathed a relieved sigh. "I know it's mean, but I'm kind of glad. I have something I need to do and my mind really isn't in the game right now."

"I could tell."

That was the thing about having friends who cared about your well-being. They paid attention to you. And while Alex appreciated Laura, she wasn't the one he wanted right now.

"I gotta go." He leaned down and kissed her cheek. "Speak to you soon." Without waiting for a response, he took off down the hallway, not stopping until he hit the pavement outside the hospital. His pulse raced and he didn't bother to stop, think or weigh the consequences of what he was about to do.

Fifteen minutes later, he pushed open the door to Rafe's clinic.

"Hello, can I help you?" The receptionist glanced down at his feet, searching for an animal he didn't have. "Do you have a question about pet care?"

"No, no. I'm a friend of Rafe's. Is the other doctor in?" He searched his memory for her name. "Jenny, I think?"

"Oh yes, I remember you. You came to visit Rafe once." She picked up the phone. "I'll tell Jenny you're here. Have a seat." She gestured to the chairs in the waiting room.

He sprawled in a seat, careful not to step on the tiny Yorkie puppy at his feet. The pink ribbon on her head probably weighed as much as she did. He smiled at her owner, who gave him a frosty, tight-ass smile.

Bitch.

Before Josh, Micah would've made some cutting remark to the woman, which probably would've reduced her to tears. Now of course he was happy and in love, thought Alex with disgust. Let the rainbows and sparkly unicorns shine bright.

"Alex? What's wrong?"

Jenny's voice penetrated his evil thoughts of the little Yorkie shitting all over her owner's cream colored shoes.

"Oh, hi. Can we talk for a minute?"

With a quizzical look, she waved at him to follow her to the back. "Come with me."

"But Dr. Esposito, I've been waiting," said the woman, her nasal whine piercing through Alex's skull like a nail.

Alex spun on his heel and clasped his hands in front of his chest. "It's a matter of life or death," he said, unable to help himself. "My Bootsie has developed an unnatural sexual attraction to men. Every man he sees he wants to hump." He winked at her, holding in his laughter at the frozen shock on her tight, plastic face. "It's pure hell trying to score when your dog has a perpetual hard-on and wants to screw your date."

He followed Jenny to the back. When he passed the giggling receptionist he grinned at her. "That'll crack her Botox, huh?"

"Stop, please," she choked out. "You'll get me fired."

"Don't worry, I know the boss."

He hurried after Jenny and followed her into a different office than the one he'd been in before with Rafe. She didn't offer him a seat and didn't look particularly friendly, either. Rafe sensed a protective, mama-bear attitude and strangely enough he was happy Rafe had people who honestly cared about him.

"What can I do for you?" She leaned against the desk, her posture as rigid as a gun dog on point. Her dark eyes took his measure and Alex sensed she didn't fully trust him. Talking to

Rafe earlier, hearing his uncertainty and the sadness in his voice rendered Alex helpless to anything but the need to find Rafe and help him make it through this time.

"Can you tell me where Rafe went? I know about his mother passing." He thought if he showed that Rafe had confided that to him, Jenny would be less suspicious of his motives.

A flicker in her eyes betrayed her surprise. "He told you? What else did he say?" She remained stiff and unbending.

"I don't think I need to reveal our conversation, it was private and meant for the two of us. But he's hurting, and I want to help him." Why was she being so overly protective of Rafe? He was a grown man after all.

"If Rafe wanted you to know . . ." She ended on a shrug. "Now I'm sorry, but I do have patients out there."

The hell she'd dismiss him like a schoolteacher.

"What problem do you have with me? I barely know you."

"Yes. But I know you, or your type at least. And Rafe is my friend and he doesn't need someone taking advantage of him when he's vulnerable."

Alex struggled to keep his temper in check but couldn't hold his tongue. "I was trying to be polite but you're insulting me without knowing anything about me, or the relationship Rafe and I might have. My type is the type to help his friend when he's hurting, no questions asked. To bring beer to get him drunk and be a shoulder to lean on when he cries."

Surprise flared in her eyes. "You care about him. I thought—"

"What? That I'm only interested in getting him into bed? That's none of your business. My physical relationship with Rafe, if there is one, is not your concern, or anyone else's, for that matter, only ours."

To his shock, Jenny's lips quirked in a little smile. "I see." She walked behind the desk and scribbled something on a pad of paper then tore it out and offered it to him. "Here. This is where he is."

Curious as to why she'd had such an abrupt change of heart, Alex nonetheless snatched the paper out of her hands before asking, in case she changed her mind. "Thanks, but what did I say to make you give this to me?"

With an even more mysterious smile than the one she had before, Jenny passed by him and opened the door to the office. "It's what you didn't say."

For about the hundredth time, Alex contemplated Jenny's words even as he sped down the NJ Turnpike. He navigated through the heavy traffic, but soon reached a stretch of highway where he could keep a steady rate of speed.

He had the paper with the address of the hotel folded snugly in his pocket and a quick glance at the dashboard clock revealed the time to be only a little past 2:00 p.m. He'd made sure the car he rented had a GPS and it showed only 50 miles left to his destination.

He blasted the radio and adjusted his sunglasses. It had been years since he'd taken a road trip of any kind; the last time was when he and Micah had gone out to the Hamptons for a weekend of summer parties. That had to be at least three years ago. Now Micah was an old married man with a husband, a dog and two grandmothers to look after.

One big happy family.

If anyone had asked Alex back in those days about settling down, he'd have laughed in their faces and bought them a drink. Now, the thought of those endless cycles of Hamptons parties beginning again, the same faces showing up year after year, a little older, a lot more jaded and desperate to make a connection, held no appeal to Alex. Mindless sex with men whose names he couldn't remember the next day seemed sad and pointless.

Alex flashed back to the other night and recalled Rafe beneath him, urging him on, taking Alex inside his tight heat until they climaxed together. It was memorable, not only for the absolute perfection of the sex, but because it was with Rafe. Alex couldn't imagine being with anyone else.

"Shit," he muttered. "I'm in fucking trouble, aren't I?" And if everything hadn't blown up with Micah the other day, Alex would've been able to call his best friend and talk to him about it; get his and Josh's perspective. Impossible now, so Alex was on his own, sailing through uncharted waters without a map or compass. And while turning around and running back to New York tempted him, Alex knew he'd come too far not to finish what he'd started.

He followed the GPS directions after he entered Pennsylvania and found the hotel with little trouble. The only problem he could see was that the desk clerk wouldn't tell him Rafe's room number. That ceased to be a problem when he watched a car drive up and park in the lot. Rafe got out of the driver's seat with a bag from Taco Bell and headed inside the hotel.

Perfect. Alex jumped out of his car and hurried after Rafe. He trailed behind him, keeping his face down until they entered the elevator. Alex moved to the rear of the elevator, even though there was plenty of space and it was only the two of them there.

"What floor?"

"I don't know, you tell me." He laughed at the look of utter amazement on Rafe's face. "Surprise."

"Alex?"

Every visible emotion played upon the canvas of Rafe's face: hope, fear, shock, joy.

"Hi."

They stood there grinning at each other until the elevator doors opened and Rafe seemed to wake up. "Oh, y-yeah. Come, I'm th-this way."

They walked down the narrow hallway. Rafe fumbled for the keycard in his back pocket and dropped it but Alex swiftly picked it up.

"Here, let me do it." The light shone green and Alex opened the door and held it, letting Rafe brush by him as he passed.

"I still don't know what you're doing here," said Rafe, setting the bag of food on the table.

"Did you get chips?" Alex opened the bag and began rummaging through it. "You are going to share, right? I'm starving."

He reached in and pulled out a smaller bag. "Aha! Chips." He crunched one and flopped down on the bed. "This is comfy." He bounced a little. "Nice give." He grinned at Rafe, who rolled his eyes.

"You didn't answer me. What are you doing here and how did you find me?"

"I went to your clinic. Boy, that woman Jenny is so suspicious."

Rafe remained silent and Alex got nervous. "Are you angry I'm here?" He got off the bed to stand before Rafe who hadn't moved from the table. Rafe's face revealed nothing to Alex. "I thought you could use a friend to be with you through this ordeal. All kidding aside. That's the real reason I'm here."

Rafe's gaze searched his face, his golden-brown eyes reflecting uncertainty. "You came all this way out here. I still can't believe it." His face filled with emotion. "No one's ever done that for me."

"It's about time they did." Alex brushed the chestnut waves of Rafe's hair off his forehead. "You do it for people; I remember how you took Lucky when Micah's grandmother was sick." He slid his hand through the silky waves of Rafe's hair before settling at the nape of his neck. Alex curled his hand around Rafe's neck and tugged him close, soaking in his warmth, enjoying the strength of Rafe's body up against his. "Now it's time to let someone take care of you."

He brushed his lips over Rafe's, testing their softness. They stood there in that hotel room, Alex teasing his lips over Rafe's mouth. He felt the soft expulsion of Rafe's breath across his cheek.

"What is it, baby?" His hands clasped Rafe's face to stare into his eyes. "Talk to me."

"I have n-nothing to say. I'm overwh-whelmed." Rafe licked his lower lip and Alex envied Rafe's tongue. He wanted nothing more than to suck its tender pink fullness into his mouth and keep kissing Rafe until they lost their breath and their minds.

"I am too. By you. You're overwhelming." Alex gave into his

spiraling desire and took Rafe's mouth in a crushing kiss. Their mouths clung and their tongues tangled. Alex's hands roamed over Rafe's body; slipping under his tee shirt to feel all that warm flesh, tracing the lean cords of muscle down Rafe's back. Rafe sank into his arms as they continued to kiss and touch each other, and Alex explored every dip and curve of Rafe's body which was becoming increasingly familiar to his hands and his lips.

He sank down to his knees and unzipped Rafe's pants, palming his straining cock. Rafe swayed and Alex wrapped his arm around Rafe's waist to hold him steady, then pulled his boxers down. Rafe's cock sprang out, flushed, swollen and beautiful to Alex's eyes. He took the entire length in his mouth, sliding down to the root then pulled up in a hard stroke. He lapped around the crown, licking up the liquid seeping from the slit.

"I love sucking you. You're my favorite popsicle." Alex slicked his fingers with saliva and pre-come and when he sucked Rafe down his throat, he inserted his fingers inside Rafe's hole, twisting and turning them. Rafe bucked his hips, shoving his cock further into Alex's mouth, but he was ready for it and relaxed his throat to take Rafe down. Alex sensed Rafe's impending orgasm, feeling the swell of Rafe's cock inside his mouth, his thrusts growing deeper and more erratic. Alex didn't forget to torment Rafe inside, curling his fingers, ruthlessly stroking Rafe's gland until with a sobbing cry, Rafe came, spurting hot and heavy down Alex's throat.

"Alex, oh God, Alex." Rafe shuddered and sagged on his feet, but Alex held him tight, letting him ride out the waves of his orgasm. Though his own cock ached, he ignored it for now. This time was for Rafe, to show him he was wanted, needed and loved.

After Rafe softened and Alex pulled away, he whispered against Rafe's thigh. "Don't worry, baby. I'm here. I'll always be here."

In this nondescript little room, Alex discovered his world as well.

CHAPTER EIGHTEEN

Inexplicably nervous, Rafe sat in the reception area of the law office of J. Frederick McSweeny Esq. and practiced his deep breathing. Having Alex next to him with his muscular thigh pressed next to his own and his soapy clean scent didn't make it easy for him to concentrate.

They were almost late because Alex insisted they take a shower together and Rafe couldn't resist a naked, wet and soapy Alex, his beautiful cock standing at the ready. Though Rafe didn't want to think too hard why Alex carried condoms with him, Rafe was damn happy he did, shivering at the memory of Alex's cock pushing into him, thrusting deep and hard until he thought they'd get thrown out of the hotel for all the noises they made.

"What kind of pompous person calls himself 'J. Frederick,'" said Alex, muttering to no one in particular. "How bad could his first name be?"

"Shh." Rafe elbowed him. "Stop it. That's mean. You don't know. Maybe he was bullied when he was younger because his name was different."

Alex opened his mouth then snapped it shut and nodded. "Yeah. You're right. I'm sorry." He placed a hand on Rafe's thigh and squeezed hard. "Do you see? You're making me nice." With that pronouncement, he laid his head on Rafe's shoulder and sighed.

Frozen with shock at Alex's forwardness in public, Rafe, for a moment, retreated back to the shy, insecure person of his youth. He began to shake and furtively looked around the room to see if anyone was watching.

His eyes remained closed, yet Alex spoke as if he saw straight to Rafe's heart. "You aren't a child anymore. Own your life and yourself."

The man was right. What did he care if anyone saw them showing affection to each other? No one would think twice if they were a heterosexual couple.

"Mr. Hazelton?"

He started in his chair and looked up at the frowning man in a dark suit standing before him. The fluorescent overhead lighting shone down on his scalp through the strands of too-black-to-be-real hair that had been plastered down to stay put until next year.

"Y-yes?"

"It's Dr. Hazelton, actually." Alex straightened up in his own seat and frowned.

How did he do it so effortlessly? With that one sentence, the attorney's haughty demeanor vanished and uncertainty took its place.

"Oh, yes, ahem. Well. Shall we step inside please?" His eyes narrowed when Alex stood by Rafe's side. "Ah. Is this a *friend* of yours?" The emphasis was undeniable as was his smirk.

Remembering what Alex had said to him when they were seated, Rafe faced the attorney down. "Yes. Mr. Stern is a very good friend of mine, as a matter of fact, and I insist he be present at our meeting."

With a withering smile, the attorney nonetheless nodded and headed to the back. "Follow me please."

He and Alex walked behind the man, and Rafe was acutely aware of Alex's presence, and his hand resting so comfortably at the small of Rafe's back. A thrill traveled down his spine when Alex's lips skimmed his ear and he whispered, "Way to go, Tiger. You told that asshole."

They entered McSweeny's office and sat down in the two chairs placed in front of the desk. Rafe waited until McSweeny had seated himself before speaking.

"When did m-my mother die and when was the funeral?"

McSweeny cleared his throat and opened the file on his desk. "She passed away quite suddenly on the 5th of June. There was no burial, however. She had left instructions to be cremated, which the Bean mortuary handled on the 10th."

"I see," said Rafe faintly. So that was that. "Did she—"

"Dr. Hazelton, let me be frank. Your mother met with me when your father died and set up these instructions. She was quite specific that you were to be notified only after cremation had taken place."

"She gave no reason? Isn't that unusual?" Alex rested his arm along the back of Rafe's chair and Rafe appreciated his close proximity.

"I'd gathered from our conversations, infrequent though they were, that you two didn't have the easiest relationship?"

Rafe nodded. "No, we didn't; however, it didn't prevent her from accepting my checks every month. But go on."

"There isn't much to say. She didn't approve of your life-style, as she called it, and didn't want you coming around." A tiny smirk appeared on McSweeny's lips, as if he knew he'd scored a hurtful point.

Alex draped his arm around Rafe's shoulder and left it there, the warmth of his palm comforting. "It's okay. Don't let it bother you."

Not bother him? "How can you say that? Parents are sup-posed to love and protect you. And a mother? She carries you inside her body." Frustrated with the burning behind his eyes, Rafe squeezed his eyes shut for a second. "How could she have rejected me like this? Even an animal would never do that to her young; abandon it the way she did me."

He'd spent his entire childhood wondering why his parents had ever decided to have children, and nothing had changed as he grew older. There'd never been a time he could recall a loving look, a gentle touch or sweet smile from either of his parents.

Why would anything have changed now?

"So why am I here? My parents didn't have much money, that I know for sure. You're not going to tell me I've inherited anything, are you?" He raised a brow in skepticism.

"Well," McSweeny flipped some pages in the file and pulled out several envelopes. "I have her bank statements here and aside from the monthly checks you sent her and her Social Security, she had no other money. And most of that was used to pay for her funeral expenses."

"So why call me out here then?" Frustrated, he pushed off the chair and began to pace the room, bewildered and hurt. "T-to look d-down on me? Sh-show me h-how I st-still don't belong?"

Knowing he was losing control, Rafe fisted his hands by his side and forced himself to stand still and take deep, cleansing breaths. Alex came to stand behind him, slipped his arms around his waist and murmured in his ear.

"Take it easy. It's going to be fine. If you want to leave, say the word, and we'll tell him 'fuck you' and walk out with our heads held high."

Warmth stole through Rafe and not because of Alex's physical presence; it was the knowledge that someone had his back and cared enough to stand with him in the face of whatever adversity was thrown in his path.

"No, I'm g-good." He inhaled sharply and drew strength from Alex and his words. "So are we finished here then, Mr. McSweeny?"

He'd mentally already prepared to leave and was halfway to the door when he was stopped by McSweeny. "Not exactly, Dr. Hazelton. Your mother left you the house. We've already got a buyer for it; it's in an area where a developer will most likely knock it down." He smoothed his moustache with the tips of his fingers. "You should clean it out as soon as possible, so we can proceed with the sale."

Things were moving at a breakneck pace; he'd never expected to have inherited a house and sell it at the same time. With rising excitement, Rafe thought of what the money from the sale of the house would mean to him; he could pay down the loan to the bank on the clinic and that would ease the worries he had over the large debt that loomed over his head.

He might also be able to put a down payment on an apartment and have a home of his own, instead of renting and pouring money out of the window each month.

The day which had started out so miserable and lonely, now blossomed and grew bright and full of dreams. "I can start after I leave here. I agree. Let's sell the house. I'll sign whatever paperwork you need."

"Good." McSweeny handed him a set of keys. "These are the front and back door keys as well as some random key. I have no clue what it's for."

The coolness of the steel in his hand as he fingered the sharp edges of the keys brought the reality of the situation into focus for Rafe and it sobered him. He'd be walking back into his house, a place he never thought of as home, for the first time in years. Hesitating only a moment, Rafe faced Alex who'd remained waiting patiently by his side.

"Would you come with me? Unless of course, you planned on going back to the city tonight."

Alex grimaced at McSweeny behind the desk and jerked his head toward the door. "Let's get out of here."

Rafe understood. Alex wouldn't want to discuss their plans in front of McSweeny. Living in New York City Rafe had become used to living his life out in the open; no hiding and no subterfuge. Here, in this conservative enclave where he grew up, Rafe knew to be more circumspect and had no problem keeping who he was to himself.

Alex, on the other hand, was never one to hide who he was, his light shining bright like a beacon cutting through the fog. Rafe couldn't and wouldn't think of asking him to change who he was. That's what made Alex so special, a stand-out. He had no shame and no fear. It's what made him so easy to love.

Not going there.

Anticipation raced through Rafe's veins. His life had moved beyond the narrow road these people traveled and along the way he'd found people like Alex, people he could trust. And in a way, he'd found himself.

"Yes, let's go."

CHAPTER
NINETEEN

There was something so relaxing about being outside the city; Alex had always enjoyed the weekends he'd gotten away to the beach in the summer. He'd never been much for the country, thinking it boring, yet when he lowered the car windows to inhale the scent of freshly mowed grass and hay, a quiet peace settled in his chest. The slight taint in the air of the manure the farmers used in the field didn't bother him and couldn't mar the sheer breathtaking expanse of open fields of newly growing corn. He had no idea Rafe came from such a rural background.

"Did you live on a farm? Like with cows and stuff?" Alex admired Rafe's handling of the car as they drove deeper into the countryside. Though he said he hadn't been here in almost ten years, Rafe certainly seemed comfortable enough on the road, and knew exactly where he was going. Alex had a hard time remembering a place after he'd left it. Thank God New York was on a grid, or he'd probably get lost in the city.

Rafe shot him a glance. "No, but I went to school with kids who did."

They passed the fields in silence. The car slowed as it made a turn down a narrow street with weather-beaten, dilapidated houses set back from the road, and open fields in the back. Without warning, Rafe pulled into the driveway of a small, wood frame house and killed the engine. Alex had his hand on the door handle, ready to exit the car.

"Wait? Please?"

The uncertainty in Rafe's voice saddened Alex. How hurtful was Rafe's childhood for him to fear entering an empty house? But Alex knew a house once lived in was never empty, no matter if anyone presently lived in it or not. It held memories, dreams and voices of the past that played a part in who you were.

"Take your time." Alex placed his hand on Rafe's which held the steering wheel in a death-like grip. "I'm not going anywhere."

"You must think I'm a fool, fearing a house." Rafe let go of the wheel, and Alex held his hand tight, letting Rafe feel his support.

"I could never think that. I think you're strong to face your past." Alex swallowed. "It's more than I'm willing to do." The admission, once spoken, couldn't be taken back and Alex fell silent, shocked he'd spoken from the heart.

A moment passed, then Rafe squeezed his hand. The silence between them remained, but it was comfortable. Birds swooped and chirped in the trees around them and in the distance, Alex thought he heard a cow lowing. It was hard to imagine anything bad happening here, with the sky so blue and the grass so fresh and green. But Alex recalled the stories Rafe had mentioned casually, of threatened beatings and whispered slurs and taunts.

"I'm ready." Rafe removed his hand and unbuckled his seat belt. Their doors opened simultaneously and he and Rafe exited the car and slammed the doors shut. Rafe mounted the sagging steps and dug for the keys in his pocket. The inner door swung in and Alex held the screen door open for Rafe.

The air smelled stale and cool. Alex hated walking into empty places; he always left the TV on when he was home to have the background noise, and turned the radio on when he left, so he'd return to voices; some form of life. Perhaps it was the result of being a twin; from conception, he'd never been alone, sharing his blood and sensing the heartbeat of his brother.

The furniture was old; there was no television, only a

lumpy-looking sofa and a vinyl recliner, worn in the seat, with tape on the arms. The kitchen, complete with a groaning avocado colored refrigerator and ancient stove, looked like a relic from the 1960s, and the dinette table was piled high with mail, magazines and newspapers. By the height of the stacks, it looked like several months' worth; one stiff breeze would send the lot toppling over.

Alex, taking note of Rafe's strained, pale face, remained close by his side and let Rafe set the pace as to how he wanted to proceed. He didn't care how long it took. Alex had no plans to leave Rafe anytime soon. If he was truthful with himself, he didn't want to leave him at all, but he couldn't face up to that fact right now, so like he always did, he brushed aside his feelings to concentrate on someone else.

"All of this has to go. I guess I can call one of those junk places and they can come and pick everything up." Rafe left his side to wander about the room, his fingertips brushing objects as he passed. "I don't want anything."

Taking that as a sign, Alex pulled out his phone. "I can look one up now and make an appointment. How's that?" At Rafe's brief smile and nod, Alex quickly found a listing of places and picked the first on the list. He called and they agreed to come the following morning at nine o'clock.

"Done." He shoved the phone back in his pocket.

To Alex's surprise, Rafe grabbed and kissed him, his lips tender yet fierce. They broke apart, panting.

Alex chuckled, and rubbed his chin. "Not that I'm complaining, but what brought that on?"

His laughter died at the intensity of Rafe's expression. There was no joy in Rafe's eyes. "I wanted to kiss a man in this house once, before I left forever, with no hope of ever returning. I wanted to prove to myself I could be wanted or desired by someone."

With a gesture that was becoming more natural every day, Alex slid his arms around Rafe's waist to hold him close. "I want you. I desire you. There's nothing to prove, baby. Look into my eyes and see it. It's right there for you. Only you."

Their kiss was softer now, sweet and searching. Alex's heart did a funny flip and he tightened his arms around Rafe, molding their bodies together. This man, with his sweet lips and gentle eyes spun him around until he ached with a hunger so profound he trembled from it. The blood sang in his ears and tears pricked his eyes.

Words rested on the tip of his tongue, life changing words, life affirming words. But he couldn't form them. They danced about in his mind, then tucked themselves away, perhaps for a later place and time.

"I want you too. Thank you." Rafe rubbed his cheek against Alex's. "Your friendship means everything to me. I don't know if I could have done this today by myself."

"Sure you could. You're strong. But you don't have to. I'm here for you."

Rafe stepped back and studied him. "This isn't a one-way friendship, you know. You understand I'm here for you as well. As much as I've been wrapped up in my own problems, I know you have shit to deal with too."

Alex's stomach clenched and up came his defense mechanisms, like prison gates slamming with a deadly, clanking sound.

"My shit is fine. Why don't we go upstairs and see if there's anything you might want to salvage." Alex took the steps of the narrow staircase two at a time. There were only two rooms upstairs with doors shut tight. Rafe trailed at his heels and Alex stepped aside, unwilling to open either door.

"This was my room." Rafe hesitated only a moment, then turned the knob. He looked inside then withdrew. His eyes were dark and anguished. "There's nothing to see. Come, let's go to her room."

Alex followed, but not before peering into the bedroom. It was completely bare; wiped clean of Rafe's existence. Late afternoon sunlight poured in through the solitary, narrow window. The stained carpet showed the imprint of furniture that had rested there for years, and faded spaces on the walls outlined missing pictures, or perhaps posters of teen crushes. How painful it must have been for a child as kind and loving as Rafe to grow up in a room and house so cold and lacking any cheer.

Bastards. Alex's anger grew at the callousness of Rafe's parents and vowed to make it up to him. He hurried to catch up with Rafe, who had entered his parents' room and stood unmoving by the dresser.

"I can't go through her personal things. It doesn't seem decent to me." Rafe opened the closet door, and Alex could see only a few items of clothing hanging. He took out two boxes and put them on the bed. "I'll go through these to see if there's anything of any importance."

"Well, I don't care about being decent or not, so if you want me to, I can look through the drawers. Maybe she won Lotto and kept all the money in her underwear."

Rafe rolled his eyes. "You're such a freak."

"Ha, but you love me anyway." Realizing what he'd said, Alex froze, then acted nonchalant and began opening dresser drawers. He slanted a look over at Rafe sitting on the bed and watched as he began rummaging through the box. A small smile played on Rafe's lips but he said nothing back.

Time passed and Rafe had only found one or two papers in the boxes he said he wanted to keep. Alex hadn't found any money, but he found several small pieces of jewelry, which Rafe said he'd either sell or maybe give to Jenny if she liked them.

The light was fading and when Alex checked his watch he saw it was almost seven o'clock. No wonder he was hungry. They'd been going at it for over two hours, nonstop.

"Hey, want to leave the rest for tomorrow? We can get here early before the junk guys and finish up."

"Yeah, sure. Let me look one last time and see if I missed anything in the closet."

Alex stretched, enjoying the sight of Rafe's ass in his faded jeans as he bent to look on the floor of the closet. He couldn't wait for tonight when they were in bed together. Deciding to finish the final drawer of the dresser before they left, he attempted to pull the drawer out but found it was jammed.

"Huh." He squatted down and yanked. The force tumbled him onto his ass, with the drawer landing at his feet. Then he saw why. There was a rectangular metal box half hidden by loads of mismatched socks, jammed into the back of the drawer.

"Rafe." He picked up the box. "Look what I found."

Rafe backed out of the closet and joined him on the floor. An attempt to open it failed. "Hmm. Locked. I wonder if that other key with the house keys was meant for this."

"Well why don't we take it with us back to the hotel and we can get some room service and open it there." He stood and slid the drawer back into the slot. "Might as well be comfortable and it's starting to get dark."

Rafe brushed off his jeans. "Sounds good to me. I'm ready to get out of here."

Alex hefted the box and followed Rafe down the stairs. After they locked up the house and got in the car, he shook the box. It sounded like papers swooshing around inside.

"Any idea what they could be?" He leaned over and placed it on the floor of the back seat, then sat back and buckled his seat belt.

Rafe shrugged and started the car, switching on the headlights. They illuminated the house and swept across the road as he backed up.

"Probably the deed for the house. What else could it be?"

But it niggled at Alex's mind the entire ride back to the hotel. Who'd bother to lock up the deed to the house and hide it? Something didn't make sense.

CHAPTER TWENTY

A good-natured debate ensued on the drive back to the hotel over best junk food. Rafe insisted candy like gummies, licorice and jelly beans were the best, while Alex insisted that French fries and potato chips ruled.

"How can you compare all that sticky stuff to the flawlessness of the fry?" Disgusted, Alex threw up his hands. "It's God's perfect food—crunchy on the outside, soft on the inside." A dreamy expression crossed Alex's face and his eyes half closed in ecstasy. "Dipped in ketchup or spicy mayo? Ohhh." He groaned. "I think I'm having a foodgasm." He lay back on his seat and whimpered. "Want fries."

"What am I going to do with you? You're insane." Rafe halted at a red light and gazed at Alex with affection. The man lay sprawled in his seat, rubbing his flat stomach and licking his lips. Alex was wildly irreverent, bold and good-looking, and Rafe knew right then he was in over his head, crazy in love with the man.

"Feed me." Alex whined. "If you take me back and feed me I'll let you ravish me all night long."

The light turned green and Rafe accelerated. They were less than a mile away now from the hotel. There was a little residual rush hour traffic but nothing like city traffic any time of the day. Though he should've been tired, the prospect of an entire night with Alex fired his blood so he was simmering, not sleepy. In the back of his mind, however, Rafe didn't believe Alex had come all this way to be with him, until now.

All the stories he'd made up in his mind about the man—his casual attitude about life, the partying and sexual escapades—they all fell by the wayside or shattered into pieces under the onslaught of Alex's gentle encouragement and helpfulness. Rafe couldn't have gone through today by himself, and having Alex there with him to lean on was an unexpected gift. He'd thought it would be a simple matter of visiting the lawyer and seeing to whatever odds and ends his mother had left unattended.

Instead he'd been sneered at by the attorney, who obviously knew about Rafe's sexual orientation and enjoyed staring at him with calculating, speculative eyes. Then there was the matter of the house. Walking into a place where he'd never felt loved or wanted was one of the hardest things he'd ever done. All the loneliness, self-doubt and insecurity came rushing back to claw at him, no matter it had been a lifetime, almost fifteen years since he'd been inside the house and in his room.

He steered the car into a space in the hotel parking lot and killed the engine but made no move to leave. "Where are you?" The back of Alex's hand brushed his cheek. "I've seen that look before. You're inside your head, thinking too much."

Rafe dropped back against the headrest. "Can't help it."

Alex cupped Rafe's face with his hand, forcing him to meet Alex's gaze. "Sure you can. You can think of me instead. And you. Us together, tonight. All night long and how fucking fantastic it's going to be."

Rafe's throat went dry and he licked his lips. "I have, I do." He covered Alex's hand with his own. "It's all I can think about actually," he said hoarsely. It was the most honest thing he'd said all day.

"Let's go," growled Alex. He ripped off the seat belt and almost flew out of the car. Rafe was only a step behind him. They'd almost made it across the parking lot when he stopped.

"Wait," he gasped. "The box. We forgot it in the car." His heart slammed in his chest. Though he hadn't run in almost a week, the adrenaline rush wasn't from the quick sprint to the hotel.

"Fuck," muttered Alex.

"I'll be right back," Rafe hesitated a second then leaned over and kissed Alex. "Don't go anywhere." He raced back to the car, retrieved the box, and came back to a still-complaining Alex.

"Go anywhere? Where the hell would I go in this place? I don't even have a room key."

"Come on. Follow me." He tucked the box under his arm.

"Well now the mood is broken." Alex's eyes twinkled. "You'll have to feed me first, since you killed all the spontaneity."

"Jesus, you're a princess."

"No, baby. I've said before. I'm your fairy godmother and me and my magic wand are going to make all your dreams come true tonight."

The earlier heavy atmosphere was replaced by lighthearted fun, which Rafe discovered he needed. There'd been so little joy in his life; as a child he'd hidden himself away and in college he'd been happy only in the dark, when whispers were to keep secrets, not for promises of passion. His love affair with Kyle was perfect, as long as it was only in the shadows.

Being with Alex was freeing; Alex knew him and didn't want to change a thing. And Rafe understood Alex in a way no one else did. That underneath the wise-ass jokester was a kind man who loved taking care of people. Alex was a nurturer, a man who took pleasure in helping others, without expecting anything in return.

Rafe wanted to give him the world.

They entered the room and Rafe placed the box on the table by the door. Alex was already on the phone with room service, no doubt ordering fries and onion rings and God knows what else.

"Try to order at least one thing that's healthy for me please."

Rafe texted Jenny and told her Alex was there with him and that he'd be cleaning out his mother's house and would be back to work on Monday.

A pair of strong arms encircled his waist. "Hi there."

Rafe leaned back against the strong planes of Alex's chest. "Hi yourself."

Alex blew his hot breath across Rafe's neck and nibbled on his ear, setting every nerve ending in his body on high alert. Maybe Rafe should've been concerned that he turned into a slut-puppy at the first touch of this man, but with Alex's lips moving across his throat and his arms holding Rafe tight against his hard body, all reason flew out the window.

"Let's go to bed. To hell with the food." Rafe arched his back, allowing Alex better access to the sensitive flesh of his throat. Desire hummed in his veins.

"Mmm." Alex sucked his neck, right under his earlobe. "I don't know. I got a double order of fries. What do you have that's better?"

Shocking himself, Rafe turned in Alex's arms facing him. "This." Rafe took Alex's mouth in a sweet and tender kiss, while rubbing against Alex and rolling his hips like one of the pole dancers he'd seen at Josh's bachelor party.

Alex reacted swiftly, cupping Rafe's ass as he walked him backward toward the bed. With what seemed like hardly any effort, Alex tossed him on the bed and Rafe bounced hard, landing in the middle of the mattress. Alex advanced on him, his eyes wild, lips reddened from their kisses.

There was a knock on the door and Rafe almost groaned aloud with frustration. "Maybe they'll go away if we don't answer it," he suggested hopefully.

Alex stared at him as if he had eight heads. "Are you crazy? Fries and onion rings, man." He raced to the door to answer the knocking.

Rubbing his aching cock, Rafe couldn't help but laugh. Bastard.

The waiter set the tray down and Rafe could see his gaze flickering between Alex standing and Rafe on the bed. Surprisingly, Rafe didn't notice disgust or hate in the young man's eyes but rather wistfulness and a touch of envy.

Rafe signed the bill and gave the kid a generous tip. Alex shut the door after him and proceeded to attack his food, rolling his eyes with orgasmic glee. For some reason, Rafe wasn't as hungry as he'd first thought, and decided he might as well see if he could open the box.

"Don't you want your food?" Alex's mouth bulged from the giant bite of his burger as well as the longed for fries. "It's really good."

Rafe took the keys he'd gotten from the lawyer out of his pocket, found the smaller key and slid it into the lock of the box. Holding his breath, Rafe turned the key and the lock opened.

"Did it work?" Still chewing, Alex had come to sit by him. "Here, have a fry." He slid it into Rafe's mouth. It was perfect; crisp on the outside, slightly salty and hot.

"Mmm. That is good."

Alex smirked. "Told ya." He gestured to the box. "So? What's in there?"

Rafe peered inside. There were some old newspaper clippings, a letter and a birth certificate. "I have no idea what any of this is." He took the whole box and sat in the center of the bed. Alex placed his burger back on the plate then joined him.

"Let's look."

Rafe looked at the birth certificate; to his shock it was his. "Huh. I have my birth certificate at my house."

"What are the other things?" Alex peered over his shoulder. "Old newspaper articles?"

"Yeah." Rafe read the first clipping. It was from thirty-two years ago, and the edges felt soft and crumbly under his fingers. The article was about a teenaged girl, seventeen years old, who'd been killed in a car crash, along with a man who was also killed. The second article was the same story, but from a different newspaper. The name of the woman was Anabelle Grant, and there was an old, slightly out of focus picture of her.

"Hmm. This is odd." He read and re-read the articles, to see if there were any clues as to why his mother might have kept them for so many years.

"What is?" Alex leaned over and gingerly took one of the pieces of newspaper and read it. "Did you know the woman?"

"No, but her last name is the same as my mother's. I mean, my mother's name was Mary Elizabeth Grant and this woman was Anabelle Grant." Rafe squinted at the picture. Even with his glasses it was hard to make out the blurred lines of her face. "Maybe they were related."

"Well there's an envelope there. Maybe it can solve your mystery." Alex reclined on the bed and watched him.

Rafe rubbed his eyes and nodded. "Yeah." He took the unsealed envelope and opened it, scanning the written words, his blood turning cold as he continued to read.

Mary,

Thank you for taking me and Raphael in but I can't stay here any longer. You and your husband have made it impossible for me to live here with your disapproval and lectures. The baby is an innocent, how can you say you hate him? I didn't set out to get pregnant, I fell in love. I thought as my older sister you'd understand and be more sympathetic, but I guess I was wrong. Why are you ashamed of us? No one has to know I'm not married. But don't worry. I love my baby more than anything in the world; I would never, ever give him up. I've made plans for me and Raphael and we'll be out of your hair, and you'll never have to see us again. Maybe one day you'll forgive me but first you'll have to tell me what I did wrong except have my baby, love him and want to keep him and give him a wonderful life.

Annie

The letter dropped from Rafe's numb fingers and all sound faded. It wasn't until he felt Alex's hands gripping his arms that he came back to that hotel room and the sight of Alex's worried face.

"Rafe, what's wrong?"

"Read the letter." His hands curled into fists to keep them from shaking.

The expressions that crossed Alex's face ranged from sympathy and surprise to shock and finally anger. When he finished he carefully placed the letter back in the box and held out his arms.

"Come here."

Rafe knew it was done out of sympathy and Alex's innate good-heartedness, but he wasn't sure he could be touched at the moment. Everything in his life was a lie and his insides felt smashed to bits.

It seemed Alex understood his reluctance. Without a word he took Rafe by the hand and tugged. Like an obedient child, Rafe followed him into the bathroom, where Alex turned on the shower, then stripped himself and Rafe.

"Let me take care of you, baby."

Rafe hadn't the strength to say no. Alex led him into the shower and with gentle, loving hands washed Rafe's hair. He then poured a generous amount of the lemony scented bath gel into his hands and slicked Rafe up. Rafe settled his back against the wall, sinking into the sensation of Alex's strong hands massaging his body.

"Shhh. It's going to be okay."

With the steamy water pouring over him, Rafe thought about the letter and its shocking contents. His mother, his real mother had loved and wanted him. He drew strength in that, and believed from that short letter, which was all that remained of her, that she would have always loved him, not matter that he was gay or stuttered. She fought for him, kept him at a time when there was still a stigma to being an unwed mother. She died, he wanted to think, trying to give him a better life.

He knew tears ran down his face at the thought of the life he missed. He'd grown up with a woman—his aunt—who hated him for the shame she believed he brought to her family. Her attitude toward him now made perfect sense. Forced to take care of her sister's illegitimate child, his mother made certain he'd never know love. And he, too young to remember his real mother, retreated into a world of books, pets and silence until he had the means to run away and not look back.

Alex turned off the water and bundled him in a large bath towel. "Let's go, baby."

Rafe was happy to lean against Alex's strength. Alex dressed him in a pair of boxers and a tee shirt and led him to the bed, where he lay down, the sheet brushing cool and soft against his body. A languorous sense of well-being stole through him.

Alex dressed himself and slipped into bed next to him. "Let me hold you now. Tomorrow we can figure out everything else, but tonight I'm here for you."

Rafe's eyelids slid shut as Alex's warmth penetrated his body. He was careful to listen for Alex's even, deep breathing, signaling he'd fallen asleep.

"I love you, Alex. I want more than only tonight."

CHAPTER TWENTY-ONE

The next morning found them at Rafe's house watching the junkmen cart out the inside contents to their Dumpster. Some of the furniture and clothing were slated for Goodwill and the rest was to be carted away to the dump. Rafe had called and made an appointment with the attorney for noontime, as he wanted to find out as much as he could about his real mother.

"Do you think he knows anything about it?" Alex watched Rafe pace the front yard. He couldn't imagine the pain his friend was going through and Alex hurt for him, knowing how badly Rafe had been treated, and what he'd missed out on in life. No matter the terrible relationship he had with his own parents, Alex was lucky enough to have had Seth in his life, and that love had never died.

"He has to," said Rafe, grimly. "They adopted me as their child and got me a new birth certificate. They needed a lawyer for that."

"You're right." Alex caught Rafe by the arm, halting his steps. "I think you're handling it remarkably well."

"You do?" Rafe's laugh came out weak. "I feel like a fucking mess."

"Well, who wouldn't be?" Alex forced Rafe to face him. "But look at you. You barely stutter anymore and you put that lawyer in his place. Keep thinking this: you never have to see these people again and they can go fuck themselves with their nasty attitudes."

Rafe studied his face for a moment and allowed himself a brief grin. "You're right."

"Of course I'm right." Alex slung his arm around Rafe's neck. "You should know that by now."

One of the workmen called Rafe over to inspect a piece of furniture, and Alex watched his lover walk away with a confident stride that hadn't been there a month ago. It had always been inside Rafe, and Alex was happy he could help Rafe discover the man he was.

"That was the last of it," said Rafe with a relieved look on his face. "We can head back, sign off on all the paperwork and have that talk." An uncertain look entered his eyes. "Unless you'd rather wait at the hotel and I can meet you there. I mean technically you don't need to come to the lawyer's office . . ." His voice trailed off.

"Don't be an idiot. Of course I'm coming with you."

Relief flooded Rafe's face. "Good. I hope you already know, but in case I didn't tell you, I really appreciate everything you've done for me. Simply showing up here to give me support was an unexpected, but happy surprise."

"I'm only doing what any friend would do." But Alex knew that wasn't true. Their relationship had shifted during this trip; from mere friends to something deeper. It wasn't anything he was willing to delve into greater depths at this time. Truth was, Alex was frightened of what he might see when all those layers were peeled away revealing what was in his heart.

Rafe knelt down to tie the laces of his sneaker. "If we leave now, we can get to the lawyer's office a little early. I'm hoping we can wrap everything up this afternoon. I'm ready to go home, how about you?"

Not really, was on the tip of Alex's tongue. It was like a little getaway, this time with only the two of them sequestered in their hotel room, without the rest of the world poking their noses in. "We could stay and go to the amusement park if you'd like. Take an extra day to have some fun."

Rafe turned a delighted face up to him. "I'd love that. I haven't been to a park in years." He jumped to his feet. "Let's get going." With one final look at the house he grew up in, he turned his back and got into the car.

It had to be hard for someone as sensitive as Rafe to walk away from a house, even one full of unhappy memories, knowing he could never return. Hopefully the lawyer could answer whatever questions Rafe might have about his past. Happier now that he'd get the chance to spend extra time alone with Rafe, Alex sang along with the radio and soon Rafe was joining him, singing to Britney Spears.

They arrived at the lawyer's office, laughing and breathless. This time they were ushered in immediately to McSweeny's office, where the attorney awaited them behind his desk.

Normally, Alex didn't make snap judgments about people; he also tended to think the better of them until proven otherwise. But there was something of the snake-oil salesman about the lawyer. Maybe it was the affected mustache or the pompous way he stood with his fingers hooked in his suspenders. Whatever it was, Alex didn't like him, or the way he treated Rafe.

"Gentlemen. What can I do for you this afternoon? Are you ready to sign the paperwork, Dr. Hazelton?" He pulled the papers out of the file. "I have an appraisal here for the home, with the comparables in the area. You can see the price is more than adequate." He handed over the papers and Rafe studied them, then put them back down.

"What do you know of my adoption?"

Alex was so proud of Rafe he could've hugged him right then. The lawyer's white face and darting eyes were a sure sign he was aware of Rafe's parentage.

"Tell me." Rafe slammed his hand down on the desk. "It's my life. I h-have a r-right to know."

Hearing how upset Rafe was, Alex stood by his side and placed his hand on Rafe's shoulder in a gesture of not only comfort, but support.

"I suggest you tell Dr. Hazelton everything." Alex folded his arms and glared at the lawyer down the bridge of his nose.

"She never wanted you to find out; she didn't want anyone to know. Her sister came to her pregnant and unmarried. They'd never gotten along. I don't know why Annie thought Mary would help her."

"Do you know who my father was?" Rafe whispered, fixated on McSweeny's face. The hope kindled in Rafe's eyes broke Alex's heart, because from the article it was obvious. Rafe must know as well, but wanted, no *needed* that validation. "Did they love each other?"

For the first time since they met, the lawyer's eyes gazed at Rafe with kindness. "From what I know, yes. Very much."

Alex put his arm around Rafe, feeling him tremble with emotion.

"But I'm afraid he died with her in the crash. They had gotten the marriage license and were coming back to your house to pick you up. It was a horribly rainy night and they skidded into oncoming traffic."

"Thank you," whispered Rafe. He cleared his throat. "Why did they—my aunt and uncle—even adopt me? It was obvious they never wanted me."

McSweeny hesitated. "Your real mother worked as a secretary in the local school system. She had some small benefits that came to her upon her death. One of them was a life insurance policy for a thousand dollars." Unable to face them anymore, McSweeny rose to busy himself with the papers Rafe needed to sign. "I'll be right back with copies." He hurried from the room, closing the door behind him.

"They used me for the money, for a lousy thousand dollars." Rafe wrapped his arms around his waist. "They stole everything from me."

"No, baby, no they didn't." Alex held him firmly by the shoulders. "They took some chump change, but the real you inside? They could never take that away."

"My real parents loved me." Rafe smiled through the

wetness in his eyes. "At least I know now I had someone who loved me once."

"I—" Alex snapped his mouth shut. "You have a lot of people who care about you. You see it now, right?"

"Yeah. Jenny and her husband are great, and so is everyone else in the clinic. I'm hoping Josh and I are still friends."

"How about me? You know I'm your friend too, right?" Alex's hands rested loosely on Rafe's waist, their faces close to one another.

Although they were almost the same height, Rafe's leaner build was deceptive, giving him the appearance of being smaller and not that strong. Recalling how Rafe held him down the first night they'd made love, the strength of Rafe's body thrusting inside him, Alex knew better, and liked that he alone knew that physical side of Rafe.

"I do. Somehow you've become my dearest friend. I hope that confession doesn't scare you off. I know we've only gotten close lately, but you've helped me as if I've known you for years."

His earnestness made Alex smile. "I know." He kissed Rafe's cheek, heedless of the fact they were in the lawyer's office and the door could open any moment. "I feel close to you as well. You know more about me than anyone."

Rafe bit his lip. "I hope I'm not out of line, but you need to talk to Micah and make up with him. You two are like brothers; I've seen you together." Rafe pulled away from Alex's hands to sit in one of the chairs by the lawyer's desk. "Look what happened to my birth parents. They never had a chance at a life with me. You don't want to lose the chance to regain a lifelong friendship because of a stupid argument."

Dread shot through Alex, his heart slamming in heavy beats. "I can't talk about Seth. It's too painful." Even now the mere thought of talking about his dead brother ripped him to shreds.

"Alex, let go of the pain. You didn't have anything to do with his death, did you?"

Rafe's gentle voice only made Alex feel worse inside.

Appalled at the question, his voice rose in the hush of the room. "No, of course not, never. I was away at college when he got so sick."

He'd already lost his brother, his parents, and maybe now his best friend. Was he about to lose his new lover because he couldn't find the words to say what was in his heart? Maybe it was time to take that step with Rafe. He'd never judge him or think him stupid.

McSweeny chose that moment to come back into the room and Rafe's attention focused on the paperwork the lawyer had for him. The lawyer promised to have a formal offer on the house by next week at the latest.

"Send the papers to my lawyer. I'll have her look them over." Rafe dug a card out of his wallet and handed it to McSweeny who glanced at it, then tucked it away in the file.

"Very good, Doctor." If Alex didn't know any better, he'd swear the lawyer looked sympathetic. "I'm sorry you found out about your parents in this manner but I'm sure it must put your mind at ease to finally know the truth."

Rafe said nothing further until they were in the car.

"Who the hell is he to say he's sure about how I feel," he fumed. His hands shook on the steering wheel. "He doesn't know shit about me nor care."

"Maybe," said Alex. "Or maybe now he's understanding the impact your adoptive mother's—"

"My aunt," said Rafe, cutting in.

Alex nodded, "Your aunt's deception had on your life." He placed his hand over Rafe's, which clutched the steering wheel in a death grip. "McSweeny was only her lawyer, Rafe. It doesn't mean he agreed with what she did."

Rafe sagged, deflated and worn like a popped balloon devoid of air. "Maybe you're right. I've never been good at reading people; I take everything at face value and can't understand why people hide or lie about things."

Alex remained silent, letting Rafe work through his problems out loud.

"I didn't always feel like that. When I was in college, I thought I was a pretty good judge of character since I'd spent so much time growing up on the outside, people-watching. I'd never get fooled by anyone, since I knew, first hand, how mean people can be."

Intrigued at this first piece of information about Rafe's personal history, Alex urged him on. A little jealous, he wanted to know who the man had dated and his old love affairs. "Someone cheated on you; your boyfriend?"

Rafe snorted in disgust. "I could hardly call him that. Kyle was a jock on the football team; gorgeous, popular." His voice grew wistful. "He was everything I thought I was missing out on all my life."

"I'm surprised he was out; most gay athletes were heavily closeted back then," Alex mused.

Rafe remained silent for a moment, tracing the edge of the steering wheel with his finger. "He wasn't. We'd only meet late at night." He stared out the windshield, and Alex watched the smoothness of his jaw tighten. "He'd only come to my room; God forbid I should be seen in his frat house. Kyle told me it was so I'd be more comfortable, but I know now it was only so he could keep hiding."

Alex's fists clenched; he'd like to punch that fucker in the face for causing Rafe such pain, even now, though it was so many years ago. "Did you get caught?"

"Not like you think." Rafe leaned back against the headrest, gazing upward. "We were talking in the library late one night, making plans. He thought we were safe, since none of his friends were studious, to say the least. But a group of his teammates had been looking for him and saw his car parked outside."

Alex placed his hand on Rafe's thigh and gave him a reassuring squeeze. "What happened?"

"They saw us and started joking around, about what he was doing talking to the fag. I decided to leave and they wouldn't let me pass."

Outraged, Alex bit out, "Did they hurt you?"

"Only my pride. They pushed me around a little, making homo jokes and a few groped me and pretended to try and kiss me. But Kyle?" Rafe huffed out a bitter laugh. "He stood there and did nothing. Didn't even tell them once to stop. He even joined in the name-calling. Finally they let me go and I went home and decided that being alone was better than being with someone who'd let me get hurt rather than stand up for who he is."

Alex caught himself rubbing Rafe's leg as if to give him re-assurance. "That must've been hard for you. Did he try and talk you out of it?"

Rafe nodded. "He'd stop by every few nights telling me it was no big deal, how he couldn't let anyone know because it would ruin his chances at becoming Pro."

"Did he?"

"Of course not. He's a pharmaceutical salesman who lives in California now. Married with children."

Alex knew the type. Closeted, but they still needed to satisfy their true urges. And if this piece of shit Kyle was a salesman, it meant he was on the road. A lot. Alex didn't know who to feel sorrier for, the man's wife, or the guys he met and fucked along the way, making them promises he never intended to keep.

"And he's tried to contact you, I bet."

"Once. I shut him down." Rafe smiled at him. "I'm ready to get out of here. Let's go hit the roller coasters."

Alex grinned. He was going to stuff Rafe full of cotton can-dy, funnel cake and everything disgusting he could find, then hold his hand tight when they rode the roller coasters.

CHAPTER TWENTY-TWO

The afternoon sun beat down on his back as Rafe surveyed the menu on the food truck. Alex was already scarfing down a corn dog, taking alternating noisy sips from a big red slushy drink. To Rafe he looked like an overgrown kid, and the joy in his face was infectious.

"I'll have a funnel cake and a frozen lemonade."

His first bite of the crunchy sweet dough, dusted with sugar, brought back some of the good memories he had from his childhood. The icy cold, tangy lemonade made a perfect accompaniment, as it counteracted the overly sweet funnel cake.

"Isn't it good? Aren't you glad you got it?" Alex nudged him and flipped his empty corn dog stick in the garbage can.

"Yeah." Rafe took another bite and licked the dusting of powdered sugar off his lips.

"Wait, you missed a spot." Alex leaned over and placing his hands on Rafe's shoulders held him still, while he licked the corner of Rafe's lips with the tip of his tongue.

Rafe stood frozen in place. It was one thing to sleep with Alex; while the sex was phenomenal, Rafe knew for Alex it wasn't permanent and they were together because of friendship.

But to stand here in the open, with hundreds of people walking by and kiss him, that took their relationship to a different level, at least for Rafe. Unfortunately Alex more than likely didn't see it that way. He was here as a friend and hadn't ever given Rafe any signals otherwise.

Alex's pulled away and his eyes lit up. "Look, let's go on that coaster."

Rafe turned around and the mass of rolling tracks and curving steel rose high before them. He'd always loved roller coasters; they made him feel free and alive.

"Yes, let's go."

Like two little kids, they ran to join the line. They discovered they both liked sitting in the first row and Rafe was ridiculously excited when they buckled him in.

"I love being the first one."

"Me too, but you're gonna have to hold my hand. What if I get scared?" Alex widened his eyes and pouted.

Rafe's lips twitched in an effort to hold back his smile. Nothing scared Alex Stern. "You're crazy." But he took Alex's hand in his and Alex smiled happily.

The roller coaster lurched, then began traveling at a slow rate of speed, gathering momentum. As they approached the first drop, Alex leaned over and kissed him as they began the fall.

Their lips clung and their hands grasped tight. When they reached bottom, Alex broke the kiss and whispered, "That's how you make me feel; like I'm free-falling, but still flying in the wind."

Rafe whispered back over the screech of the wheels, "You make me feel reckless too."

Their fingers remained firmly laced together as they screamed in pretend fright through the rest of the ride. The violent ups and downs of the roller coaster didn't bother Rafe; he clung to Alex and they held onto each other through the twists and turns. They stumbled out of the car, laughing so hard they couldn't catch their breath.

Alex slipped his arm around Rafe's neck and Rafe, accustomed to his overt displays of affection now, naturally fell into the embrace. He ignored the sideways looks from some people; Rafe could care less what anyone here had to say anymore.

Pressed up against the hardness of Alex's chest, the smell of carnival food drifting through the air and the screams of the people on the rides, Rafe had never felt as alive as he did right now.

There was a buzzing in his pocket and he reached in to pull out his phone but it came up dark. "Must be yours."

Alex dug into his pocket but by the time he wrestled it out, it had stopped ringing. His face darkened as Rafe watched him check the missed calls.

"Bad news?" Rafe asked hesitantly. All the positive energy drained from Alex and his dancing eyes turned flat.

"Someone I have no desire to talk to, that's all." He walked away, still clutching the phone in his hand.

Micah, it must be Micah. Here was his chance to be as good a friend to Alex as the man had been to him these past days. Even though Micah had made some horrible accusations, totally unfounded and cruel, Rafe knew how much Alex loved his friend. And Micah loved Alex.

"Alex." Rafe hurried over to Alex who stared down at the blank phone screen. "It's time to end all this stupidity between you and Micah. You have to make up. Yes, he was wrong to jump to assumptions and say those stupid things, but friends make mistakes. And you were wrong for hiding things, important things from him from the beginning of your friendship."

"Rafe—"

"No," Rafe cut Alex off. "It's time you listened to me. Don't throw away the best friend you've ever had over some dumb argument. You aren't children anymore. Sit down and talk to each other. Share your brother with Micah." He touched Alex's shoulder. "You know he loves you, Alex. And I know how much you love him."

"It wasn't Micah." Alex spun the phone in his hand.

Rafe looked back at him, confused by Alex's reaction to the phone call. "Oh." He waited for Alex to say something, elaborate further on who it was but the silence dragged on. Finally, when he couldn't stand it any longer he asked, "Who was it?" He wasn't doing it to be nosy but rather to try and help Alex who, from the desolate look in his eyes, needed him whether he realized it or not.

"Would you mind if we left?" Alex slid the phone back into his pocket. "I'd like to go back."

"Sure." Rafe gave a tentative smile and waited for one in return but none was forthcoming. He and Alex walked silently through the park, not speaking until they reached the car. Rafe had just pressed the button to deactivate the alarm when Alex's phone rang again. This time he was quicker and answered it right away. To Rafe's surprise he hurried away from their car and stood under a tree to talk.

Hurt that Alex felt the need to hide whoever he was speaking with, Rafe slid into the car and turned on the engine so he could open the windows. He wasn't eavesdropping but he did hear Alex's voice raised in frustration and a little anger. Rafe decided to turn on the radio; if Alex wanted to tell him who it was, he would. This was a good reminder to Rafe that he and Alex were friends, nothing more.

Alex opened the door and slid inside the car, his face tense with anger. Rafe, mindful of Alex's desire for privacy, said nothing and started driving. They joined the line of cars waiting to leave the parking lot. Normally, Alex would be flirting and joking with him, but he maintained the silent treatment. They finally entered the main road and drove off to their hotel.

After a few miles went by with nothing but the radio announcer's annoying voice, Rafe couldn't stand it anymore. "It's not that I want to pry, but is everything all right?" He shot a glance over to Alex who, to his shock, seemed on the verge of a breakdown. Making a quick decision, Rafe pulled into the empty parking lot of a diner that was out of business and shut off the engine. "Alex, talk to me."

The desolation in Alex's eyes when he turned his face hit Rafe like a punch in the stomach. His blue eyes held none of their earlier sparkle, and Rafe could see the sheen of tears building, as Alex struggled for composure.

"Tell me," he begged. "Let me help you like you helped me."

After hesitating long enough that Rafe thought he might punch his hand through the windshield, Alex spoke. "It's my mother." His voice caught for a second. "She's in the hospital. They think it might be a heart attack but they're not sure."

"Alex," Rafe breathed, sliding his hand up Alex's arm. "I'm so sorry. Are you guys close, or—"

A harsh bark of laughter ended on a sob. "We haven't spoken in years. She . . . she hates me; hates me because I'm gay and hates me because I lived while Seth, her favorite, died." The tears now came in earnest, trickling down Alex's face.

"Oh, no, no." Rafe undid his seat belt and moved closer, thankful for the bench seat in the rental car. "I'm sure that isn't the case."

Alex tried to smile amid his tears. "That's you, Rafe. Always seeing the good in people, not the bad. That was my father on the phone, telling me—*ordering* me—to come home and see her."

Rafe gave Alex's shoulder a squeeze. "When do you want to leave? We're all finished here, so once we get back to the hotel room we can be packed and ready to leave within a half hour."

He rebuckled his seat belt, started the car and began the short drive back to the hotel.

"I'm not going."

"Oh?" Rafe knew Alex well enough now not to push him, but let him talk it out.

"I know you think I should. But what for?" Alex raked his hands through his hair and flipped down his sunglasses in what Rafe saw as a defensive measure to avoid facing Rafe's disapproval.

"Because she's your mother, whether you like it or not."

The silence between them grew as they traveled.

"You can't know," Alex began. "All the heartache and pain I went through to try and be what they wanted, what I could never be, but tried no matter how much of myself I gave up."

"So tell me; talk to me. I'm here for you, the way you've been for me. Friendship is a two-way street you know."

"No, I don't know. I've never managed to have a friend like

that."

"You do now."

Rafe drove into the hotel parking lot. Alex had his hand on the door, unlocking it and pushing it open as soon as Rafe turned off the engine. He was halfway across the parking lot before Rafe caught up with him. Unwilling to continue such a personal conversation in public, Rafe waited until they were safely back in their room with the door closed, before he spoke.

"Tell me what you're thinking. Let me in. I couldn't have made it through these last few days without you." Rafe stood before Alex, who'd slumped into the standard hotel club chair.

"She doesn't really want to see me. My father thinks she does because he said she mentioned my name once or twice." Alex gazed up at Rafe. "She wouldn't want to see me, her gay son."

"But maybe you should. Attitudes change, people change."

"The only thing they ever wanted was for me to change. To become who Seth would have been; a straight doctor. Well I'm not either one of those things. I'm their living disappointment."

Rafe sat on the arm of the chair. "Alex, when was the last time you saw them?"

He shook his head. "Years ago."

Rafe's lips curved in a small smile. "Years ago you and Micah were best friends, screwing around. I was a stuttering mess. Now Micah is married and in love, and you two don't even talk."

"And you barely stutter anymore." He rested his hand on Rafe's thigh, its comforting weight pleasant. Rafe covered Alex's hand with his own.

"What would I give to have a chance to see my real mother and father. To maybe hear from their lips that they loved me." Rafe drew in a breath. "What if she dies without you ever seeing her. There are no second chances if that happens. You're lucky because you're being given that chance. How can you refuse?"

Alex sat mute and Rafe stood up, went into the bathroom and began packing. There was no need to stay anymore no matter what. He heard Alex's step behind him and caught his gaze in the mirror.

"I have a question for you."

Rafe faced Alex, gripping the smooth countertop between his fingers. "Yes?"

"Will you come with me? If I decide to go to my parents and the hospital. I know it's asking a lot and you have to get back to the clinic—"

"Shh." Rafe put his fingers over Alex's lips. "Of course I will. You don't even need to ask. Don't you know by now how much I care for you?" He brushed his lips over Alex's, the faint taste of his cherry drink still sweetly present in Alex's mouth.

"You're the only one who does," said Alex, before he slid his tongue into Rafe's mouth. They remained in that little hotel bathroom, kissing, until Rafe broke away with a gasp.

"We should leave. We can drop off your car at the rental place here and come back in my car."

Alex reached for him, pulling Rafe up against his chest. "I'd rather get into bed and make you scream."

"Alex," he sighed, the familiar pulse of desire throbbing wherever Alex touched him. "We should go. Stop distracting me."

"I like distracting you." His lips nibbled down Rafe's jaw. "You get all flushed and you make all these crazy sounds."

He was about to make another one of those sounds if Alex didn't get his hands off his ass. "You'll thank me for this." With a determination he didn't know he had, Rafe wrenched out of Alex's arms and pushed him away. "We need to leave." This time he sidestepped Alex's grasp and left the bathroom.

"Tease." He threw himself down on the bed and watched Rafe pack. "Hey, Rafe?"

Rafe zipped up his duffel bag and placed it on the floor. "Yeah?"

"What you said before, that you cared for me?" Alex's gaze searched his face anxiously. "You know I care about you too, right?"

A subtle difference in terminology, and Rafe wondered whether it was a deliberate choice of words. There was a difference, at least in his mind. He cared *about* many people and the animals he treated. But Alex was the person he cared *for* in his heart.

"Sure." He managed a casual smile. "We should get going; it's a long drive and you need to tell me where we're going."

Rafe hefted his bag and waited for Alex to throw his few things into his overnight bag. Perhaps when they got back home and Alex had sorted out his family issues, Rafe would be able to pull away a bit so the ache in his heart wouldn't be as great when they inevitably parted ways.

CHAPTER TWENTY-THREE

The drive back to New York was endless. Maybe it was the traffic on the Turnpike or the fact that the same ten songs played on the radio for the entire three-hour trip. Rafe didn't speak much, Alex noticed, and even though he asked several times if things were okay, Alex suspected Rafe wasn't telling the truth.

They stopped briefly to use the restroom, where once again, Alex attempted to find out why Rafe had become so reticent.

"Hey, if you're having second thoughts, I can do this alone." He offered a potato chip to Rafe from the bag he'd bought inside the gas station's convenience store.

"No, thanks." Though Rafe's face remained a mask of neutrality, Alex heard the hurt in his voice. "Is that what you want? I don't want to intrude if you'd rather do this alone."

"God, no." The words burst out of Alex. "I need you there. I thought maybe you regretted the offer to come."

Rafe gazed at him with speculative eyes. "I would never regret helping you, especially after what you did for me these past few days. You're my friend, Alex. I'll do anything I can to help you."

He didn't care if it held them up or if it was inappropriate with his mother in the hospital, but the need to kiss Rafe overwhelmed everything else. To his delight, Rafe took control, holding Alex tight, delving and exploring Alex's mouth with his tongue until both were left gasping for air when they finally broke apart.

Alex rested his forehead against Rafe's. "I like your kind of help."

It seemed Rafe was about to say something, then he smiled faintly and said, "We should get going."

The GPS was set to Alex's parents' home on the North Shore of Long Island. The area was chock-full of beautiful Tudor mansions with their half-timbered fronts setting the stage for magnificent lawns and gardens, as well as massive colonial brick homes, their pillars reminiscent of southern estates. In the years since Alex had been in this area, very little had changed on the outside. He was all too aware of the beautiful façades not matching the inner ugliness they hid and wondered how many other families had painful secrets they weren't willing to accept.

When they pulled into the driveway of his parents' rambling brick home, the dread that he'd managed to keep at bay until this moment took control, insinuating itself through his bones and blood. He wasn't aware he was shaking until Rafe slid over on the seat, took him in his arms and held him for a moment.

"It's going to be fine. I promise."

"You don't know my father," Alex whispered.

"But I know you," Rafe replied with his sweet, calm smile. "You're strong and kind and full of heart. You won't let him make you anything you aren't."

He really didn't deserve a friend like Rafe.

"I'm so glad you're here with me. Thank you." He cupped Rafe's jaw and kissed him, leisurely exploring his mouth, enjoying Rafe's sighs of pleasure. With great reluctance he drew back, savoring the sight of Rafe's reddened lips and sated smile.

"Into the lion's den we go." He got out of the car and stood for a moment, breathing in the scent of newly mowed grass and damp earth. It was late and relatively quiet here in this pastoral-like enclave his parents had ensconced themselves in. Even as a child, he'd longed for more excitement than playing on the swings in the large backyard, and had talked his brother into making up stories of dragons and kings and pirate treasure.

The front door opened and Alex's stomach cramped as the tall figure of his father stepped out under the lights of the front porch. With shock, Alex noticed his father had turned white, but that did nothing to detract from his overall commanding appearance. Alex often thought his father would make a perfect general in the army; his posture was never anything less than poker straight and when his cold blue eyes flicked over you, you could feel the frost in the air, even in the dead of summer.

"Alexander."

How welcoming. What did he expect, a hug and a kiss? Open arms and an "I love you"? He could've laughed at the ridiculousness of that situation.

"Father."

With deliberate steps his father descended the stairs, like a king descending from his throne. His gaze flicked dismissively over Rafe who'd come to stand near Alex in a show of support.

"I'm glad to see you didn't allow your activities to prevent you from doing the right thing and coming to see your mother."

"Good aftern-noon, Dr. St-Stern. I'm Dr. Rafe Hazelton." Shit, Rafe's stutter had returned, which meant he was nervous. He gave his lover an anxious look, but he needn't have worried. Rafe held out his hand and Alex held his breath, waiting to see what his father would do.

"Hmm, yes. Dr. Hazelton. What's your specialty?" He ignored Rafe's outstretched hand.

"I'm a veterinarian."

His father sniffed. "A dog doctor? Priceless."

"Rafe is my friend, Father."

That was enough to set his father's lip curling in disgust. "Friend." Once again that cold, hawk-like gaze touched Rafe, but now there was a hint of derision in his eyes as well as disgust. "Is that what you call it nowadays?"

His father seemed about to continue, then remembering they were outside and subject to possible scrutiny by the neighbors, turned around and strode back up the stairs. He entered the house, leaving the front door open behind him.

"What do we do now?"

Alex smiled slightly and signaled to Rafe to open the trunk. "We take our bags, head inside and show my father what a gay couple looks like."

Rafe made a face as he popped the trunk. "I'm not here to throw my sexuality in your father's face. He's nothing to me."

Shame-faced, Alex conceded. "You're right. That was childish of me." He lifted his bag out and waited for Rafe to do the same before slamming down the hood of the trunk. "And because of that, I want to put our bags down and go directly to the hospital to see my mother."

Rafe's eyes glowed. "I'm proud of you." A hesitant look entered his eyes. "Do you want me to come with you?"

Alex draped his arm around Rafe's shoulders. "I wouldn't leave you here with him, but more importantly, I need you with me."

Rafe sagged against him in relief. "Thank God."

Alex kissed his head. "Let's go."

They walked up the steps and into the house.

His father had disappeared, which made it easier to escape to the hospital after he and Rafe put their bags down in what used to be his room, now used as a guest room. He was silent on the short, ten minute drive to the hospital. His mind was full of memories of Seth and the short life they'd shared.

The same hospital smell permeated the air here, like at his hospital. He hadn't been back to this place since his brother died. Rafe's steady presence by his side was the only thing holding him together. They found his mother's room and walked inside, seeing the private duty nurse sitting in the corner. Once in the room, however, Alex only had eyes for his mother.

Alex was dimly aware of Rafe greeting the nurse and explaining who they were. He slowly approached the bed where his mother lay, the beeping noise of the machines poking at his brain. The translucent paleness of his mother's face and hands was only a shade lighter than the sheets they rested upon. With a pang, he noticed her once luxurious dark hair had turned gray.

"Mother?" His voice creeping up in tone, slightly above a whisper, yet not strong enough to carry far. "Mother, it's Alex. Can you hear me?" He ached to touch her, the years falling back as he remembered her kisses when he was young. Before he changed from the child she'd loved without condition into the man she rejected for whom he loved.

Giving in to his need, he rested his hand on top of hers, its coolness welcome against his overheated skin. He sensed someone next to him and knew it was Rafe. Sweet Rafe with his kind eyes and perfect heart. Too good for a man like Alex, but he couldn't give him up. Rafe had become his lifeline back to a world Alex wanted to rejoin.

"The nurse said she's been resting more comfortably today than yesterday."

"Thank you," he whispered. "I never knew she had a bad heart."

They stayed like that for several minutes, Alex merely staring at her face, remembering all the times he and Seth snuggled on her lap when they were little. It served no purpose now to dwell on the bad times. Even their last bitter conversation left no lasting imprint on his mind.

Her eyelids fluttered and her head moved on the pillow.

"Mother can you hear me?" Alex was careful not to disturb any of the wires or her IV drip.

She opened her eyes and held his gaze. Her mouth moved but no sound came out. The nurse approached the bed and Alex smiled through the fear in his heart.

"Can she have a sip of water?"

The nurse nodded. "Why don't you give it to her?"

"Is that you?" Her hand moved on the pillow and her voice sounded fretful. "Seth, is that you?"

Rafe held him around the waist. "She's confused. She was asking for you yesterday, remember?" He barely heard Rafe through the pain.

"Mother? It's me. Alex."

Several minutes passed and she continued to study his face. Her lips began to tremble and tears spilled from the corners of her eyes. "Oh, Alexander. I'm so sorry."

"It's okay. You were confused—"

"Not about that." Her voice, though weak, was firm. "I made a mistake. A horrible one, about everything; you, your life. I know how much I hurt you but can you forgive me?"

So many years, so much pain. Could he let it go?

"How can you deny her, Alex? You're her only child, all she has left." Rafe whispered to him. "Most of us don't get that second chance."

Her hand lifted on the sheet and he took it gingerly in his. "Is this man next to you someone special?"

Alex was about to answer when Rafe took away his chance. "Hello, Mrs. Stern, I'm Rafe. A friend of Alex's."

Her gaze traveled between his and Rafe's faces. "I see. Thank you, Rafe, for bringing him back to me."

"Mother, you should rest. I'm going back to the house now and I'll be back tomorrow." He leaned over and kissed her forehead.

"I never stopped loving you. Even when you left and said you'd never come back, I held out hope."

"It'll be okay. Rest easy."

They left and Alex gratefully allowed Rafe to lead him to the car and drive him back to his parents' house.

The house was quiet and they settled down in the family room with drinks, Alex unable to wrap his head around what his mother said. Actually, he could hardly believe he was sitting here, in this house he swore never to step foot in again after their last terrible fight.

"Are you all right?" Rafe sat next to him on the love seat. "I'm sure you must be overwhelmed by everything; being home, your mother in the hospital and the way she welcomed you."

Alex shifted in his seat and toed off his sneakers. "Care to give me a foot rub?" Without waiting for an answer, he swung his legs up and placed them in Rafe's lap. He almost groaned when Rafe began to massage his feet. "Christ, you have amazing hands."

"And you're only noticing now?" Rafe joked. "I must be slacking off."

Alex wiggled his toes. "If you do a good job on my toes, I'll let you rub something else."

Rafe rolled his eyes. "You're incorrigible."

Alex chuckled and was about to respond when his father's icy voice cut through the air.

"Disgusting is the word I'd use, if you ask me. I didn't expect to come into my home and find this."

Rafe pulled his hands away as if Alex's feet were on fire. Alex hated seeing Rafe uncomfortable and his anger grew at his friend's embarrassment.

"What's disgusting about a foot rub between friends?" He swung his legs down and sat up straight. "Don't be so uptight, Father."

Dr. Herbert Stern stood by the bar and poured himself a straight scotch. Alex watched his father's practiced moves and braced himself for whatever grenades and missiles were to be launched in his and Rafe's path.

His father sat in the leather club chair near the loveseat and stretched his legs out, staring into the amber liquid in his glass.

"You saw your mother?"

"I did. We spoke."

That granted him full eye contact for the first time. "She woke up? What did she say?"

Alex crossed his ankles and studied his feet. "That's between Mother and myself."

"I have a right to know."

"Why?"

His father stared at him, seemingly stymied by that question.

"I think, Dr. Stern, Alex and his mother need time to heal and get a chance to reconnect."

Alex threw Rafe a grateful smile.

"Excuse me, young man, but I don't give a damn what you think about my wife, or son, or anything for that matter." His father set down his tumbler on the coffee table.

Rafe stiffened and tried again. "I-I didn't m-mean to insert m-myself in your pr-private affairs. My c-concern is Alex."

Alex wanted to hug Rafe and tell him how much he admired his courage for speaking up no matter how nervous Alex's father made him.

His father stared at Rafe for a moment then focused on Alex with an amused grin. But Alex knew there was no humor, only malice, in that smile.

"Is this the best you can do for a man? Someone who can't get a word out without tripping over his tongue." His grin morphed into a full-blown laugh. "Even as a faggot you're a loser." He picked up his drink and drained it. "Where'd you find him, Alex? Some seedy bar you go to?"

There was a roaring in Alex's ears and his breath came in short pants. "Apologize." He stood, fists clenching while he trembled in a cold sweat. "Apologize to my friend."

Rafe sat still as an Easter Island statue. His face was pale yet his eyes burned with a fire Alex had yet to see.

"I d-don't need his apology. I f-feel sorry f-for him."

"Sorry for me?" His father's white brows drew together in anger. "Who the hell are you to feel sorry for me?"

"B-because you h-have no idea h-how wonderful y-your s-son is."

"What do you know about him; you're a nobody, someone he most likely picked up in a bar."

"Stop it." Alex advanced on his father, wanting nothing more than to rip his face off for insulting Rafe. "Rafe is ten times the man you'll ever be. He's a respected veterinarian, owns his own business. But most important is how he cares for people. He's kind and loving and has the biggest, most wonderful heart I've ever known."

That snide smirk flickered on his father's lips as he glanced between Alex and Rafe, who gazed wide-eyed at Alex.

"Jesus Christ. You sound like you're in love with the man."

Like the air washed clean after a hard summer rain, it all became clear to Alex. He'd never known it before, so how would he have recognized it? And more importantly, would Rafe believe him even when Alex said what had been hiding in his heart for a while?

"I am," said Alex and hearing the sharp inhalation of Rafe's breath, walked to his side and drew him close. For a moment he rested his cheek against Rafe, soaking in the peace this man gave him. It was like returning home, when all you wanted was to wrap yourself up in the comfort and warmth of familiar acceptance; a safe harbor to rest after a long, hard journey. Rafe's strength and love was what Alex craved.

"I love you," he whispered, but knew Rafe heard. "Come with me." Without a backward glance at his father who stood scowling and red-faced, Alex took Rafe by the hand and walked out.

CHAPTER TWENTY-FOUR

Rafe allowed himself to be led up the wide staircase and back into the bedroom where he and Alex had earlier dumped their bags. His heart pounded and it was hard to catch his breath. Surely Alex meant what he said as a means to shock his father.

Alex didn't turn on the overhead light; he let the moonlight shine in through the large wall of bay windows behind the bed. Rafe had more time now to take in his surroundings and saw this must have been Alex's room when he was a child; the bed was queen sized and had a dark blue comforter, the headboard was padded in the same dark blue material. His desk and bookcase, still filled with the classics as well as science books were on the opposite wall. Little league trophies crowded the shelves as well as swimming ribbons. In the center of the desk sat a large framed picture of Alex and his twin brother Seth at what must have been age sixteen or seventeen. Fraternal, yet still so similar in looks, they could, at first glance, pass for identical. Rafe could pick out Alex in a second by the devilish glint in his eyes. Seth had a more peaceful, calm expression on his forever youthful face.

Alex's strong arms slipped around his waist. "Hi."

Rafe turned to face him. "Hi yourself."

"So, about downstairs."

"Don't." Rafe shook his head and forced a smile. He knew

what was coming. Alex had said what he did to anger his father and nothing else. "I'm not going to hold you to it. I understand why you said it."

Alex stepped back, his face creased with hurt. "Is that what you think? You think I said it to upset my father?"

"Well, yeah. I mean why else?"

"Because of this." Alex's mouth covered his in a bruising kiss. Rafe stiffened for a moment then moaned, pressing his mouth to Alex's, matching the thrust of his tongue, stroke for stroke. They kissed with increasing fervor, Rafe's mind spinning in a thousand pinwheels of light, wishing beyond hope that Alex's words could only have been true.

Alex continued kissing him, his mouth, hot and wet, traveling down Rafe's cheek to nibble at his jaw, only stopping when he reached Rafe's ear. "You can't think of another reason?"

Rafe, weakened by the desire pouring through him and the harrowing events of the long day, sank into Alex's arms. "N-not really."

Alex pushed him back so that he fell onto the bed. Even in the moonlight Rafe could see the emotion blazing from Alex's eyes. "After all this time together you still don't know?" He loomed over Rafe, a shadowy figure except for those fiery eyes.

"Look how I fell apart in front of your f-father." Rafe struggled to keep his voice steady. "Even now I have to think before I speak so as not to get caught up in the words and what I want to say."

"I don't care about that." Alex pulled his shirt over his head and threw it in the corner.

Rafe licked his lips. "You don't?"

Alex undid his pants and kicked them off to join his shirt, then joined Rafe on the bed. The mattress dipped and they faced each other. "I don't. I don't care about any of that shit. You're the only one who defines yourself by what you think of as a limitation. It's all part of who you are and what makes you special." Alex propped himself up on his elbow, facing Rafe. "When you let go of the perception, you free yourself. The only thing I care about is you."

"I care about you too," said Rafe, carefully. "You've become my best friend."

"That's good," Alex said, slipping his hand behind Rafe's neck. "Because you're supposed to be best friends with the person you love." His smile faded. "I wasn't saying it for effect downstairs or to shock my father, Rafe. It took me years to get past the hurt of his abandonment and disapproval. None of it mattered though when I heard him attacking you. It was like a slap in my face, waking me up to see reality."

"Reality?" Rafe's heart pounded so loud he almost couldn't hear himself speak.

"You. Me. Us." Alex leaned over and kissed him. "I love you, Rafe. You're the reality I'm looking at. I never had someone stand up with me, defend me."

Alex stroked his back and Rafe arched into his touch. "Alex—"

"No." To his surprise, Alex looked pained; not like a man in love. "You don't have to say you love me because you think I want to hear it. I understand you may not believe me or think I'm still doing it to prove a point to my father."

Rafe shook his head. "That wasn't what I was going to say."

"Oh."

Wanting to do this right, Rafe needed to sort it all out in his head before he put it into words. He sat up and faced Alex who lay on the bed next to him.

"All my life I wanted to be what I perceived as normal; to be able to speak without stuttering, and have friends. Being gay was something I hid and was ashamed of until I went to college. There, I thought I was in love, but being someone's closet lover, hidden in the dark wasn't a life I was willing to lead."

"You're worth so much more than that."

"When I met you and your friends, I thought you were a guy without much depth; all good looks but no substance. It put me on my guard again not to trust and not to believe."

"It was easier to play the part than face my real life."

Rafe held out his hand and Alex took it, toying with his fingers. Who really knew anyone? People hid behind their masks, pretend playing, living half a life. Looking at a man like Alex, always full of life, jokes and smiles, one would never imagine he had any demons hiding. What looks perfect on the surface is often the most broken inside.

"I learned that about you. And I learned that I was guilty of making the same snap judgments about you that people always make about me."

"I gave people reason to, though." Alex laced their fingers together.

"You know what I also learned about you? You're a man with an amazing capacity to love. I've never known someone so open and so willing to give of himself. You overwhelmed me, consumed me and now I can't imagine life without you."

Alex's hand tightened around his. "That's how I feel about you."

"Do you know how much I love you?" Rafe pushed Alex down and gazed into his handsome face. "I never thought it was like this. There aren't words enough to tell you."

"Then show me, baby. I don't need the words. Show me how much you love me, so I can give all the love right back to you."

Rafe straddled Alex and kissed him, their open mouths meeting in a clash of teeth and tongues. Rafe plunged his tongue deep and Alex greedily sucked it, their breaths merging, his hand sliding behind Alex's neck to hold his head steady while he bit and nipped his lips. The hot rush of Alex's breath against his face, coupled with Alex's breathy moan sparked a fire within Rafe he'd never before experienced. He wanted to take Alex hard, claim him for his own, live inside him and never let him go.

He rubbed his cheek with Alex's, relishing the scratchy bristles of his late night beard. "Let's take a shower."

Alex jumped off the bed and took his hand. "You're wearing too many clothes." Rafe tugged his shirt over his head and shucked his jeans and boxers in seconds flat.

"How's that?" He stroked himself, drawing Alex's hungry gaze.

"Not good enough. Come here." Alex yanked him close and Rafe melted into his chest, wrapping his arms around Alex's neck. The air brushed up against his naked body and his cock rubbed against the damp cotton of Alex's boxers. Rafe's cock twitched and it was almost enough to set him off.

"Alex, fuck. Stop or I'm gonna come."

Alex chuckled in his ear. "I can't control myself around you."

"Good 'cause I plan to have you begging by the end of the night." He smiled at Alex's hiss of indrawn breath. "Let's take that shower."

They entered the large marble bathroom and Rafe could only gape at the size of the shower. "You could fit five people in there." He walked inside and turned on the taps. The rainfall shower head spilled hot water over him and he stood under the spray, enjoying the beat of water on his naked skin.

Alex joined him and Rafe couldn't help but admire all the naked, muscled flesh. He stepped close and ran his hands over Alex's broad chest. "Let me wash you?"

Alex merely nodded and Rafe led him to the center of the beautifully tiled shower stall. From a shelf built into the wall, he pulled out a bottle of shower gel and a wonderful scent of coconut emerged as he poured some into his hand. Rafe spread it over Alex's torso, running his hands over the corded muscles in Alex's arms, stomach and thighs.

"Turn around."

Alex opened his eyes and blinked then obeyed and faced the wall. He spread his legs without being asked. Rafe couldn't resist and smoothed his hands over the sweet mounds of Alex's ass, and trailed his fingers in the crease between them.

"Baby, please." Alex's strained voice echoed.

Rafe covered Alex's body with his own but didn't move; he let the water beat down on them as he grasped Alex's hard cock with a slippery, soapy hand. It didn't take him more than five or six strokes before Alex climaxed hard, his sharp cry muffled as Rafe pressed his wet mouth to the edge of Alex's lips. "I love you."

Feeling more in control than ever before, Rafe turned off the water and led a shaky Alex out of the shower. He wrapped himself first in a towel then Alex, drying them both off with brisk rubs. Alex stood placid as a child, coming willingly when Rafe brought him back to the bedroom. He took the tube of lubricant from Alex's overnight bag and put it on the bed, deliberately leaving the condoms where they were.

"I love you, Alex. I hope I made myself clear before. I love your good nature and your kind heart and I don't ever want you to have cause to doubt my feelings."

Alex's sated smile told Rafe everything as he reached up and pulled Rafe down in another bone-melting kiss. Rafe trailed hot kisses down Alex's chest then stopped and whispered, "Turn over for me."

Alex complied immediately and lay flat on the bed. The only sound in the room was his steady breathing.

"Spread your legs." Alex obeyed and Rafe, enjoying the sight of Alex's firm, muscular ass, couldn't resist kissing each cheek's roundness. Alex sighed into the pillow, shifting restlessly and Rafe smiled continuing to press kisses until he reached the crease, separating the two beautiful globes. Though he'd never done it before, he wanted to give this to Alex, show him how firmly he held him within his heart.

"Baby," Alex moaned.

"Shh." Rafe spread the cheeks and swiped his tongue against the slightly damp hole. Alex choked back a cry but spread his legs wider. Rafe bent down again and with more confidence, lapped and licked at Alex's hole, then with his heart pounding, dipped his tongue inside. It tasted hot and dark and Rafe's cock hardened painfully. He pointed his tongue and drove in deep then fluttered it, enjoying how Alex whimpered beneath him.

Alex bucked and cried out, twisting the sheets in his fists. "Fuck, Rafe."

Rafe continued lapping and laving at Alex's hole until the

man was a trembling, writhing mess. Sitting back on his haunches, Rafe smiled and stroked his cock. The sight of Alex lying beneath him was enough to get him off.

"Fuck me, damn it," growled Alex. "Now. Come on."

Rafe placed a hand on the small of Alex's back, feeling the muscles jump and bunch under his hands. All that power at his fingertips was a turn-on and Rafe couldn't wait to get inside Alex. "No condom, Alex. I want to feel you take me all the way."

Alex groaned. "When you talk like that I could almost come again. I want you now, any way I can have you."

Rafe lubed his cock quickly and guided himself into Alex, pushing past the tight ring and into the wet furnace of Alex's body. He loved that his flesh and Alex's touched now. They'd said "I love you" to each other for the first time and for the first time ever they were bare, skin touching skin. He sank himself deep and it was incredible; the increased heat, the wet friction, sensations sweeping through him, burning a path of fire from his spine down through his cock.

"Alex," he sobbed, as he thrust in and out, each roll of his hips bringing him closer and closer to that all-encompassing moment of oblivion. "Alex." He lunged in deep and came hard and strong, stars dancing before his eyes, his body shaking with release. He flattened himself against Alex's body, his lips buried in the damp curls at Alex's neck.

After a moment he pulled out, hissing slightly at the drag against his sensitive cock, but loathe to leave the enveloping heat of Alex's body. He took one of the towels they'd dropped on the floor and wiped the liquid trickling from Alex, as well as his own sticky body. Rafe crawled back into bed with Alex and kissed his cheek. Alex opened his eyes and smiled at him.

"Come under the covers, baby."

Rafe slipped in next to Alex and welcomed the warmth of his bulk. Alex put his arm around Rafe, pulled him close and whispered, "I love you. Let's get some sleep." Drowsy and satisfied, happier than he'd ever been in his life, Rafe closed his eyes and slept.

CHAPTER TWENTY-FIVE

He could get used to this. Alex gazed down at a sleeping Rafe who lay curled on his side, mouth slightly open. His hair lay in messy waves across his brow and his lips were full and pouting. Christ, he looked good enough to eat, all disheveled and warm with sleep. Last night had opened Alex's eyes to many things; he and his mother might have a relationship, built from the ashes of his brother's death, but he and his father would not.

But most important—whether or not he made peace with his family or with Micah—was that he'd be doing it with Rafe by his side. They'd been fooling themselves in the beginning, thinking they could have a relationship without getting serious, that friends could have sex and not involve their hearts.

Alex curled himself around Rafe's naked body, loving the feel of the man as Rafe instinctively settled into his arms. They'd made love again during the night and Alex hadn't known how much he would crave the sound of a lover calling out his name in ecstasy, until he had Rafe under him crying out his name as he came.

He gently kissed Rafe's cheek.

"I can tell you're watching me and thinking nefarious thoughts." Rafe wiggled his ass into Alex's groin, settling himself firmly.

Alex thrust himself into the crease of Rafe's ass, while he

grasped Rafe's stiffening cock and stroked him, giving a little squeeze to the sensitive head with every few pulls. They rocked together, and Alex buried his face in the sweet curve of Rafe's neck as he came against Rafe's back, while Rafe shuddered his release, spilling himself within Alex's palm.

"Mmm. That's the best morning wake-up call I've ever had." Rafe rolled over to face him and they kissed, their tongues languid and sweet in the early morning hours. It would be a trying day as he came face to face with his father once again, in addition to visiting his mother. Having Rafe by his side with his encouragement made it far easier than he'd thought.

"Me too." He traced Rafe's full lips with the pad of his thumb. "Can we talk a minute?"

Rafe nodded and sat up against the headboard, a wary look in his eyes.

Alex pushed the hair off his face. "I want to tell you about Seth."

Rafe scooted over and put his arm around him. "You don't need to if it causes you too much pain. It's enough for me to know you want to share." He pressed a kiss to Alex's shoulder.

"You should know. I can handle it now. Knowing someone loves me for who I am, not what I should or could have been—" he kissed Rafe's cheek, "—nothing can really hurt me anymore." He climbed out of the bed and went to the desk where the picture of him and Seth sat. He picked it up to study the photograph taken at the beach. Their arms around each other, faces alight with laughter; who knew three years later Seth would be gone, their world shattered to pieces, never to be the same.

Still holding the photograph, Alex returned to the bed and sat in the middle cross-legged. "This was Seth." He pointed to the right. "We were fraternal but everyone confused us. We looked very similar."

"I know," said Rafe, a grin teasing his lips. "I could spot you instantly. You had the look of laughter in your eyes."

Alex's smile was wistful. "You say laughter, they called it troublemaker." He traced Seth's face with his fingers. "We'd figure out ways to trick people and switch places with each other."

"It sounds like you two had a wonderful relationship." Rafe squeezed his shoulder and kept his hand there, rubbing his back, offering him comfort.

"The best. Seth was funny and smart and everyone loved him. He was captain of the baseball team and a great swimmer. He loved me, even when I told him I was gay." Alex brushed aside the tears. "He was the first person I told and he hugged me and laughed."

"Laughed?"

"Yeah." Alex remembered as if it were yesterday. "Seth said it was good I was gay, since we were twins, now he could get all the girls and I wouldn't be hogging in on his territory."

"That's what you need to have. Unconditional love." Rafe took the photograph from his hands. "What happened?"

"Leukemia. He got the diagnosis not even two months after this picture was taken. One of the most virulent forms. My parents tried everything, every treatment, every specialist. He went through chemo, bone marrow transplants, whatever drug they offered." He drew in a breath and shuddered. "He'd go into remission for a month or so and then it would come roaring back. By the end . . ." He couldn't go on to describe what his big beautiful brother had looked like.

"Shh." Rafe took him in his arms and held him as he cried. "He's at peace now and no longer in any pain."

After several minutes he wiped his eyes and lay his head on Rafe's shoulder. "I prayed to God to take me instead of him. He was the good one; he could get married, have children . . ." Alex shook his head. "Why? Why him? He never hurt anyone."

"I don't have an answer, baby," Rafe smoothed his hair back and Alex saw the sympathy in Rafe's eyes and knew Rafe must be thinking of his own parents, his real mother and father who were killed so senselessly and so young.

"I'm sorry. I'm being selfish and insensitive."

"You mean because of my parents dying? It's not the same.

I never knew them; I couldn't miss what I never had. And—" Rafe stopped and he blinked rapidly, but not before Alex caught the glitter of tears, "—I have to think they loved and wanted me. But with you and Seth, God, what a cruel thing to have to live through, especially since he was your twin. That made your connection so much deeper and more intimate."

Alex nodded. "He told me before he died to follow my dream." He recalled Seth's pain ravaged face smiling weakly at him from his hospital bed. He'd lost all his hair by then and his body had dwindled to skin and bones, but the fire in his eyes burned fierce and bright. He fought until the last breath of hope that still remained in his body.

"Do it Alex. Go find what makes you happy and do it. I know you'll be the best at it, whatever it'll be. I have faith in you. And I'll be there cheering you on, no matter what it is. And wherever I am, I'll always be with you, right by your side."

Two nights later Seth died.

"I didn't have a dream then, but I knew he wanted to be a doctor, so I thought, I'll be like Seth. I'd make him proud and maybe my parents would be proud of me too. They'd always seen how much better Seth was at everything than I was."

The warmth of Rafe's words flowed over Alex like forgiving wine. "Oh Alex, I'm sure that isn't true."

But it was. Alex concentrated on his studies to the exclusion of everything else in college. He excelled at his medical boards and got into the Yale Medical School. Everything he did was to be the best, as good as Seth would have been. While his mother sat by, immersed in her own private sorrow, his father would question him about his classes and endlessly discuss how Alex would eventually join his practice. And all the while, the noose tightened around Alex's neck.

"You don't know, Rafe. All the time I was in medical school with Micah, the only thing I could think of was if Seth would do it this way. How would he handle it. What specialty would he have chosen. Until I woke up one morning and it came to me that I wasn't living my life; I was living Seth's. I tried to be Seth, but I was failing at it."

"That wasn't what Seth meant was it?" Rafe took his hand and laced their fingers together. "He didn't want you to take his life."

"No," whispered Alex. "He wanted me to find myself, find what made me happy."

"And?"

"I love being a surgical nurse; I interact so much more with the patients and that's what I like. Although sometimes I wish . . ." Rafe squeezed his hand.

"What, baby? Tell me what you're thinking."

"Sometimes I think of going back to medical school, not to practice, but to do research." He swallowed hard and stared at the floor. "Cancer research."

"Oh baby." Rafe slipped his arms around him. "You'd be amazing at it. But only if it's what you want, not what you think others might want you to do. Make your own path."

Dreams put aside rushed back to the forefront. He'd long ago made peace with himself over leaving medical school, but every once in a while Alex wondered what it might be like to spend his time trying to find a cure for that bastard disease that killed his brother.

"And it isn't something you have to decide right now. I'm sure any medical school in the city would be happy to have you with your work experience."

"You're a nice ego boost." He put the picture down and fluttered his fingers across Rafe's thigh. Alex grinned at the instantaneous reaction of Rafe's cock, which jerked and began to swell to rather useful and interesting proportions.

"Alex, we need to get dressed and go see your mother." Rafe tried to wriggle away but Alex jumped on him and smothered him with kisses, and grabbed Rafe's now fully erect cock.

"It's too early for visiting hours." He bent his head and looked up with an innocent smile. "I'm sure we can find something to do to pass the time."

Rafe groaned and lay back, but he had a smile on his face.

"Like I said. Incorrigible."

"I only hope when we go visit my mother we find last night wasn't an aberration. I won't hide who we are to each other. I know she's ill, but if she can't accept us together, there will be no happy reunion." They'd finished breakfast and had walked around the grounds where Alex pointed out his and Seth's favorite places. No longer wracked with pain, Alex could look at the past with the clarity of love.

Driving to the hospital with the radio blasting and the sun shining, Alex could almost make himself believe he wasn't missing Micah either.

His mother was sitting in a chair this morning, still pale, but a far cry from last night's scare.

"Mother?" When did he stop calling her Mom? When she said nothing as his father railed against him for leaving medical school? Or was it when he told them he was gay and his father laughed at him and said he always knew there was something wrong with him. Or at the funeral when, gray and broken, his father looked at him and said the wrong son was taken from him. That was something he'd never tell anyone. He'd keep the agony of those words tight to himself. Now he would use them as a mantra to push forward and achieve, instead of lying down and licking his wounds.

Her eyes widened and her hands twisted round each other in her lap. "Alex. It *is* you." An uncertain smile flickered on her lips then vanished. "I thought I saw you last night. I'm so happy to see you."

"How are you feeling? Did the doctor come by to check you?" Still holding Rafe's hand, he walked closer and Alex could see her attention was focused on their clasped hands.

"Um. Yes. He said it was a mild heart attack. I can go home tomorrow, but have to take it easy and exercise and watch my diet."

"That's wonderful."

They were dancing around each other like strangers. Which, after all these years, they were. But it was time, like Rafe said, to take that step back toward life.

"Mom, this is my partner, Rafe Hazelton. He was here with me last night." He squeezed Rafe's hand.

"Hello, Mrs. Stern. I'm so happy to hear you're on the mend and going home."

"Hello, Rafe." Her wobbly voice had Alex wondering if she was as nervous about talking to him and meeting Rafe, as he was to speak to her after all these years. "Tell me a bit about yourself. How long have you known Alex?"

Rafe, bless his sweet and good-natured heart, tried to put her at ease. "Alex and I met about a year ago through a friend, then recently, it's become more serious between us."

Enough pussy-footing around. He'd never go back to hiding who he was, not even if it meant losing his mother again. "I love him. This is the man I'm going to spend the rest of my life with, Mom. Can you accept that?"

"Bravo, bravo." Sounds of clapping from behind him caused both him and Rafe to spin around. "How melodramatic; a performance worthy of at least an Oscar nomination." His father's smirk did nothing to hide his anger, which reddened his face and darkened his blue eyes to nearly black. "Have you no concern for your mother's welfare? Upsetting her with this news while she's recovering could set her recovery back." His jaw tightened. "Leave."

"No, Herb. I want him to stay. He's my son, our son." His mother reached out her hand and Alex took it. Rafe had moved to stand by the windows. "I broke down completely after Seth died; I couldn't stand up to you, or help Alex through his own pain, and for that I need to beg his forgiveness. Since then, I drifted through the years, on antidepressants, merely taking up space. It's only recently I've felt a pull to return to living."

Alex knelt at her side. "Mom. I'm sorry I caused you so much pain, but I can't change who I am." His voice caught in his throat. "I tried, but I can't be Seth."

"Oh, sweetheart, I never wanted you to be him. You're so special in your own right; as wonderful and beautiful a person. I couldn't love you any more. And for all the years you thought different, I hope you can forgive me." Her hands gripped his with surprising strength.

Years wasted. Perhaps not, however, if he'd needed those years to learn about who he was. Tears ran down his face, wetting his cheeks and her hands. He'd done it, finally. The first step, always the hardest, had been taken.

His father's bluster remained as hateful as ever, "This is ridiculous. He walks in here after years away, flaunting his relationship in front of my peers, determined to make me a laughingstock."

Alex opened his mouth but to his shock, Rafe cut him off.

"No one fl-flaunted anything. W-we came to see your w-wife and for Alex to m-make peace with his m-mother. He'd do th-the same with you, but you're more intent on holding on to past hurts and prejudices than moving forward."

Alex let go of his mother's hands and stood, needing to hold Rafe. The smile on his lover's face spurred Alex on and he yanked Rafe hard against his chest.

"God I fucking love you." Alex glided his hands down Rafe's face, tracing the jut of his cheekbones, coming to rest on his shoulders. "You have no idea." He wanted to bury himself in Rafe's warm scent forever.

His father snorted. "This is disgusting. Dolores, are you going to allow this display?"

The tentative smile on his mother's lips had blossomed to a full-blown smile. "He's happy. I haven't seen Alex truly happy since before Seth became sick. And if the reason is that young man, then he can kiss him in a Macy's window for all I care."

Alex watched her color anxiously, but her voice remained strong and her eyes clear and bright.

"I have my son back for the first time in years." She craned her neck. "Rafe, come here, please."

Rafe went to her, concern etched on his face. Alex hovered

by his side.

"Do you love my son? Really love him?"

The beautiful smile he loved to see broke across Rafe's face. "I've never known a man like Alex. When he enters a room, all eyes are on him and he doesn't need to say a word. He consumes me, engulfs me and I can't imagine my life without him. He's my best friend, my lover and the only man I've ever loved."

"Well," she responded weakly. "That answers that. Now come give me a kiss."

Love such as he never knew filled Alex. To have his mother and his lover together was a present he'd never expected to receive. "Thank you, Mom." He bent and kissed her cheek.

"I love you, sweetheart, and thank you for the kiss, but I was talking to Rafe." She winked at him and the three of them shared a laugh.

"Dolores, you're sick. I'm going to speak to the doctor about this and he'll probably want to increase your medication."

Blind fury descended over Alex. "I see what you're doing, you bastard." He spat out the bitter words he'd waited a decade to release. "You'd rather keep her drugged and half-alive than have a relationship with me. Why do you hate me so much? I tried everything to make you love me as much as you loved Seth. I tried to help him stay alive; I gave him my blood, my marrow. If I could, I would've ripped my heart from my chest."

Rafe's arms came around his waist to hold him, and he leaned into him for balance, to keep him centered.

All the hurt he'd carried inside him for years spilled out and he broke the promise he made to himself earlier not to reveal his father's hateful, hurtful words.

"How could I ever forget my own father telling me he always knew something was wrong with me because I'm gay? That he wished it was me who died instead of Seth?" His chest heaved and it hurt to breathe, yet somehow, held within Rafe's arms, he was freed from pain.

He could hear his mother weeping quietly and it nearly killed him to hurt her, but the words tumbled out.

"I wanted to fucking die for Seth, but I'm sorry, I lived and you've made me pay for that with your hatred every single day since."

Stricken and shaking, his father deflated. His lips moved but no sound came out. Without a further word, he turned and left the room.

Rafe had returned to his mother's side and held her hand, speaking softly to her. Alex noticed with relief her tears had dried.

"I'm sorry, Mom. I tried, but—"

"Don't be sorry. One day I hope he comes around but that's his problem not mine anymore. The fog I've lived under has lifted and I'm ready to take back my life." She bit her lip. "I'd love to get to know Rafe." She smiled up at the two of them as the tears spilled down her cheeks. "Can we start again, Alex? I've missed having two boys in my life."

Alex's heart swelled. His mother in his life and his lover at his side. His life was almost complete.

"We already have, Mom."

CHAPTER TWENTY-SIX

The ride back to the city was a completely different one from the tense and somber ride to Long Island the day before. Alex sat with his feet out of the window, belting out '80s tunes, while stuffing jalapeño potato chips in his face.

There was little traffic on the road at this late hour. They'd spent the remainder of the day with Alex's mother, speaking with her doctor, and Rafe was proud to see Alex step up and let the doctor know Dolores was not to be given any increased dosages of antidepressants.

Alex's mother surprised him. He'd expected a cold, indifferent woman, not one who showed her affection as easily as she did all afternoon. Rafe understood the power of the mind and how it can lead you down the darkest of paths. It was a testament to Dolores' inner core of steel how she pulled herself back up, and now with Alex and his help, she would return to her family.

Whether or not that family would include Alex's father, remained to be seen. He hadn't returned to the hospital room and when he and Alex went back to the house to pack for the trip home, the housekeeper told Alex his father hadn't been home all day.

"Turn down here." Alex hoisted his feet inside and sat up straight, brushing the potato chip crumbs from his lips. Rafe wanted to taste the tangy saltiness of his mouth and looked forward to later and another night spent wrapped around each other. He'd gone from a man stuck in neutral, used to his solitude, to someone who craved the physical touch of another.

"Why?" But he complied, knowing from the smirk on Alex's face he was up to no good. And Rafe was only too happy to follow down Alex's path of destruction.

"Park here." They pulled into a parking lot and Rafe was able to make out the sign that said "Beach Parking."

"The beach?" He hadn't been to the beach in years. "But we're on the North Shore."

Alex waved his hand in the air and they walked toward the lapping waves. "A mere technicality, my good man. The Long Island Sound is much superior to Jones Beach."

"I've only been a couple of times." It was beautiful at night; mysterious and a bit awe-inspiring.

Even in the dark Rafe could see the amazement in Alex's eyes. "What?"

Rafe shrugged. "I lived inland, remember? When did I have the chance to play on the beach?"

Somehow he found himself in the sand, the air knocked out of him, with Alex lying on top of him. "Wanna play now?" Rafe sucked in a breath as Alex's tongue traced patterns down his throat, sucking the tender skin under his ear.

"Alex," he moaned. "We're in the open. Anyone can see us." But his protests didn't stop him from arching up into the cradle of Alex's pelvis and rolling his hips, desperate for friction against his throbbing cock.

"Who—" panted Alex, "—a peeping seagull?" He reached between them and swiftly popped open Rafe's jeans and pulled down his zipper. Rafe struggled out of his pants and Alex did the same.

The soft night air blew a warm breeze against Rafe's aching cock. How was it that this man could get him hard even while sand crept up his ass? Then all thoughts fled when Alex grasped both their erections and proceeded to rub and stroke them together, collecting the wetness from their leaking heads to smooth the way down their shafts.

"Mmmm." Alex hummed, leaning down to give the head of Rafe's cock a quick kiss.

It was messy and wild as he thrust upward, Alex's wet fist rubbing them together; first hard and slow then faster and faster as their hips moved in unison. "Fuck, oh fuck, Alex." Sand flew everywhere as Rafe's hands dug beneath him, and his head thrashed back and forth. A crazy kaleidoscope of colors burst behind his eyes as he keened a high-pitched cry of release, shaking and trembling. Alex never ceased his movements until Rafe lay still, limp and boneless, incapable of moving.

A moment later Alex came with a groan and afterward they lay together, the rolling waves and their heavy breathing the only sounds in the quiet night.

"I've been dying for you all day, baby." Bright-eyed, Alex went on, "Watching you stand up to my father was sexy as hell." He crawled up on his elbows to kiss Rafe on the mouth and Rafe savored the sharp jalapeño taste on Alex's tongue. Their kisses turned gentle, mouths caressing, soft and sweet. It made Rafe think of their bodies merging, their souls becoming one.

Not that he'd ever tell Alex that. He'd probably look at Rafe and laugh at his mushy behavior and make kissy noises, then tease him mercilessly. Alex wasn't romantic, Rafe didn't think. Then he remembered that evening, when all this had started between them, and their dance in Micah's kitchen. Suddenly Rafe wasn't so sure.

"Alex?"

"Hmm?" They snuggled next to one another, uncaring of the grit in their pants. Thin clouds scuttled across the glow of the moon and the waves continued their infinite rolling toward shore, their steady shushing on the sand a comforting sound. Tiny lights winked from across the water.

"I really love you. More than anything."

"I really love you too. More than everything."

Contentment seeped through Rafe. By mutual agreement they rose and despite a valiant effort to shake and brush all the sand from their clothes and their bodies, Rafe knew he'd be finding sand in some pretty interesting places later tonight when he showered. Plus, he'd have to take the car and have it vacuumed before returning it to the rental place.

By the time Rafe opened the driver's side door to get into the car, Alex had his head stuck in the back seat, rummaging around in his overnight bag. When Rafe started the engine, he heard a triumphant, "Aha!" and Alex straightened himself out from his contorted position and slid back into the front seat, clutching a bottle of Glenfiddich scotch.

"A going-away present from my beloved father." Alex opened it and took a healthy swig. "Ahhh." He held it up in the air. "Thanks, Daddy dearest." He took another.

"Alex," Rafe hissed. "Put that down. I can't drive on the highway with you waving a bottle of scotch. The cops will pull me over." Even now, his gaze darted from side to side hoping the local town police were busy with some nuisance crime this late at night and didn't stop them.

"I'll keep it between my legs." He waggled his brows. "With all the other good stuff."

"You're really certifiable, aren't you." Rafe stopped at a red light, leaned over and snuck a quick kiss. The scotch burned his lips, leaving a fiery taste.

"But so tasty too." Alex snickered and Rafe suspected he was going to have his hands full by the time they got to his apartment if the man was quoting old lines from "I Love Lucy" at one o'clock in the morning.

Rafe headed for his apartment in Brooklyn, rather than Alex's in the city because he knew there was a garage right near him and his building had an elevator. The last thing he wanted to do in the early morning hours was lug a big, drunk man up three flights of stairs.

Instead, after dropping the car off and dragging the bags out, as well as a giggling, totally wasted Alex, Rafe had to lead him down the block and into the elevator of his own building, shushing him, hoping he didn't wake the neighbors.

"Mmm. You're all cute and sexy when you're annoyed." Alex flattened Rafe against the elevator wall. "Makes me want to fuck you."

"Everything makes you want to fuck me."

Alex stopped to think, his brow furrowed and scratched his head. "Well yeah, but that's 'cause you're so fucking cute." He cackled with laughter. "Get it?"

Rafe shook his head in disgust. "You're drunk. Let's get you inside. I'll give you some aspirin and put you into the shower."

"Only if you take it with me, baby."

The door slid open and Rafe tugged Alex and their bags into his apartment. Once inside, he threw the bags on the floor and turned on the light.

"Ow, that's bright." Holding his hand over his eyes, Alex winced.

Ignoring him, Rafe went to the bathroom and got the aspirin and after pouring a glass of water, handed both of them to Alex. To his surprise, Alex didn't protest, merely took the aspirin and washed it down.

"Come." Rafe took his hand and led him to the shower. "Take your shower. Use any towel."

"You're leaving me here alone? What if I slip and fall?" Alex pouted. "You know, most household accidents happen in the shower."

A twinge of guilt hit Rafe. "All right," he grumbled. "But no funny business. This is strictly a get clean shower."

Alex blinked. "Of course."

Yeah right. As soon as they got naked and under the water, Alex tried to grope him. But Rafe didn't want a drunk Alex. He knew Alex took the expensive bottle of scotch from his father as a final "fuck you" to the man who couldn't stand the sight of him. And Rafe didn't want to be any part of that.

"Alex, let me clean the sand out of your ass."

Alex kissed his neck. "You always say the sweetest things, baby."

Even Rafe couldn't help but smile.

The shower revived Alex but Rafe could see he was tired and beginning to fade. He pushed him into his bed and lay down next to him. The sight of the naked, sleepy Alex cuddling his pillow set Rafe's heart fluttering in his chest. He loved Alex so much and wished he could take away the sting of rejection from both his father and Micah.

An idea formed in his head.

"Close your eyes and get some sleep."

"Hmm." Alex cracked one eye open. "Give me a goodnight kiss first." He pursed his lips and made kissing noises.

Rafe took Alex's face between his hands and kissed him hard and deep, pouring all the love and passion he'd held within him, waiting for the right man to come along.

Alex wrapped his arm around Rafe and kissed him back with the same fervor and it hit Rafe then that Alex had never mentioned being in love before or even dating other men. Perhaps they were two of the lucky ones in this vast city, who'd found love. Their kiss turned sweeter and softer, and Rafe imagined how empty his life would be if he hadn't taken the chance of that extra step to open his heart to love.

The steady breathing next to him indicated Alex had finally succumbed to sleep. Rafe slid out of bed and put on a pair of shorts and a tee shirt. Tomorrow he needed to get back to running, especially after hanging out with the junk food king.

Sneaking a quick look at Alex to make sure he was still safely asleep, Rafe pulled up Josh's contact on his phone. He typed out a text and waited. There was only a moment's hesitation before he hit the send button and waited for a reply. Keyed up and anxious, Rafe paced about the apartment. He wasn't being disloyal to Alex. He was helping him. Rafe had seen the quiet sadness in Alex's face at odd moments of the day and knew he was thinking of Micah. However much of a bastard the man had been to Alex, he was also his best friend.

His phone vibrated and Rafe swiped at the screen with a somewhat shaky finger. He smiled at the response.

About time someone pulled their head out of their ass to get these two back together. Micah's been a worse asshole than usual. Almost like the old days.

Rafe typed out his plan and he and Josh worked out the logistics. Still smiling, he left his phone on the table and slid back into bed, curving himself around Alex's warmth. To his surprise, Alex rolled over and pulled him into his arms, but Rafe could see he was still mostly asleep.

"Don' wanna sleep without you," Alex grumbled. "No more."

Rafe curled himself into Alex's embrace and kissed his scruffy jaw. "I'm here. I'll always be here for you."

Rafe blinked awake and saw it was only a little past ten in the morning. Alex was sprawled across the bed, dead to the world. Rafe stared at him in sympathy, knowing the man was going to wake up with a massive hangover.

Live by the scotch, die by the scotch. Besides, a hangover might prevent him from killing Rafe when Alex found out what he'd planned behind his back.

Sliding out of bed soundlessly, Rafe changed into running shorts and tied his sneakers. After quickly brushing his teeth, he scribbled a note and left it propped up by the clock. He grabbed his wallet, phone and keys and headed out the door. The fresh cool morning air hit him, quickening his pulse, and the green leafy park across the street beckoned to him.

After spending the past few days back home and even on Long Island, Rafe had rediscovered how much he missed the country. He crossed the street and entered the park, noting it was already pretty crowded for a Saturday morning and joined the runners on the path. Easily falling into his rhythm, he turned the music up louder and began to run.

An hour later, feeling better than he had in days, Rafe walked into his apartment. He'd stopped at the local bagel store and picked up fresh bagels, two different kinds of cream cheese and some lox. As luck would have it, Alex was still asleep, so he put everything in the kitchen and headed into the shower to wash off the sweat from his run. It was only eleven o'clock and he predicted after all the alcohol Alex had downed last night, he wouldn't be waking up until noon. Which was a good thing.

Knowing that, and the hangover Alex would probably have when he did finally awaken, Rafe put on a big pot of coffee, thankful he'd never invested in a one cup at a time coffeemaker. He drank his first down quickly, then poured a second to sip slowly as he stretched out on his sofa.

He hoped Alex would understand why he did what he did. For Rafe, friendships were sacred, not to be taken lightly and certainly not to be discarded in anger and haste. He'd learned this after never having anyone to rely on growing up. Life was lonely enough if you chose to go through it alone. But when you pushed away people you loved because of misunderstandings and stubborn pride . . . Rafe stared into his cup. He couldn't go back to that person he was before.

Meeting Alex, getting to know the person underneath the façade had changed Rafe irrevocably. He saw the tears of the clown, and knew the pain Alex hid from everyone else and why. More than anything else, Rafe wanted to help Alex shed his past and always be the effervescent man who lit up a room and Rafe's heart simply by walking in with a smile.

He went into the kitchen to throw the dregs of his coffee into the sink. It was still early and Rafe yawned. It wouldn't do him any harm to climb back into bed and cuddle. He slid in next to Alex, burrowing into his warmth, slipping his arms around Alex's waist and kissing his neck. He threw his leg over Alex's muscular thigh, loving its hairy scrape against his own.

Alex's morning erection rose thick and strong and Rafe knew it would be a terrible thing to waste. He grasped Alex in his hand and slowly jacked him off, pressing his own groin into Alex's ass. Rocking the two of them together in a slowly undulating roll, Rafe knew the second Alex came awake by the hand joining his own holding Alex's cock. Together, they stroked Alex to a shuddering, sweet release, his groan of completion echoing against the walls of Rafe's apartment.

After a few moments to catch their breath, Alex rolled over and grinned sleepily. "Morning. That was a nice way to wake up."

"I thought I'd give you a nice dream." Rafe kissed him. "How's your head?"

"Still attached." Alex flopped back on the pillows. "Where were you?" He squinted and rubbed his face with his hands, wincing a bit. "You smell all clean and fresh." He grabbed Rafe and pulled him on top of his chest. "I love the way you smell." He nuzzled Rafe's neck and that tingling feeling, the sweet agony of desire rushed through Rafe. "I love the way you taste." He nipped Rafe's neck and Rafe moaned into Alex's sleep-rough hair.

"I'm so loveable." Rafe breathed, finding it hard to speak, his heart was so full.

"You are, baby," Alex framed Rafe's face with his hands and Rafe's heart thumped so loud, he was surprised Alex didn't hear it. "I don't know all the right words, I've never said them before and God knows I've never felt it. But after being with you, loving you every night and day, I want this. I want your breath to be the last sound I hear at night before I go to sleep. I want to feel your heart pounding like it is right now every morning when I wake you up with a kiss." Alex kissed him, not hard and searching, but tender and soft. "I want you. Only you."

Unable to move or breathe, Rafe could only nod, then gulped in air. "Those words couldn't be any more perfect. I want that too, want you. I never thought I'd find someone who'd look beyond my surface. I'm so glad it was you. I love you, Alex."

"Love you too, baby. Let's have a lazy Saturday in bed." He glided his hands down Rafe's back, fondling his ass. "I want to make you scream." Alex teased the crease of Rafe's ass with his finger and began to kiss his neck in earnest, "Where's your lube?"

A few more kisses and touches and Rafe wouldn't remember his name. Fuck, he had so little willpower. Rafe snuck a quick look at the clock. Shit. Almost noon.

"Um, how about we have a lazy Saturday night instead?" He wriggled off Alex, leaving the bed and remaining out of grabbing reach. "We have to get up and get dressed."

Pouting and looking extremely annoyed, Alex sat up. "Why? It's only like noon? That's practically morning." He patted the spot next to him. "Come back and I'll make it worth your while. I'll let you have your way with me."

Now that he was up, Rafe refused to let himself be tempted, even if the temptation was a big blond Adonis, naked in his bed.

"I, uh, invited company to come." Before Alex could ask a question, he hurried into the kitchen. "I got bagels and everything. Even lox." He glanced over his shoulder to catch Alex's puzzled look.

"Who's coming? Do I know them?" Alex got out of bed and yawned, stretching his arms out.

Rafe couldn't help but stare. Silhouetted by the sun streaming in from the window behind him, Alex's shadowed body was all dips and hard planes. Hopefully, Alex would understand why Rafe did what he did and take it with the love it was meant and not as meddling where he didn't belong.

"You could say so." Rafe took plates out and set them on the table.

"I don't know why you're being all mysterious. Is it Jenny? Oh man, I don't think she likes me too much." A pained expression crossed Alex's face. "I'd better shower and shave and try to look halfway decent." He gathered up his stuff and rushed into the bathroom. "How much time do I have?"

"About half an hour. Don't worry princess, you look gorgeous no matter what."

Alex stuck his head out of the bathroom, his face already half covered in shaving cream. "You're only saying that 'cause you love me."

Rafe laughed, "You're right."

Being in his kitchen and hearing Alex splash around in the bathroom gave Rafe a feeling of home and permanency he'd never imagined. He made the bed, loving how his sheets now smelled like the two of them, instead of only him and his laundry detergent. With Alex's belongings scattered about and his larger than life presence already imprinted in the apartment, Rafe could no longer think of a time without Alex and wondered where their next step would take them.

The bell rang downstairs, and he buzzed back to let them in. Fuck, he was nervous.

"Is that her?" Alex came skittering out of the bathroom, buttoning his jeans. "Do I look okay?"

Rafe put his hands on Alex's shoulders. "It's not Jenny and her husband. Don't be mad at me."

The doorbell rang and Rafe, looking back at Alex's confused face, went to answer it.

"Hi guys, come on in."

Josh came in first holding Lucky, then Micah walked in. Rafe watched Alex's puzzled expression change to dismay, hurt, then anger.

"You tricked me. You let me think it was Jenny. How could you not tell me they were coming?"

"Because I know you and I know you'd have run away. It's time already for you two to stop acting like childish idiots and clear the air." Rafe glanced at Micah, noting his wary face. He'd never seen the man so sad and lost. "You both said some hurtful things that need forgiveness."

Josh too looked sad and upset. "I've tried to speak to him every day, I begged him to call Alex and talk." He shook his head. "Two stubborn assholes."

The men reminded Rafe of big angry cats; Micah a sleek black panther and Alex a large golden lion, circling each other, cautious and unsure if they should attack or retreat.

Lucky nudged his leg and he petted her. The dog, perhaps sensing the tension, walked over to Alex and after licking his hand and him petting her, barked at him, then looked at Micah and barked as well. She stood in between them, her plumy tail waving and barked again.

"I think we get the message girl." Rafe gave her a chew toy from when he watched her the year before for Josh and Micah. She took it and lay down in the corner with it.

Taking Lucky's place in between the two men, Rafe pointed at the table. "Sit, both of you." At their hesitation he raised his voice. "NOW."

Alex raised his brows but complied. Micah silently followed.

Josh whispered in his ear. "Now what?"

Rafe had no fucking clue.

CHAPTER TWENTY-SEVEN

How could Rafe have done this to him? Angry as he was though, the more he thought about it, Alex wasn't surprised. It was Rafe's inherent nature to resolve conflicts. Alex couldn't be mad at him, since he himself didn't understand what the hell had led them to this point.

He stared at Micah as if seeing him for the first time. It hit him like a punch in the stomach how much he missed his friend. The sadness in Micah's eyes mirrored the desolation Alex allowed himself to sink into late at night when no one else was around and he could mourn the loss of his friend.

"Alex, I—"

"Micah, I'm—"

They broke off and laughed self-consciously then fell silent.

"You first," said Alex softly. Rafe and Josh settled into the chairs next to him and Micah.

"I'm sorry." Micah spoke bluntly, but Alex knew it was his way. "I've been a miserable fucking idiot. You're my best friend. I overreacted with Lucky and then hearing you had a brother?" He reached across the table and took Alex's hand. "What the hell, Alex? A brother?" Micah's voice flowed sadly, but without condemnation. "How come you never told me?" He squeezed his fingers. "What happened?"

This time there was no yelling or accusing tone. Only quiet sorrow and a healing touch. The only sound was Lucky's gnawing on her toy. At least someone was having a good time.

"I couldn't deal with it, to be honest. It wasn't only that I had a brother. Seth was my twin, but in life he was everything I should have been. He was straight, knew he wanted to be a doctor like our father and never got in any trouble. When he was seventeen he was diagnosed with leukemia and nothing they did could save him. He died our first year of medical school." The pain was still there, but bearable now. That sense of peace when he thought about Seth surrounded him, as if his brother was present at the table.

After years of hiding, it suddenly became imperative Micah hear the truth from his lips. "It was never my dream to go to medical school; it was Seth's dream and my father's for both of us. I thought if I could take his place my parents would forgive me for being gay and maybe love me like they did him. I didn't tell you because you had enough on your own head to deal with."

A light dawned in Micah's eyes. "That's why you dropped out. You never wanted to be a doctor after all." He shook his head in sadness. "Alex, you idiot." But it was said with affection and years of love and friendship behind it. "You didn't think I cared enough about you to put my own problems aside to help you or be there for you?"

"I didn't want that. It was easier to hide it all and pretend away the pain." Under the table, Rafe took his hand and laced their fingers together. No more hiding the pain. Never again.

"I've been a lousy friend then for you to accomplish it for all these years."

"You were the best. Because deep down, I knew I could tell you and you'd still love me. That's why it hurt so much when you said what you did and lashed out at me." In all their years together he and Micah had never sat down to talk to each other. Maybe if they had neither would've been as screwed up as they were. But it wasn't their way. And then again, Micah might never have met Josh, nor he, Rafe.

Micah flinched. "I'm sorry. You're right, you should've been able to and for that I can't tell you how much I regret being that selfish bastard."

They smiled at each other from across the table. "No more hiding, okay Alex?" Micah's gaze turned troubled. "It was crap not having you around."

"I won't. Promise. I'm even talking to my mother again. We came from seeing her this weekend. She was in the hospital for a mild heart attack."

"But she'll be fine, right?"

Alex smiled at the genuine concern on Micah's face. He knew how sensitive Micah had become to illness after taking care of his grandmother. "Yes. I'm going to call her in a little while to check on her, make sure everything went well with her release and going home. How are Ruth and Ethel by the way? Did they enjoy the Hamptons?"

"They loved it. Ruth even remembered some stories from when she and my grandfather would go there for some summers. But never mind that." A speculative gleam entered Micah's eyes and Alex braced himself. He knew what was coming.

"So tell me, now that we've cleared the air." Micah leaned back and drummed his fingers on the table. The gold from his wedding band caught a shaft of light and gleamed. How would he look with a band, Alex wondered, glancing to his own hand. The thought of marriage and wearing a wedding ring didn't seem laughable or silly anymore. He'd be free to show his love for a man who loved him back.

"What's the story with you and Rafe?" Micah's teeth flashed white against his tanned face. "You've gotten rather, umm, chummy, shall I say?"

"Chummy? I haven't heard that word in years. You must be hanging around too many Golden Girls, my friend. Besides." He stood and braced his arms on the table leaning over to glare in Micah's face. "You owe Rafe an apology as well. You talked to him like he was some random bar hook-up instead of the man who came, no questions asked, and saved your dog's life."

Micah's grin faded. "You're right again." He focused his

attention now on Rafe. "I'm sorry, man. I owe you a huge apology and a world of thanks. If not for you, we might have lost Lucky and I don't know how I would've been able to handle that."

Josh took Micah's hand, exactly like Rafe held his, and Alex marveled at a human being's ability to find that one person who made their fractured life whole. Josh had done that for Micah and by some twist of fate, he'd found a man like Rafe who saw past his insecurities and fear, beyond the false bravado and smiles and loved him for who he was inside.

Who that was, Alex was still discovering. It was good to know Rafe would be by his side for the ride.

"I accept your apology, Micah. And you should know your friend has been as miserable without you as you were without him."

"Hey." Alex whined in mock protest. "I wasn't miserable all the time."

Rafe gave him a sweet smile with a hint of the devil behind it. "No, you're right. Not all the time."

"All right you two." Micah growled. "Spill it or it's gonna get ugly."

"Bagels anyone?" Alex held the plate up. "We have a lovely assortment."

"Alex. Are you two a couple or what?"

Before Alex had a chance to answer, Rafe chimed in.

"Go ahead, Alex. Put the poor man out of his misery already. He's suffered enough, I think."

Alex understood. Rafe wanted this validation of their relationship, in front of their closest friends. Maybe deep down he questioned Alex's true feelings, maybe it was simply his own insecurities. Whatever it was, Alex had no qualms revealing his feelings. What he said now wasn't for Micah and Josh's benefit. What he said right now came from his heart.

"Rafe and I, we're a couple, yes. But it's more than that. I love him. I'm hoping he'll want to spend the rest of his life with me. Maybe it happened fast, but it doesn't take long to recognize when someone becomes as important to your life as the air you breathe and the water you drink."

"Alex." Rafe's smile threatened the brightness of the summer sky. "I-I d-didn't know . . ." He bit his lip, his eyes brimming with emotion.

"I'm not sure even I knew how much you meant to me." He took Rafe's hands in his, Micah and Josh fading from sight. All Alex saw was Rafe. "But the thought of waking up without you now is unthinkable. When I lost Seth my heart broke apart and it took me years to find the pieces to put it together again. If I lost you now—" Alex drew in a deep shuddering breath, "—I wouldn't have a heart left to break."

Rafe kissed his cheek. "There's not a chance in the world I'd lose my way back to you. Wherever you are is where I belong."

Suddenly self-conscious, Alex remembered his friends were there with them. He needn't have worried. Perhaps sensing the deeply emotional moment, Micah and Josh had left the table to give them a bit more privacy. But when he and Rafe stopped talking, Josh smiled at him from his seat on the sofa, where he'd been leafing through Rafe's running magazines. Micah's head was pillowed in his lap and they made the perfect picture of domestic bliss.

"I told you, Alex. I said all you had to do was open your heart and you'd find love. See?" He smirked. "True love conquers all."

Alex groaned. "Micah, haven't I told you to stop Josh from watching *The Bachelor?*" He headed for the coffeemaker, but not before snagging another kiss from Rafe, who was busy slicing the bagels. Josh may be right about something after all. When Alex opened his heart, he not only found love with Rafe, but rediscovered a passion within himself, a yearning to help he'd put aside many times in the past as foolish or unattainable.

And in his head and his heart he heard his brother's voice cheering him on, urging him to take the step, push himself further than he'd ever gone before.

"I've been thinking about things lately and I've come to a

decision."

Rafe set the knife on the plate and leaned his hip on the table. "What is it?"

These three people had all in some way helped shape his life. The fourth person missing, the one who left a hole in his heart that only now was beginning to mend, was with him in spirit. Though Seth was gone for these past fifteen years and not a day had passed without Alex mourning his absence, Alex would make sure his brother would be remembered.

"I think I want to go back to school."

Micah and Josh stared back at him in shock, but Rafe came over to him and hugged him tight.

"I'm so proud of you."

Micah posed the first of what Alex knew would be a thousand questions. "School? What school? Medical school? You're going to go back to med school? Seriously?" Alex could see the growing excitement in his friend's face and he caught some of the enthusiasm as he explained his decision.

"If I do this, and I am serious, I'd go into research, cancer research. I want to beat this fucking disease. I want to avenge my brother's death, to be the one to finally have that *aha!* moment."

"It will take years, you know," Rafe pointed out. "Plus grants are hard to come by."

"I'm willing to take as long as I can."

It didn't matter if it took him the rest of his days. For the first time, Alex was happy with where his life was. He had a lover, he had his friends and he even had his mother back in his life. That reminded him to call her. Maybe the news of his decision would give her some added strength in her recovery.

A troubling thought occurred to him and he took Rafe by the arm and led him off to the living room to talk more privately.

"Are you bothered by my decision? Do you think I'm doing the right thing?"

Rafe curled his hand around Alex's shoulder and tipped his head back to gaze straight into his eyes. "I think," he paused for a moment, "No, I *know*, you'll be an amazing doctor. You have the passion and the drive to accomplish whatever you want."

"It's going to be tough haul for a few years. Going back to med school at my age . . . there'll be long hours and it will be really rough. We aren't going to see each other as much as we'd like."

This was the hardest thing he'd ever thought he'd say, but he owed it to Rafe. He loved him too much. "I'd understand if you wanted to walk away now. I'm hoping you want to stay with me because I am nothing if not a selfish bastard and I don't want you to go. I sprang this on you with no notice and I'm sorry."

"I thought you loved me, Alex." Rafe's face grew hot with anger. "Do you think I can walk away because times get tough? I thought we were through with that running from problems bullshit."

"I do love you. You know that."

Rafe spun away from him to walk to the windows overlooking the park. Micah and Josh had gone and hidden themselves in the bedroom with Lucky.

"So, love means sticking with a person no matter what. Life isn't God damn roses and sunshine. I'm the first one to tell you that. But if I could have picked anyone to choose to spend the rest of my life with, no matter what obstacles there were, I'd pick you. You brought light to my life and taught me not to be so serious. You showed me what the true meaning of friendship is. I've never met another person like you and I don't want you to think twice about your dream. Your dream makes you who you are and that's the man I fell in love with and will always love, no matter what."

Could he have gotten any luckier than this man? Alex stood behind Rafe and slid his arms around his lover's waist, loving the way their bodies molded against one another. "I'm sorry, baby," he whispered in Rafe's ear. "I'm not used to having someone in my life who cares about me. But you have my heart and no matter how many nights I may have to be away, I'm always coming back home to you."

"I'll never leave you, Alex." Rafe gave him one of his open, beautiful smiles. "I love you with my life. Besides," mischief sparked in his eyes, "you still haven't conceded the inherent superiority of jelly beans to French fries." Rafe kissed him then, his mouth delicate and sweet. Alex was the only man who knew, underneath Rafe's sweet and mild exterior, how scorchingly hot his kisses could turn and how wickedly his lips and tongue moved over and inside Alex's body.

"You haven't convinced me yet." Alex whispered, holding Rafe close to his heart. "I think it will take a lifetime of persuasion."

EPILOGUE

TWO YEARS LATER

"Is everyone here?" Rafe looked around the apartment, scanning the crowd. Jenny, her husband and their baby were there, talking to Josh and Micah, who was holding one of their twins in his arms. Little Rebecca was only three months old but already a beauty with her silky black hair and round eyes. Josh had a sleeping Jacob in the carriage next to him and was pushing him back and forth in a steady, soothing motion. As Rafe watched he had to laugh as Josh's grandmother Ethel stood before him with a scowl on her face.

"Sorry, Granma," he heard Josh say as he handed her the carriage. A proud smile erased her frown and she walked over to where Ruth sat; the two of them leaned over to stare and cluck over their great-grandson.

"Sweetheart, don't be so nervous." Dolores patted him on his shoulder. "Alex will be here any moment."

Dolores Stern had fully recovered from her mild heart attack and Alex and Rafe had spent many of their weekends on Long Island with her. Alex had taken him to the cemetery and he'd held Alex as he cried over Seth's grave. Initially Rafe encouraged Alex to try and make amends with his father, to forge some sort of understanding and peace, even if it was an uneasy one. Each time they met was more awkward than the last, with Alex's father completely ignoring Rafe, and only showing interest in discussing Alex's medical school classes.

The last straw was a dinner Rafe had arranged for the three

of them. He and Alex were at the restaurant and Alex's father walked in with a beautiful young woman. She was the daughter of a new colleague and, Dr. Stern explained, as she sat mortified, understanding immediately how she'd been used, he'd invited her to meet his son. He ignored Rafe completely.

Alex apologized to the woman and he and Rafe left the restaurant.

Rafe gave up on any reconciliation after that. It was no surprise to either him or Alex when Dolores announced she and Alex's father were separating and she moved into the city to be closer to her son.

"I can't help it, Mom. I've never thrown a surprise party before. I want everything to be perfect."

"Oh it will be, love. I'm so proud of you and of Alex."

Rafe loved Alex's mother. Next to hearing Alex tell him he loved him for the first time, the happiest day of Rafe's life was when Dolores took him aside and told him to stop calling her Mrs. Stern.

"I feel like my mother-in-law and she was no favorite of mine." She took his hands in hers. *"I'd love it if you'd call me Mom."* Her eyes shone with hope.

Rafe's heart squeezed in his chest. "I couldn't think of anyone better."

"Well I haven't done anything. Alex is the one to finish his second year of medical school and with honors, yet." They shared a proud smile.

"Sweetheart, you've been by his side, encouraging him, and being there for him, all the while running your own practice." She patted his cheek. "I haven't heard any complaints from you about anything. You're wonderful. My son is lucky to have you." She left his side to coo over Micah and Josh's babies.

Rafe wondered how true it all was. He and Alex loved each other but they spent so little time together now. After the sale of his mother's house, he'd poured most of the money into his practice and with the rest they'd bought a small house in Brooklyn. The weekends found him renovating the various little things that always needed to be done, while Alex studied. Rafe had taken to feeding the stray cats in the backyard for company while he cleared the garden, and he'd put out several birdfeeders, high enough so the cats couldn't get to them.

There was a scrape in the lock and then the door opened. Alex stood in the doorway in shock as everyone yelled, "Surprise!"

Rafe, though, was surprised himself as Alex had a big bouquet of flowers and what looked like a bottle of champagne, as well as a few other bags in his hands.

"Hi, baby. Happy last day of classes." He kissed Alex's cheek.

"Hi yourself." Alex scanned the group of people in his living room, his gaze resting on Micah and nodding. Confused, Rafe watched as Micah, Josh and Dolores hustled everyone out of the living room and into the backyard, before he had a chance to say a word.

"Alex?" But Alex paid him no attention and took him by the elbow, leading him to their little living room, where they'd put all the pictures of their friends and family. "What's going on?"

"What's going on is that I love you." Alex pushed him down on the sofa and lay down on top of him. Immediately, a surge of want and longing rolled through Rafe. With Alex's studies, their sex life had been on hold for the past two weeks and he was horny as hell.

"I love you too, but we have guests."

"They can wait." Alex gazed into his eyes and Rafe saw desire, want and love. "All I could think about when I finished was I couldn't wait to come back here to you. To see you and hold you." Alex nuzzled against Rafe's neck and Rafe, helpless as always against Alex's touch, pressed up against his lover, relishing his strength. "I missed you so much and I'm sorry for all the time I've taken away from us."

"I've missed you, but I know how important this is for you. I won't do anything to stand in the way of your dream."

From the garden, Rafe could hear the birds and the murmurs of their guests, milling about. All he'd ever wanted in his life was here in this house and with this man in his arms.

Alex held him by the shoulders, the fierceness of his gaze shooting a thrill through Rafe. "I have no dream if you aren't part of my life. Without you, it all becomes a nightmare. And I won't let that happen. I know what it's like to be neglected and I promise you, you'll always be first in my life."

"You haven't neglected me." Rafe rubbed his cheek to Alex's and kissed the corner of his mouth. "Having you as my partner is one of my life's greatest rewards, but I also love how our work infuses us with a sense of purpose. Never think I feel neglected because you have a passion for your job."

The old, devilish smile, the one that had been missing while Alex worked so hard to catch up at school, returned now to his face. "My one true passion is you and I plan on making it up to you in the weeks to come." With the tenderness Rafe loved about him, Alex kissed his lips, then slipped off the sofa. Rafe's eyes widened. "Now, I had my own surprise planned as well." He pulled out a box from his pocket. "Marry me?"

Rafe sat stunned and speechless. "Wh-what?" He blinked and rubbed his eyes. Maybe his new contacts were making him see things but it looked like a gold band in a box.

"I want it all, baby. We have the house already, and now I want the rest. The kids, the dog and cat, Thanksgiving dinners." Alex took the ring out of the box and held it out. "I want it all with you. A family. Forever. I love you, Rafe."

With fingers that only shook a little bit, Rafe took the ring from Alex and looked inside. It was inscribed: *The other half of my heart.*

"I love you too, more than I thought possible. Of course I'll marry you."

Alex put the ring on his finger. "I got a matching one for me but I'll let you inscribe it. You'll probably want to put, 'To the most amazing lover.' Or something like that."

"Modesty becomes you, Alex."

Startled, Rafe looked up to see everyone crowded at the door. Micah grinned at them, and his eyes gleamed with happiness.

Alex's mother stood in front with tears in her eyes. "You said yes, right?"

Rafe took Alex's face between his hands and kissed him. "Of course I said yes, Mom. How could I say no to him?"

"I'm irresistible."

"You're impossible." Rafe kissed him again. "Impossible to resist," he whispered.

"I love you too, Rafe."

THE END

ABOUT THE AUTHOR

Felice Stevens has always been a romantic at heart. She believes that while life is tough, there is always a happy ending just around the corner. She started reading traditional historical romances when she was a teenager, then life and law school got in the way. It wasn't until she picked up a copy of Bertrice Small and became swept away to Queen Elizabeth's court that her interest in romance novels became renewed.

But somewhere along the way, her tastes shifted. While she still enjoys a juicy Historical romance, she discovered the world of Male/Male romance. And once she picked up her first, she became so enamored of the authors, the character-driven stories and the overwhelming emotion of the books, she knew she wanted to write her own.

Felice lives in New York City with her husband and two children and hopefully soon a cat of her own. Her day begins with a lot of caffeine and ends with a glass or two of red wine. She practices law but daydreams of a time when she can sit by a beach somewhere and write beautiful stories of men falling in love. Although there is bound to be angst along the way, a Happily Ever After is always guaranteed.

www.felicestevens.com

OTHER TITLES BY FELICE STEVENS

Made in the USA
Middletown, DE
21 January 2022

59291833R00139